Acclaim for the authors of
Regency Reunions at Christmas

DIANE GASTON

"[Gaston's] insightful way with characterization will win over readers who like their romances served up with a generous measure of historical realism."
—*Booklist* on *Secretly Bound to the Marquess*

LAURA MARTIN

"Excellent book that caught my interest from the beginning and held it to the end."
—*Goodreads* review on *A Match to Fool Society*

HELEN DICKSON

"In this Regency romance, Dickson creates a beautiful, character-driven story vaguely reminiscent of *10 Things I Hate About You* and *The Taming of the Shrew*."
—*Library Journal* on *The Earl's Wager for a Lady*

Diane Gaston's dream job was always to write romance novels. One day she dared to pursue that dream and has never looked back. Her books have won romance's highest honors: the RITA® Award, the National Readers' Choice Award, the HOLT Medallion, Golden Quill and Golden Heart® Award. She lives in Virginia, USA, with her husband and three very ordinary house cats. Diane loves to hear from readers and friends. Visit her website at dianegaston.com.

Laura Martin writes historical romances with an adventurous undercurrent. When not writing, she spends her time working as a doctor in Cambridgeshire, where she lives with her husband. In her spare moments Laura loves to lose herself in a book and has been known to read from cover to cover in a single day when the story is particularly gripping. She also loves to travel—especially to visit historical sites and far-flung shores.

Helen Dickson was born and still lives in South Yorkshire, with her retired farm manager husband. Having moved out of the busy farmhouse where she raised their two sons, she now has more time to indulge in her favorite pastimes. She enjoys being outdoors, traveling, reading and music. An incurable romantic, she writes for pleasure. It was a love of history that drove her to writing historical fiction.

REGENCY REUNIONS AT CHRISTMAS

Diane Gaston
Laura Martin
Helen Dickson

HARLEQUIN
HISTORICAL

HARLEQUIN®
HISTORICAL™

Recycling programs for this product may not exist in your area.

ISBN-13: 978-1-335-59582-9

Regency Reunions at Christmas

Copyright © 2023 by Harlequin Enterprises ULC

The Major's Christmas Return
Copyright © 2023 by Diane Perkins

A Proposal for the Penniless Lady
Copyright © 2023 by Laura Martin

Her Duke Under the Mistletoe
Copyright © 2023 by Helen Dickson

For questions and comments about the quality of this book, please contact us at CustomerService@Harlequin.com.

Harlequin Enterprises ULC
22 Adelaide St. West, 41st Floor
Toronto, Ontario M5H 4E3, Canada
www.Harlequin.com

Printed in U.S.A.

CONTENTS

THE MAJOR'S CHRISTMAS RETURN

Diane Gaston

To the talented writers gathered
together at the Inn at Narrow Passage.
My thanks to you all.

Dear Reader,

There is something about isolation that fosters
closeness. That is certainly true of the gathering of
my writer friends for a weekend once a year. It was
true in 2020, too, when the isolation of COVID made
us all create Christmas celebrations of a very modest
sort. In this story, the isolation caused by another
disease and a snowstorm give Caroline and Nash a
second chance at love.

Enjoy!
Diane Gaston

Chapter One

Caroline Demain peered out the carriage window and caught a glimpse of the stately yellow-brick country house. In mere minutes she'd be in the embrace of her dear friend Sybella.

Dear, *dear* Sybella. What would Caroline have done if Sybella's letter had not reached her, inviting her to come for Christmas and stay as long as she liked? Without Sybella's invitation Caroline would be knocking on the door of the poorhouse in a matter of weeks.

Sybella had bought her more time. She'd even provided funds for the travel from London. Caroline was grateful.

Her brow furrowed. Perhaps the full newspaper accounts had not reached Sybella, the accounts that implied she'd killed her husband.

Caroline again saw Percy tumble down the stairs, his face alarmed, his body twisted and eyes vacant after he hit the bottom step.

She *had* killed him.

The carriage drew up to the main entrance to the house. The yard was eerily quiet, no signs of life at all.

One of the coachmen helped her climb out of the carriage, the other unloaded her trunk, portmanteau, hatbox and bag. He set them down in front of the door. Caroline thanked them, gave them each a coin for their efforts. They pulled on their forelocks and climbed back onto the carriage. It pulled away, leaving her alone.

She expected the door to open—surely someone had heard the carriage—but it did not.

Squaring her shoulders, she climbed the stone steps and sounded the brass knocker. After a minute's pause, the door opened and she stepped into the Marble Hall.

The door was held by a young dark-haired footman, no older than seventeen, perhaps. Behind him were two maids even younger than the footman, huddled together. The smallest, and perhaps youngest, was a girl with black skin and brown eyes, a white cap covering her hair and wearing the apron of a kitchen servant. The other maid was taller, red-haired and freckle-faced. All three gaped at Caroline wide-eyed, as if in shock.

'I—I am Mrs Demain.' How she hated that name. 'Lady Bolton is expecting me.'

The footman closed the door and handed her a folded sheet of paper.

She opened it and immediately recognised Sybella's handwriting:

Dear Caroline,
Please forgive us. We've had to flee to my parents'
house. You see, a friend of Jeremy's, a guest here
for a few weeks, was supposed to be gone by now
but—please do not be alarmed—he has contracted
typhus. We had to leave for the children's sake, you
understand.
*   We've left a footman and a maid to attend you,*
and a kitchen maid to prepare meals. They will also
attend the patient. You must not enter the patient's

room. Do not go anywhere near it! I should not for-give myself if you also became ill.

I am sure Mama will insist we stay until Twelfth Night. Expect us after, if there is no more illness there. Send word if there is.

I did so wish to see you, but we simply had to leave. Yours,
S.
PS I would have had you come with us, but you know how my mother is.

Caroline stared at the letter, trying to let the words sink in. She was to stay alone in this country house with an outbreak of typhus and only these three youths to care for the place and the patient?

Well, at least she had a roof over her head and food to eat. Some day soon it could be so much worse.

She glanced up at the three young servants. It looked as if the kitchen maid was about to burst into tears.

'When did Lord and Lady Bolton leave?' she asked.

The footman responded. 'Not more than a half-hour ago.'

So this situation was almost as new to these young servants as it was to her. 'Were you told what was in the letter?'

The three nodded.

'The sick man has typhus!' the kitchen maid cried.

The footman looked bleak. 'We've seen typhus. We've seen friends die of it in the orphanage.'

'We could die, too!' The girl burst into tears.

The footman and other maid rushed to comfort her.

Now Caroline understood. 'You fear catching typhus.'

The red-haired maid's eyes flashed. 'Lord and Lady Bolton left us here. They do not care if we get sick and die.'

'Hush, Molly,' the footman said. 'She will tell Lady Bolton.'

'I will not tell Lady Bolton,' she assured them. 'After all, they left me here, too.'

'Yes,' the red-haired maid countered. 'But you are to stay *away* from the gentleman. You are safe and we are not!'

'We'll manage, Molly,' the footman said.

How could Sybella be so cruel to these poor young people, adding this cruelty to what must have been a lifetime of cruelties? Most of Caroline's life had been carefree and full of abundance. Now she had nothing to lose.

If she contracted typhus, who was there to care if she lived or died?

'May I know your names?' she asked.

The footman bowed. 'I am Elliot, ma'am.' He gestured to the maids. 'This is Molly and Lucy.'

Caroline smiled at each of them in turn. 'Elliot. Molly. Lucy. I am pleased to meet you. I have a small trunk and other luggage outside. Do you suppose you could bring it in? Then we can decide what to do.'

Elliot and Molly hurried out the door.

Lucy stared at her.

Caroline smiled at her again. 'What are your duties here, Lucy?'

The girl gazed down. 'The kitchen, ma'am. The scullery.'

'Then you will be feeding us?'

The girl nodded.

The door opened again. Elliot carried in the trunk and Molly, the portmanteau, her hatbox and other bag—all her worldly possessions.

Caroline turned to them. 'Thank you, Elliot. Molly. You may put them down here for the time being.'

They placed her luggage on the black and white chequered floor.

Caroline took a fortifying breath. 'Here is what we shall do.' There was no other choice really. 'I will care for the patient. Only me. You three will have enough to do tending to this house on your own.'

'But my lady said—' Molly's eyes widened.

Caroline put up a hand. 'Lady Bolton is not here. We are. We four will decide what is to be done.' She turned to the kitchen maid. 'Lucy, you will tend the kitchen. I am certain the rest of us know nothing about cooking food.' She faced Molly. 'And you must tend to the house. Whatever cleaning and laundry needs doing.' Finally the footman. 'Elliot, you are the only one who can perform the heavy tasks.' She pointed to herself. 'I am experienced at nursing, so I will care for the patient.' She'd certainly tended to Percy often enough—although most of those times were when he'd imbibed too much drink.

She only now removed her hat and cloak. The footman rushed forward to take them from her.

With a resolve more forced than secure, she lifted her chin. 'Now, show me to the patient.'

Elliot shoved her hat and cloak into Molly's hands. 'This way, ma'am.'

He led her up the staircase past the library and the lord and lady's bedchambers to a wing of lesser bedchambers. Molly and Lucy followed but held back as they reached the doorway to one of the rooms.

Elliot gestured to the door. 'He is in here.'

She opened the door and entered.

The room's curtains were drawn and the room dark. The air smelt stale. Prominently in the room was the bed and the sleeping figure in it. The only sound, his raspy breathing.

Her eyes adjusted to the dim light. He lay still, tangled in the bedsheets, his back to her. His bare back.

The man wore no shirt.

Was he naked?

She took a step back.

Wait. She was no green girl. She'd seen Percy naked before, tended to him before.

She approached the bed. As she got closer she could see the patient's dark hair was damp with sweat. She reached over and placed her fingers on his back. His skin burned with fever.

He stirred, groaned and turned over in bed.

Caroline gasped.

His eyes opened, barely focusing on her. 'Caro?' he mumbled. 'Caro.'

He rolled over again.

Her legs threatened to give out.

The sick man lying in the bed, whose care was solely hers, was Nash.

Major Guy Nashfield.

The man who left her standing at the altar on their wedding day seven years before.

Chapter Two

Caroline bolted out of the bedchamber door, unable to breathe.

Nash was here. Here! He was ill and she alone must care for him. How could she bear it?

A memory of that day flashed through her mind. She stood at the altar upon which the vicar tapped impatiently. Their few guests shuffled and whispered together in the pews. Nash was late. Where was he? What could have happened? They all turned at the sound of the heavy wooden door opening. Not Nash. Percy.

'He is not coming,' Percy said as he strode towards her. 'He is on a ship to Portugal.'

Caroline felt that pain again, that dagger in the heart.

'Ma'am?'

She blinked and saw the three worried faces. The poor orphaned servants. Abandoned as she had been.

She took a breath. 'Yes. Right.'

Compose yourself.

'He—he is feverish. Sleeping.' Except when he opened his eyes and spoke her name. 'I will settle myself first. Change my clothes.' She glanced down the hallway. 'Is there a suitable bedchamber on this wing that I might use?'

Molly nodded. 'This way, ma'am. I will show you.'

* * *

Soon Caroline settled in a room two doors down from Nash. Molly found her an old work dress to wear, an apron and a cap, which would save the few clothes she still possessed. Elliot brought her a scuttle of coal, a jug of fresh water, a pail of soapy water, mops, scrub brushes and fresh chamber pots.

She stood at the bedchamber door. The only thing to do was pretend it was not Nash, merely some stranger, as she'd expected. Another deep breath and she turned the latch, opened the door and entered. Nash did not move. His raspy breathing filled her ears. Thank goodness he slept.

She went to work, first opening the curtains and the windows, letting fresh air and light fill the room. The room was in disarray. A food tray sat on a nearby table, its food half consumed. Clothes were scattered on the floor and other furniture. A breeze from the window lifted the corner of a napkin and raised gooseflesh on her arms. She put more coals on the fire, but it did little to warm the chill she'd let in. Better the cold than the stale air.

She turned to Nash. He'd thrown off his blankets and the light from the window showed more than his chest was bare. Gritting her teeth, she approached the bed and gingerly untangled the blankets from his bare limbs.

She gasped. A scar went from the top of his thigh to his knee. His back was riddled with smaller scars. She felt tears sting her eyes. What had he endured? So many scars.

No. She would not waste her sympathy on this man. He chose war. He was supposed to have worked in the War Office, not boarded that ship to Portugal.

She covered him, tucking in the corners to help keep him covered.

She replaced the water in the pitcher with fresh water and then mopped the floor. Already the room smelled bet-

Fresh water. Mopped floor. Clean smell.

He'd already imposed on Bolton enough. He was supposed to be gone. Yesterday? The day before? He was not exactly sure how many days had gone by since he fell sick.

He poured another glass of water and downed it. The effort exhausted him, and he lay back down, shivering again, his head spinning.

Nash covered himself with the blanket and closed his eyes.

Would he dream again? Of her?

Caroline.

Damn the illness that brought her back into his dreams. He'd thought battle and pain and death had finally erased her from his memory.

Maybe if he stayed awake.

It was no use. He was too sick.

She came back in his dreams.

Sitting next to the bed, wiping his brow with a cool damp cloth, putting a white nightshirt over his head, guiding his arms through, feeding him broth.

Her voice sounded the same, but different. Weary. Her lovely face did not smile.

He missed her smile.

'Dreaming,' he mumbled. 'Dreaming.'

'Drink more.' She lifted the cup to his lips.

Vivid dream. The broth tasted good.

He drank it all. She faded from view. He dreamt no more.

Caroline let herself out of the bedchamber and leaned against the closed door.

He'd not been lucid. No speaking her name. Barely focusing on her. Still so very sick. So very pale. Still hot with fever.

And she was solely responsible for him, for keeping him alive.

ter. As soon as she could manage, she'd change
linens, find him a bed shirt.

He stirred in the bed and she whipped aroun
sound, hoping he did not wake. As long as he sle
could keep the illusion he was anybody. He rolled o
the blankets slipped off him. The breeze from the wi
made her shiver.

She walked over to the windows.

Snow fell in large flakes, lacy and thick enough to
scure the view. Caroline paused and simply admired
beauty of it, frosting the ground, the shrubbery, the tre
There would be no leaving Bolton House today, even
she had another place to go.

She closed the windows, gathered her mop and pail an
exited the room.

She'd check on her 'patient' again later. At the moment
she felt in great need of a soothing cup of tea.

Nash caught but a fleeting glimpse of the maid as she
carried the bucket and mop from the room. The room
smelled of wet wood and soap and for the first time since
he became ill he felt he could breathe. She'd left the curtains drawn, letting in the light. It was daytime; that much
he knew. What day, he had no idea. How long had he remained feverish? After Waterloo it had been days and
he'd been out of his head. This time he was not that sick.

He remembered the doctor visiting. The man certainly
fled from the room as quickly as he entered.

Nash forced himself to sit up in bed. His mouth tasted
foul. He picked up the pitcher on the side table, his hand
shaking. He managed to pour himself a glass of water and
bring it to his lips without spilling most of it. It felt cool
on his throat. And fresh.

The maid must have brought fresh water.

She'd instructed Elliot to look among Bolton's clothing for a clean nightshirt for Nash. She did not feel even a twinge of guilt for using anything of Bolton's. Or of Sybella's. They were the ones who'd left her in this position.

Did Sybella truly think she would not tend to Nash? That they would not cross paths? What a terrible trick to play on both her and Nash.

Caroline took a breath and carried the cup back to the kitchen where Lucy was putting the finishing touches on dinner.

At least they would eat well. A large roast of beef had already been cooking on a spit when Caroline arrived. They would make many meals from that. Lucy said there were potatoes and turnips and carrots and preserves. They'd do fine with the food.

There was only Nash to worry about. And not becoming ill herself.

'How are you faring, Lucy?' Caroline asked as she carried the cup to the scullery.

'I think it is all right,' the girl answered.

Caroline dipped the cup in the soapy water and rinsed it in the clean water before placing it on the draining board.

She dried her hands on her apron. 'How may I help?'

The kitchen maid gaped at her. 'Oh, ma'am. I cannot ask you to help.'

Caroline smiled. 'Lucy, I assure you I have been in a kitchen before.'

By necessity. She'd learned to fix some food after being forced to let her cook go.

Lucy still looked uncertain. 'Would it be too much to take the potatoes out of the fire?'

'I can do that.'

Elliot came through the door, carrying a load of wood which he stacked near the huge fireplace where the beef was roasting. 'The snow comes pretty thick now. It'll be hard going to bring the stable workers their food.'

'Stable workers!' Caroline had not given thought to how many others were on the estate. 'How many?'

'Two, I was told,' he responded.

'Are there any other workers on the estate?' she asked.

'Only the tenants and their families, but they should be able to take care of themselves.'

Molly entered the kitchen. She curtsied to Caroline. 'I've set a table in the small sitting room for your dinner, ma'am. It will be warmer in there.'

'Thank you, Molly.' Caroline really did not wish to be alone, though. Alone with her thoughts and memories. 'How smart of you to use a small room.'

The maid flushed with the compliment.

Caroline tried to scoop a potato from the fire with a long-handled spoon, but it rolled off.

'I'll do that, ma'am,' Molly said, taking the spoon from her hand.

Caroline wanted to keep busy. If she were busy, she would not think. 'Perhaps I can pack up some food for the stable workers. We should send them enough for tonight and tomorrow morning. If it keeps snowing like this, it will be even harder to reach them.' She turned to Elliot. 'Will you be able to carry food to them now?'

'Yes, ma'am.'

Lucy found two large baskets and cloth to line them with.

'Bring them some drink, as well,' Caroline suggested. 'Surely there is some beer or gin or something.'

Elliot looked sceptical. 'I thought the spirits were only for you and the sick gentleman.'

She glanced at them each in turn. 'We are all in this to-gether, remember. We will use whatever we desire to try to make this as pleasant for all of us as we can.'

Chapter Three

Nash had the dream again. The dream of Caroline, her arm around him, helping him sit and drink some broth. She faded away again, only to reappear with a cool cloth to his head. The room was dark now, the only light shining on her face, floating in front of him.

She disappeared again and it felt as if he'd sunk into oblivion, only to wake up in hell.

No. Not hell. Battle. Smoke all around him. Screams of the wounded. Air filled with the scent of gunpowder, blood and rage. He was trapped in the centre of it.

Had to save his men. Save his men. One by one they fell, shot by cannon, impaled by steel.

'No!' he cried. 'No!'

She appeared again. Caroline. 'Nash! Nash! Wake up. You are dreaming.'

He tried to rise. To fight. To try to keep his men alive. She held him down by his shoulders.

'It is a dream,' she said. 'Only a dream.'

She was dressed as an angel all in white. Where was he?

'Am I dead? This is hell?' He seized her. 'If this is hell, why are you here, Caro? This place is not for you.'

He could still hear the horses charging towards him and the French drums. And always the cries of his men.

'This is not hell, Nash,' her apparition told him. 'You are at Bolton House. You are ill. Typhus. Lie down. Try to sleep.'

'Why does my mind conjure up you? I left you behind long ago.' He'd tried to forget her. Forget what she'd done.

'Lie down.' There was an edge in her voice now. 'You need rest.'

He shoved her away and lay back against the pillows. 'Leave me,' he murmured. 'Leave me again.'

But Caroline did not dare leave him, not with him delirious with fever. She moved one of the brocade-cushioned chairs to where she could easily watch him, but not be directly in his sight, should he wake.

She feared he would die.

She watched his chest rise and fall, seeing that face that still made her heart skip a beat. He must not die.

Not Nash.

She'd studied the lists that were printed in the *Gazette* after the battles, the lists of the officers killed and wounded. She'd searched for his name and breathed a sigh of relief when it wasn't there. She'd read he'd been wounded at Waterloo. Was the scar on his leg from that injury?

A pain deep inside her ached thinking of that wound.

'Nash,' she whispered low enough so he could not hear her. 'Nash, why did you leave me? Why did you send Percy to tell me you did not want me? Why did you not come?'

He mumbled something and turned fitfully, throwing off his covers again. She moved closer and touched him, His skin still burned. She straightened his blankets and tucked him in again.

'Do not die, Nash,' she begged louder. 'Please do not die.'

There was nothing to do but sit and wait.

And hope.

* * *

Nash opened his eyes to daylight streaming through the windows. The room was cold, but he did not mind. It felt good to fill his lungs with cool air. He could breathe easily now. The fever had left him.

How long had he been he ill? He rubbed his chin. More than a day's worth of beard. He could remember very little. Dreams, mostly. Lord, he'd even dreamed of Caroline.

His stomach spasmed with hunger. Let it please be morning, because then breakfast would still be on the sideboard and he could eat right away. He'd ring for a footman, get dressed and eat.

Nash sat up and swung his legs over the side of the bed. It was then he saw her. In the chair, curled up, asleep, a blanket wrapped around her.

Caroline.

'What the devil are you doing here?' he shouted.

She jolted awake. Jumped to her feet. 'Nash?'

Her hair tumbled over her shoulders. A white nightdress billowed around her body. She looked thinner.

Why would he notice that? As if he cared how she looked.

'Well?' he demanded. 'What are you doing here?'

Her grey eyes flashed—that is, he remembered them being grey; it was not that bright in the room. 'I am tending to you. Making sure you didn't die.'

'Die?' He laughed.

She put her hands on her hips. 'The fever was very bad. You were delirious.'

He sat back on the bed. 'Never mind. Ring for a footman. I want to dress.'

'No.'

'No?' How dare she refuse him. 'Then I'll ring myself.' He rose again, angry that he must walk past her looking dishevelled, unshaven and wearing night clothes that were not his.

'Sit down, Nash,' she ordered. 'You cannot call for a footman. No one will come. You are in quarantine.'

'Quarantine?' That was nonsense. 'For what?'

'The doctor said you have typhus and are very contagious.'

He laughed. 'Nonsense. I've had typhus before. This was not typhus.'

She raised a sceptical brow.

He rose again and faced her directly. 'Get Bolton for me. He'll listen to me.'

She did not waver. Instead, she spoke slowly, as if to an infant. 'Bolton and Sybella and their children and most of their servants have gone. They fled the typhus.'

He threw up his arms. This was outrageous. 'Get me somebody, then! Anybody but you!'

If his words wounded her, she did not show it. She responded calmly. 'I cannot. The three servants Bolton and Sybella left here are terrified of typhus.'

'I don't have—' What was the use? He peered at her. 'Wait. Only three servants?'

'Three servants and me,' she clarified. 'And two stable workers.'

Unbelievable. Bolton had left Nash with Caroline and damned near no one else?

He rubbed his face. 'Tell the servants I do not have typhus.'

'I cannot do that,' she protested. 'These servants are very young, Nash. Barely out of the schoolroom. They're orphans and have seen friends die of typhus.'

He'd not known Caroline to take such an interest in the servants. Not that she was ever unkind to them. She was never unkind to anyone.

Except him.

'Very well, Caro.' He slipped into using the diminutive of her name as he used to do. 'I'll dress myself. Perhaps one of the terrified servants could request my horse be saddled. I am not staying here.'

She walked over to the window and extended her hand. 'You are not going anywhere, Nash.'

He let out an exasperated breath and dutifully shuffled over to look outside.

It was white. Nothing but white. Snow covered the shrubbery, the trees, the paths. He judged its depth to be at least a foot. Maybe two.

'Blast,' he murmured. He was snowed in with Caroline.

Her voice turned low, almost sympathetic. 'I will leave you to dress. Shall I bring you breakfast?'

His hunger came rushing back. 'I cannot go down to the breakfast room?'

'No. You must stay here.' She avoided looking at him.

They were standing next to each other at the window. He remembered that his lips could kiss her forehead without bending down. He remembered thinking they fit perfectly together.

How wrong he'd been.

Nash glanced at her face. Lines of stress touched the corners of her eyes, yet she remained otherwise unchanged from when he last saw her seven years before.

She glanced back but quickly averted her eyes. 'I'll bring you a tray of food directly.'

She turned and walked to the door, her white nightdress flowing around her as she walked.

Nash waited in a chair by the window, his feet resting on the sill. The wind rattled the panes of glass and the air felt fresh near them. He'd spent weeks shut away in a sick room and the idea of more confinement—with Caroline, no less—put him on edge. He'd shaved, washed himself and combed his hair. He chose comfortable clothes—his buckskin breeches, stockings and a shirt.

A knock sounded at the door.

'Come in,' he said.

She entered carrying a tray, placing it on a table.

Nash lowered his legs and stood. His wounded leg ached, but the aching would go away after he walked for a while. He limped over to the table.

Caroline's eyes widened, then turned sympathetic. He wanted no sympathy from her. He wanted nothing from her.

Except maybe breakfast.

'My leg is stiff after I sit,' he said curtly as he sat.

She nodded as if understanding his pain. 'I saw the scar.'

She had seen the scar? Of course she had. She must have been the one who helped him into that nightshirt.

He bit into a piece of toast. 'I am shocked, Caro. You. Gazing at a man's naked flesh.'

'I hardly had a choice,' she countered. 'You had no clothes on when I first tended to you.'

She walked to the door.

He wanted to get a rise out of her, or maybe he simply did not want her to leave. 'What would Percy say about you gazing at a naked man?'

She looked at him over her shoulder. 'Percy's dead, Nash. Did you not know?'

'Dead?' He dropped his piece of toast. 'When?'

'Last July.'

Last July. Last July he'd still been in Belgium, ill with a fever that made this one seem tepid. His wound had been infected and he'd been fighting for his life, certainly not reading London papers.

'What happened?' he asked. 'Did he become ill or die of drink?' Not that Nash cared he was dead.

She turned and looked him directly in the eye. 'Neither,' she said. 'I killed him.'

She opened the door and left.

Chapter Four

Caroline spent as much time as she could avoiding Nash's room. She was certain he had finished breakfast ages ago and that the room needed tending. She'd run out of excuses.

Laden with clean linens, she approached his door, resolute in simply performing her tasks and leaving.

Caroline knocked and heard Nash's voice, so familiar even after all these years.

'Come in.'

Nash reclined on the two chairs, sitting on one and elevating his feet on the other. Both were near the window positioned so he could look outside.

The room was very cold. Caroline immediately set the linens aside, feeling guilty. She'd forgotten to check the fireplace. She immediately hurried over to it. 'Did the fire go out? Did you run out of coal?'

'Don't fret, Caro,' he responded in a chiding tone. 'The fire is fine. I opened the window for a while. Fresh air, you know.'

That had been her first impulse the day before, as well. To open the window and fill the room with fresh air.

'You should not be so chilled,' she scolded. 'It cannot be good for you.'

He smiled—gracious, she'd forgotten how wonderful

his smile was. 'I feel quite well, actually. A bit weak, I admit, but not feverish. Quite out of my mind with boredom, however.'

'Well, I'm not ready to release you from quarantine, if that is what you are after.' She picked up his food tray and carried it to the door.

'Leaving already?' He turned to sarcasm now.

'Not yet.' She made herself respond matter-of-factly. 'I have more cleaning to do.'

He sat up straighter. 'Put the tray down. I can do that. You are acting like a common chambermaid.'

'Do not be nonsensical, Nash.' She placed the tray just outside the room. 'For you I am the chambermaid and the kitchen maid and the footman. Besides, Elliot will be good enough to remove the tray from the hallway.'

'Elliot?' His brows rose.

'The footman who was left here.'

He laughed. 'I wonder what he did to be left behind.'

She walked over to the bed and pulled off the blankets and linens. 'Merely being an orphan, I suspect. He and the two maids are all from the Lincoln orphanage.'

'Ah.' Nash nodded. 'Expendable then. No harm done if they caught this typhus and died.'

He'd grasped the essence of it. She was unsure why she both resented and was gratified by his quick understanding.

'It is certainly how they feel about it,' she said.

Caroline balled up the linens and set them out the door as well.

When she came back in, Nash was rising from his chair. 'So, the orphans refused to tend to me and then you were forced into it?'

She spread one sheet over the bed and tucked it in the

mattress. 'I volunteered,' she said, adding, 'Of course, at the time I did not know it was you I must tend.'

He picked up the second sheet and handed it to her. 'No doubt you would have refused the task, then.'

'I would have been tempted to refuse, I assure you,' she said.

He helped her spread the bed linen and tuck it in. 'And you are not afraid of catching typhus?'

She shrugged. 'Not as much as they.'

He spread the blankets over the bed, and she put the pillows in the pillowslips. After that was done, he collapsed in the chair again. She just stared at him.

He looked annoyed. 'That should not have exhausted me.'

'Perhaps you are not as recovered as you think you are.' She fluffed up the pillows. 'I'll leave now, unless there is something else you wish me to do.'

His gaze softened 'Stay, Caro. Tell me what happened with Percy.'

She glanced away. 'I meant was there any other task you require of me?'

'Require of you?' He used his hands to lift his scarred leg onto the other chair. 'Perhaps some ale later? And something to read? I am going mad with nothing to do.'

'As you wish.' Caroline hurried out the door.

It was churlish of her to hurry away, she knew, but her emotions were in total disorder. It was easier when he taunted her, easier for her to feel her anger towards him then. But when he helped her make the bed? That confused her. That was too much like the man she'd thought she'd been in love with.

She heaved a heavy sigh and opened the door again. 'I'll bring you the ale and some books.'

His gaze remained on her. 'A book soon, Caro? I need to stop thinking.'

She nodded, unsure of what he meant.

So she went directly to the library and for the second time that day, scanned the bookshelves. She selected *Travels in China: from Pekin to Canton* by John Barrow, Esq. That ought to be absorbing. And to rattle him she chose *The Castles of Athlin and Dunbayne* by Ann Radcliffe. Because he'd used to roast her for reading novels.

Her eye caught the title of another book. She pulled it off the shelf.

Observations on the Typhus or Low Contagious Fever by D. Campbell MD.

The very first page of the first chapter said:

A particular species of fever is apt to be produced in consequence of persons residing in apartments where there is not a sufficiently free circulation of air, especially if crowded together and accompanied with neglect of clean linens and a deficiency of proper food...

There certainly had not been free circulation of air in Nash's room and his linens were unclean because of his illness, but there were no crowds and no lack of proper food. Perhaps Nash was correct. Perhaps he did not have typhus.

She put the book in her apron pocket and took the two other volumes back to Nash's room. Entering after a quick knock and leaving as quickly. Managing not to say a word.

Caroline could not stay one minute? Was his company that objectionable to her?

It now made sense why Bolton had insisted Nash be gone by yesterday instead of remaining the four days until Christmas. Nash had planned to be in London before Christmas anyway. A position in the War Office depended on it.

Bolton had helped him regain his strength and conquer his limp. They'd spent many hours riding, shooting, walking the estate. Nash wanted to be in top shape when he appeared at the War Office. He'd just begun to feel almost himself again when that damned fever caught him.

Now he could not even put a blanket on a bed without exhausting himself.

He gazed out of the window at the snow-covered ground. Even if Caroline freed him from his quarantine, he'd not make it back to London in time.

Nash closed his eyes, trying to calm the restlessness that truly was driving him mad. This room, this confinement reminded him of that bare windowless room in Brussels where he lay in bed, unable to even stand on his injured leg. He'd suffered fevers there, too, from infections of his wound. Confined again, those memories refused to leave him alone. He'd come so close to death, he fancied he'd seen its face taunting him, mocking him.

He shook that thought away.

Better to think of Caroline.

She was altered from the Caroline he knew seven years before, the Caroline he'd been about to marry, the Caroline who betrayed him. She'd been so bright then, filling his days with a glow of happiness unlike any he'd known before. That flame that glowed so brightly in those days seemed to have burned out.

Or maybe it was merely that she resented having to care for him when she'd hoped never to see him again.

He reached over and picked up one of the books. He opened the cover—*The Castles of Athlin and Dunbayne. A Highland Story* by Ann Radcliffe.

Nash smiled. This book had not been chosen by accident. Perhaps Caroline remembered those happier days as well when he'd tease her about reading Ann Radcliffe's Gothics.

He opened the book and started to read.

Chapter Five

At Caroline's suggestion Molly and Elliot had spent most of the morning closing off rooms and covering furniture. Caroline needed only one sitting room, leaving only the kitchen rooms, the servants' hall and their bedchambers to be tended to and to heat. Lucy had had some panicked tears that morning, but Caroline assured her they would only eat meals she knew how to cook and that they would all help.

Keeping them fed and warm. That was of the utmost importance. Things Caroline had taken for granted growing up.

She entered the kitchen.

Lucy stood on a stool in a corner of the kitchen, her hand on the round object wrapped in the cloth and hanging on a hook.

'Lucy?' Caroline asked.

The girl immediately jumped down. 'Sorry, ma'am. I was just sniffing the plum pudding. It smells so nice and sweet.'

Caroline did not know how she could smell anything but the wonderful aroma of the bread, obviously just out of the oven. 'The bread looks fine,' she told Lucy. 'You've done a wonderful job.'

Lucy frowned. 'The loaves are not the same size. And some look almost burnt.'

Caroline leaned down to one loaf and inhaled. 'I do not think it matters what size the loaves are, and almost burnt is not burnt.'

The girl looked a bit mollified. 'Would you taste a piece?'

Caroline smiled. 'With pleasure!'

Lucy sliced off the heel of one loaf and was about to discard it.

'I'll eat the heel.' Caroline extended her hand.

Lucy looked reluctant but handed her the piece. The bread was still warm from the oven. Caroline held it to her nose for one last sniff before biting into it.

'Oh, Lucy,' she exclaimed. 'It is delicious!'

The kitchen maid beamed, but she turned wistfully towards the plum pudding. 'I helped Cook make the pudding on Stir-Up Sunday. She said the servants always had a taste of it on Christmas. I never had plum pudding before.'

No plum pudding on Christmas day? 'Well, you shall have some this Christmas. We all will.'

Lucy's eyes grew wide. 'Lord and Lady Bolton would not be angry at us?'

'I doubt they would give it a thought.' They would have their fill of puddings and cakes and flummery at Sybella's parents' estate.

Lucy tossed another glance at the pudding. 'A Christmas pudding.' She sighed.

'In fact,' Caroline said decisively, 'let us plan a proper Christmas dinner with all the special foods.'

Lucy's brown eyes sparkled. 'Oh, ma'am. A proper Christmas dinner!'

'Molly and I will help,' Caroline assured her.

She took another bite of the bread. 'I believe I will bring the small loaf of your bread to Major Nashfield. He's asked for ale. Where shall I find the ale?'

'Elliot has the key to the cellar,' Lucy said. 'He and

the stable boys are making a path from the stable to the kitchen.'

A reprieve, then. She would not have to return to Nash's room until they were finished. It gave her time to read the typhus book.

'I'll be in the sitting room. Have Elliot let me know when he is finished.'

In the sitting room Caroline picked up the typhus book and settled in a chair by the fire.

Nash poured himself a glass of water. It had been over two hours since Caroline left him. He suspected she was delaying his request for ale to annoy him. Like leaving him the Radcliffe book.

He'd read it and he had to admit he had not thought once of his present situation or the past while turning its pages, reading how the two heroes of the book risked their lives for the women they loved. He would have done so for Caroline once.

He downed the water and resumed his trudge around the room. If he persisted, his limp disappeared. He could feel the fatigue threaten as he completed another rotation. He'd push through it.

A knock sounded at the door and Caroline entered carrying a tray with a pitcher of ale and a plate of bread and cheese.

'I apologise for the delay.' She placed the tray on the table. 'The footman had the key to the spirits and he was busy clearing a path to the stable.'

Her unexpected apology kept him speechless.

'I found a book about typhus,' she went on. 'You do not have it.'

She'd actually investigated? 'I know.'

She cleared her throat and did not face him directly. 'So

you are free. But, if you do not mind, I'd like to talk to the servants first. I want to reassure them.'

'I see,' he managed to say.

'You might come down for dinner,' she said. 'Then, whenever you wish.'

He was surprised at how relieved he felt. And how grateful. 'You give these servants a great deal of consideration.'

Her eyes flashed. 'They deserve it. They were forced into a very difficult situation.'

He spoke softly. 'I meant it as a compliment, Caro. It seems a great kindness to them.'

She flushed. 'They deserve kindness.'

He gestured to the bread and cheese. 'Thank you for the food, Caro. You are kind to me, as well.'

Her gaze flew to his, as if trying to judge if he meant his words. Neither of them was willing to trust the words of the other, apparently.

When it was time for dinner Elliot led Nash to a small drawing room off the grand parlour and near the servants' stairway, not the breakfast room where Nash had shared meals with Bolton and his wife. The room was warmly decorated in reds and golds, but not the latest style of the more formal reception rooms and drawing rooms. There was a seating area near the fireplace, where a warm wood fire burned. An old spinet graced one corner and a table set for two people, the other.

For Caroline and him.

The footman bowed and left the room. Nash chose one of the chairs at the table and gratefully sat, the walk through the house having fatigued him.

A wine bottle and glasses were on the table. Nash poured himself a glass of wine. As he sipped, he glanced out the room's small window which looked out upon the garden at the rear of the house. Wind had blown some of the snow from the cone-shaped shrubbery in the formal garden, but there was little if any melting. The sky was darkening.

Footsteps sounded on the servants' stairs and Caroline entered the room. She'd not dressed for dinner, but neither had he. She wore the same rather plain dress he'd seen her in all day.

She lowered herself in the chair across from him. 'Elliot will be bringing the food directly.'

He sat again and poured wine for her.

The only sounds in the room were the ticking clock on the mantel and the hissing of the burning wood in the fireplace. The silence unsettled him.

Finally Elliot walked in carrying a large tray with two covered dishes, a plate of bread covered with a napkin, and butter. He placed the bread and butter in the middle of the table and the covered dishes in front of each of them. When he removed the cover, Nash was greeted with the tantalising aroma of beef stew.

'The food will not be fancy,' Caroline explained in clipped tones. 'Lucy, the kitchen maid, is barely out of the school room. She is doing the best she can.'

'I have no complaints.' Nash glanced at Elliot who seemed to be looking for his reaction. 'Give my compliments to the cook, Elliot.'

Elliot gave a slight nod, bowed and left the room which became silent again.

Nash snapped, 'Are you never going to speak?'

Caroline glanced up at him. 'I do not know what you and I have to talk about.'

The past. They could talk about the past. About what she did to break off their plans to marry. Or of what happened with Percy.

But she looked so distressed, sitting so still and not eating, that he did not have the heart to press her.

He softened his voice. 'Caro, I am sorry you and the servants have been stranded here because of me. I fear I have ruined your Christmas.' He took a spoonful of stew and swallowed it. 'Elliot, the footman, led me to believe they expect nothing at all on Christmas day.'

Christmas and the servants. Surely those were subjects upon which they could converse.

She lifted her wine glass and took a sip. 'The three servants did not have Christmas celebrations at the orphanage. Lucy said they had never tasted plum pudding.'

They fell silent when Elliot re-entered the room. 'Would you like brandy, sir?'

'Very much,' Nash responded.

Elliot turned to Caroline. 'I will bring the next course, ma'am.'

She smiled at him. 'You are doing well, Elliot.'

His face shone with pleasure before he walked out.

Nash finished the wine left in his glass. 'I'm appalled Bolton left one inexperienced footman to do the work of half a dozen men. And only two maids.'

Caroline averted her gaze and was silent again. She said nothing until after Elliot brought in a plate of dried fruits, biscuits and the brandy.

'I am sorry for this simple dessert,' she said, as if he'd made a complaint. 'Lucy is quite overwhelmed.'

'What do you take me for, Caro?' he snapped. 'What have I said or done that makes you think I expect anything more?'

His upbringing had not been as lavish as hers. He was a mere younger son of a baron of no great wealth. And in the army he'd done without comforts many a time.

She waved a dismissive hand. 'A habit, merely.'

'What do you mean a *habit*?' he asked.

She clamped her lips together and looked away.

What forbidden topic had he stumbled upon this time?

But he'd lost his patience with her. He stood and leaned over the table. 'Caro, I have tried to be cordial, and you refuse to do likewise. You once were not like this. Or I thought you were not like this. I do not deserve this treatment.'

She half stood as well, her eyes flashing. 'You do not deserve it?'

'I do not.' Nash grabbed the bottle of brandy and his glass. 'You chose Percy, recall.'

He strode out of the room.

Chapter Six

The next morning Caroline kept herself busy. When she was busy, she did not think about Nash—or anything else.

His storming out after dinner the night before disturbed her. She'd been childish, she knew, for not being more gracious with him, but did he really expect they could engage in typical dinnertime conversation?

Much better they avoid each other.

So, she'd come down to the kitchen at the crack of dawn to help Molly and Lucy plan for a proper Christmas feast to go with the plum pudding. Mince pies. Mussels. Roast goose. White soup. Parsnips and Brussels sprouts. Wassail. They might even try a fancy jelly to put some colour on the table.

Sybella's cook owned a copy of *The Art of Cookery Made Plain and Simple*. They looked through the book, picking the dishes they wished—and could manage.

Today they would make mince pies.

Caroline had learned some very simple cooking skills after being forced to let her cook go. She quite liked dipping her fingers in flour and butter to mix the pie crusts. By mid-afternoon she'd gone hours at a time not thinking about Nash at all. Or even about Percy.

At first Molly and Lucy deferred to Caroline in everything, but she eventually convinced them that they needed to guide her in the kitchen. Quickly after working together as equals, Molly and Lucy relaxed enough to laugh with Caroline as friends.

They were about ready to assemble the pies for baking when there was a clatter at the back door. A cold breeze and men's voices blew down the hallway. Caroline and the maids stepped into the hallway to see what was happening.

Elliot and the stable workers carried in armfuls of evergreens from the back door.

Molly ran towards them. 'What are you doing, Elliot? You are tracking in snow and mud.'

'These are for Christmas decorations,' the young man replied.

One of the stablemen added, 'We've got holly and pine and ivy and—'

'Mistletoe,' the other stableman finished for him.

'We cannot bring that in here,' Molly protested. 'What will Lord and Lady Bolton say?'

Another man entered, his arms laden as well, his face flushed with colour from the brisk air.

Nash.

'Lord and Lady Bolton will not be troubled by it.' He smiled. 'We are going to celebrate Christmas with decorations and games and singing. Why should we not?'

Lucy clapped her hands in excitement. 'A proper celebration?'

Nash smiled at the young maid. 'A proper celebration.'

Caroline walked over to them. 'Put the greenery in the still room. It can dry there.'

Elliot and the stablemen took two more trips each to bring in all that they'd gathered. Nash leaned against the wall.

'Major,' one of the stablemen said after he dropped his last load. 'We forgot a yule log.'

His fellow stableman broke in. 'Clem and me can go find one.' He gestured to the other man. 'C'mon, Clem.'

They left as quickly as they'd arrived.

Elliot walked out of the still room, removed his wet coat and boots and put on dry shoes. He inclined his head towards the maids. 'Major, this is Molly, one of the housemaids, and Lucy, the kitchen maid.'

The two maids curtsied.

Nash smiled at them. 'I suspect you are responsible for my comfortable accommodations and the fine meals I've been served. I thank you.'

Molly beamed. Lucy blushed. They both fled back to the kitchen.

Nash gestured to the floor's puddles and clumps of mud. 'Find me a mop and bucket and I'll clean this up.'

'I'll do it, Major,' Elliot said. 'I'll get the mop. You should sit a while, I think.'

As Elliot walked past Caroline, he murmured. 'I think he did too much work, ma'am.'

Caroline noticed the strain around Nash's eyes. 'Would you like some tea, Nash?'

He gave a wan smile. 'Tea would be welcome.'

He took off his hat and hung it on a peg near the door. He started to remove his greatcoat but leaned against the wall again.

Caroline walked over to him. 'I'll get your coat. Your boots should come off, too.'

She tugged the coat off his shoulders, once again touching him as she'd done when he was with fever. She hung the coat on another peg and knelt down to pull off his boots. Like Elliot, he'd left a pair of dry shoes there as well.

She looked over her shoulder as she started down the hallway to the kitchen. 'I'll bring your tea to the drawing room.'

He used a hand braced against the wall as he followed her. 'May I take my tea here?' He entered the kitchen and lowered himself carefully in a chair by the long table. 'If I will not be in your way.'

A momentary unguarded expression on his face was so weary, she said. 'We can serve you here.'

'I'll bring the tea things,' Molly said.

Caroline put the kettle on the fire. Molly brought the pot and a cup and saucer, and Caroline unlocked the tea caddy and spooned some tea into the pot. Nash seemed to watch her every move. She tried not to let it rattle her. Why should it, after all?

When the tea was ready Caroline joined Molly and Lucy in assembling the mince pies. She glanced over at Nash who had poured his tea and sipped. His eyes seemed to lose their weariness.

As she moved to fix the next pie, she asked, 'Would you like some biscuits with your tea?'

He put down his cup. 'I would,' he said. 'But do not interrupt your work. I can wait.'

She turned her attention back to the pies. When they finished, Molly left to tend to the fireplaces and Lucy to making bread.

Caroline filled a plate with biscuits, fixed herself a cup of tea and joined Nash.

'Are you feeling better?' she asked.

'Much.' He took a biscuit. 'But I would happily sit here a while longer and devour these biscuits.'

He had not yet rested enough, she realised. 'Whatever possessed you to go out and gather evergreens?'

He took a bite of the biscuit and swallowed. 'I am fine, I assure you. Just tired.' He popped the rest of the biscuit in his mouth. Finishing it, he added, 'I also was desperate to be out of doors. Since my injury, I've developed a loathing of confinement.'

She wanted to ask why, but this was Nash. Why should she care?

He told her anyway. 'I was confined in Brussels after the battle. For quite a while.' He consumed another biscuit. 'It would have been easier if there had been windows in the room.'

That sounded dreadful. 'How long?' she asked.

'Two months.' He took another sip of tea.

So long? Even more dreadful. 'Your recovery was difficult, then?'

He shrugged. 'My leg was saved. That was worth it.' He smiled. 'And an urge to be outside is not a bad consequence.'

Nash would have hated needing to walk with a stick, using a false leg. Caroline had seen many amputee former soldiers begging on the streets of London. Picturing him as one was wrenching.

Instead of sympathy, though, she scolded, 'You could have merely stepped outside, you know. You did not have to go off gathering greenery.'

His eyes flashed. 'Gathering the greenery was a pleasure. It was I who suggested it. What would Christmas be without decorations?' He leaned closer so that Lucy could not hear. 'The least I can do for all the trouble I've caused is let these servants have a real Christmas.'

It was her thinking exactly. That was why they were making pies, after all.

She could not back down, though. 'But you did not have to go. You could have sent Elliot and the stablemen to do the chore.'

He glared at her. 'I *wanted* to go.' He gestured to the

area where they'd been assembling the pies. 'The pies are obviously for Christmas. You are helping make them.'

She pursed her lips. 'The food is all here. There is no reason not to make a Christmas feast.'

He leaned back. 'Admit it, Caro. You had the same idea I had. To give these servants a holiday celebration. Do not fault me for my part in it.'

He stood but had to brace himself against the table for a moment to get his balance. 'Thank you for the tea and the biscuits.'

He made his way to the door, favouring his bad leg. Caroline felt pain at his every step.

She rose from her chair and caught up to him. 'I'll help you,' she offered.

He waved her away. 'No. My leg gets better with moving it.'

She watched him make his way to the servants' stairs and it did not seem that his leg was working any better. She turned back to the kitchen and saw Lucy staring at her. The girl quickly averted her eyes.

By dinnertime Nash's fatigue had eased and his leg was nearly pain-free. He'd considered asking for his dinner to be served in his bedchamber, but he neither wanted to create more work for the servants nor did he want to spend any more time in the room than he had to. So he'd make another stab at having civil discourse with Caroline.

Like the day before, he waited in the drawing room at the table set for two. This time when he heard footsteps on the servants' stairs he expected Caroline to walk in.

She wore the same dress as she'd worn earlier when he caught her making pies. She seemed comfortable in the kitchen with the servants. When he'd known her before, he'd guess she'd only visited the kitchens as a child, begging for a sweet. It made him unexpectedly warm to her.

No matter. She'd remained cool to him.

He stood at her entrance. 'Good evening, Caro.'

'Nash,' she responded.

Elliot followed with their food which started with pea soup and slices of beef with dishes of potatoes and carrots. Nash poured the wine.

'There is beef again,' Caroline said. 'It was what they left us an abundance of, I am afraid.'

Nash put down his spoon and faced her directly. 'Do not apologise, Caro. I told you before.'

At least she looked chagrined. 'Yes. You have been quite obliging, I must admit.'

He tried smiling at her. 'Obliging? A compliment, Caro?'

She lowered her gaze. 'Deserved.'

He could taunt her more, but did he want to?

She raised her eyes again. 'How are you feeling, Nash? Were you able to rest enough?'

Nash would have preferred she not attend to his weakness, but at least she was cordial. 'Yes. I am all restored, I assure you.'

After Elliot removed the soup, he left the room and Nash and Caroline were alone.

Nash chose a safe subject. 'It seems we are likeminded in wanting to make a Christmas celebration for the servants.'

They used to be likeminded in everything—years ago.

This time Caroline continued the conversation. 'Molly told me at Christmas the children from the orphanage would walk back and forth from the Cathedral to the Castle, singing in the streets for alms, and being dazzled by all the wares for sale at the winter market. They earned money by singing, but there was no special dinner at Christmas, certainly no gifts.'

'Can you imagine it?' he responded. 'Too bad we cannot shop at the Lincoln winter market for gifts.' Not with snow covering the roads.

'They are expecting nothing,' she said. 'They won't be missing gifts.'

He took a sip of wine. 'I'll give them their vails early.' It was customary to give money to the servants after a visit. 'Could you find some cloth and string or something to put the coins in?'

'I am certain I can find some,' she said.

Nash relaxed a bit.

'I went in search of ribbons and things for the greenery. I found plenty,' she said.

'What else should we do tomorrow?' he asked.

'If Clem and Will find a yule log, we must have a lighting ceremony,' she said. 'And a Christmas candle.'

He smiled. 'And wassail. We must have wassail.' Could he actually be looking forward to this Christmas? With Caroline?

They continued to talk of plans for the holiday. Where to place the greenery. Which fireplace for the yule log. What foods would be served. Nash was not only tolerating the dinner with Caroline; he was actually enjoying it. For several moments at a time he forgot everything but the pleasure of being with her again.

After they finished the dessert course, gingerbread with whipped cream, they sat in the chairs near the fire. Nash drank brandy and Caroline sipped tea. They were easy with each other, almost like it had been seven years before.

Nash's leg started to ache, and he pulled a small stool over to prop it up.

Caroline stared at him. 'Tell me what happened to your leg.'

This was another change in her demeanour. Nash had

an impulse to refuse to answer, like she refused to answer about Percy's death, but he did not want to shut down the conversation as she had done the night before.

'A French soldier's sword,' he responded. 'During the battle.'

He could say more, but already he was hearing the roar of the battle, the pounding of the French drums, the screams of the horses and the men.

She looked at him with genuine sympathy. 'Was the battle horrendous?'

'Worse than any other,' he responded. 'Except perhaps Badajoz.' He waved a hand. 'Badajoz was terrible in a different way. Waterloo was...' He paused. 'So long and so uncertain.'

'I read of it,' she said. 'So many died.'

He drained the brandy from his glass and poured himself another. 'Yes. I dream of them sometimes.' And wake up shouting and in a cold sweat.

Her voice turned soft. 'I think you must have dreamed of the battle when you were ill.'

Had he? He dreamed so many things. He dreamed of her. Or had he? Perhaps she'd been real.

'Did I wake you, Caro?' he asked.

She smiled kindly. 'You did, but you were ill.'

And he remembered she touched him, spoke to him. And he shoved her away.

He finished his drink in silence, as she finished her tea. Resisting the urge to pour another, he rose. 'I believe I will retire now.'

She looked up. Disappointed? He could not tell. 'Good night, then, Nash.'

He managed a smile. 'Tomorrow. We are rising early. We have a busy day.'

She smiled back.

Chapter Seven

He loomed large again.

Percy.

Face distorted with cruelty and pleasure.

With all her strength she shoved him away.

And watched him fall...

Terror on his face...

'Wake up, Caro! Wake up. You are dreaming.'

She opened her eyes. It was Nash.

Without thinking, she wrapped her arms around him and clung to him and shook.

He held her. 'Shh... It was only a dream. I am here. You are safe.'

The dream faded and realisation struck. She pulled away. 'Forgive me. How stupid of me.'

He remained seated on her bed. Close. His handsome face illuminated by a candle flame.

'No more stupid than my nightmares.' His gentle hand swept a lock of hair off her face.

That simple touch calmed her.

He stood and took the candle in his hand. 'Wait here a moment,' he said. 'Don't move.'

As if she weren't afraid to move. When he was gone the emotions and images from the dream returned.

After a moment a faint glow appeared in the doorway. She watched the glow grow brighter as his footsteps sounded in the hall. The candle appeared, Nash a mere silhouette behind it. As he walked closer to her, she could see he held the candle in one hand and a bottle and glass in the other. He set the candle on the bedside table and poured some contents of the bottle into the glass.

'Brandy.' He handed the glass to her. 'I brought it to my room in case I have one of my dreams.'

She gratefully sipped the mellow liquid, letting it warm her throat and chest as she swallowed. 'Your dreams are of battle, you said.'

He averted his gaze. 'Not the battle so much. I see the faces of the dead.'

She took another sip of brandy and waited for it to warm her again. 'The faces....' She saw Percy's face.

He gestured to the bed. 'May I sit?'

She nodded, finishing the brandy. He poured her another and stretched out his wounded leg. Now she could see he wore only a shirt and drawers. Of course, she wore only her nightdress. What did it matter? He'd worn less when he'd been ill.

'I dreamed of Percy,' she murmured.

He faced her but said nothing. It was as if he left it entirely to her whether to say more or remain quiet. She chose to speak.

'You asked me about Percy,' she said. 'I will tell you.' But how to tell him?

She took a breath. 'My—my marriage was not a happy one. Percy was delighted with my money—until it was gone—but I do not think he liked me overmuch.'

His brows rose. She averted her gaze.

'That day—I do not know why—he lured me to the second floor of our house, then looked at me with such loathing, it frightened me.' She shuddered to remember it. 'He lunged at me, seized my arms and pushed me to the stairway.' She looked into Nash's eyes. 'He intended to kill me.'

She glanced away again. 'I fought him. I hit him. Kicked him. Twisted away. He thrust me to the edge of the stairway.' She closed her eyes, seeing it all again. 'And let go enough to push me down the stairs. I swung away from him.' She squeezed her eyes shut against the memory. 'And when he came at me again, I shoved him with all my might. He fell down the stairs. A—a spiral staircase. He fell all the way to the bottom.' She turned her gaze to Nash again. 'I killed him.'

Nash's face looked grim in the candlelight. 'He tried to kill you.'

She covered her face with her hands and wept. Not for Percy. For herself. Before she knew it, she was enveloped in Nash's arms. He held her close and let her cry. She let herself cry, as well. To weep over how foolish she'd been to marry Percy, foolish to believe his declarations of love. She wept for her girlish hopes and dreams. For losing Nash.

She wanted to pretend none of it happened and they were still young and full of the joy of being together.

But she did collect herself, pulling away and letting his embrace end.

She wiped her face with the bed sheet. 'I—I might have wound up in Newgate prison, but one of the moneylenders to whom Percy owed a great deal of money barged in our door to collect. He witnessed everything. Of course, the *ton* preferred to believe I deliberately killed him…'

Everyone loved Percy. He was so generous, so charming, so enjoyable to be with. Ladies loved to dance with him at balls and have secret trysts with him; gentlemen loved to hunt with him or gamble with him. But word had been circulating that he was not paying his debts and some people were no longer believing that Caroline was at fault.

Her death would have solved all that. He could have said anything he wished about her after her death. Best of all, he'd be free to remarry any one of the wealthy widows who'd already shared his bed.

Nash stared at her, all curled up in the bed, making herself small. Hiding from the memories. How he understood that.

Curse Percy! Nash thought he could not detest the man more for marrying Caroline, but for trying to kill her…? He'd kill the man himself if he could.

Nash moved closer to hold her again. She leaned her head against his shoulder and her lovely hair tickled his face. It felt so comfortable to hold her like this, as though she was always meant to be in his arms.

But she'd chosen Percy's arms, he could not help thinking. Percy had held her—until Percy tried to kill her.

He held her until she fell asleep again, then gently lay her down in the bed and covered her with the blankets. He picked up the bottle, glass and candle and padded back to his bedchamber. Instead of going back to sleep he sat by the window and poured another glass of brandy. He blew out the candle flame and gazed at the garden, illuminated by moonlight shining on the white snow.

For all that he'd tried to wipe her out of his life, his mind, his soul, the emotions came rushing back. He could still see her, young and vibrant, her smile lighting up his heart like a thousand candles. She still was that to him, even now, even though she looked weary and sad.

He still loved her.

By morning Nash told himself he'd be content being in her company this Christmas. He'd not expect more. She'd been through enough.

He rose, washed, shaved and dressed himself, then made his way down to the drawing room for breakfast. The stiffness and ache in his leg eased quickly and, even with little sleep, he felt increased energy. It encouraged him.

Caroline was already seated at the table.

'Good morning,' he said, trying for the right tone of cheerfulness.

She looked wary. 'Nash,' she said quietly.

He sat across from her and surveyed the table with its simple fare of bread, butter, jam, cheese, cooked eggs and slices of ham. Respectable breakfast, he thought. Caroline had only a slice of bread and butter and a cup of tea.

'I am famished,' he remarked as he placed ham and cheese and eggs on his plate. 'Lucy did very well with this fare.'

Caroline seemed pleased at his words. 'I'll tell her you said so.'

That encouraged him. 'The servants work hard. I hope they enjoy this Christmas Eve.'

'Will you help decorate?' she asked uncertainly.

He poured himself a cup of tea. 'Of course I'll help. I look forward to it.'

Her frown disappeared. He felt unexpectedly glad of that.

'Nash, I—I am so sorry about last night,' she blurted out.

'Sorry?' That surprised him. 'Caro, you did the same for me when I was ill. We are even now, are we not?'

'I suppose.'

He leaned forward and spoke sincerely. 'What happened to you was harrowing, to say the least. I wish you had not experienced it.'

She glanced away and he feared she would become ensnared in the memory again.

He lifted his chin. 'Come, Caro. We must be happy for the servants. We want nothing to spoil their Christmas Eve.' He too quickly downed an egg and sparked a coughing fit.

She laughed.

It was worth almost choking.

Chapter Eight

Caroline nearly relaxed through the rest of breakfast. Nash was so like she remembered him that it almost felt as if no time had passed, yet so much had happened since— since he abandoned her. She found she did not want to think about that. She wanted to think about how warm and comforting his arms had been the night before, how safe and cherished she felt in his embrace.

He looked so handsome this morning, the pallor of illness gone. His blue eyes glowed in the sunlight from the window, so startling against his dark brows and hair. He'd grown magnificently into a man over these years while her youthful beauty, if she'd ever possessed any, had turned haggard and wan.

If he had not loved her then, how could he love her now? She was beyond love.

She took a last sip of her tea.

She could at least enjoy the happiness of sharing this Christmas with Nash and making this a Christmas Elliot, Lucy and Molly would never forget.

Caroline stood. 'We should start. I will collect the ribbons and other fripperies we found yesterday. Would you and Elliot begin cutting the branches into usable pieces?'

He stood as well. 'As you wish, Caro.'

At first she'd resented him calling her Caro. Now it merely seemed familiar. 'We'll meet you in the still room after we've gathered our supplies.'

She walked towards the door near the servants' stairway.

Nash hurried over and held it open for her. 'I'll probably find Elliot below stairs.'

His nearness heightened her senses. 'I'm going up. It is faster by these stairs.'

After climbing a few steps she turned to watch him going down until she could see him no more.

Caroline met Molly as she entered the hallway outside the servants' hall. Caroline carried a huge basket filled with ribbons of all colours and thin strips of white lace.

Molly gaped at it. 'Are you sure Lady Bolton will not be angry about taking the ribbons?'

'I am sure,' Caroline said. 'We'll put them all back, neat and clean, so no harm done.'

Molly riffled her fingers through the silken strands. 'They are so pretty.'

At Molly's age Caroline would have had as many ribbons as she wished and would not have given them a thought.

'Our Christmas decorations will be even prettier. Wait and see,' she said.

From down the hallway she could hear Nash's laughter. Her heart skipped a beat at the sound, so familiar, so dear.

They reached the door to the still room.

'We are ready!' Caroline lifted her basket with its colourful ware.

Nash flashed her a grin, then turned to Elliot. 'Are we ready, my friend?'

Elliot peered out from behind a stack of holly laden with red berries. 'I've never seen so much greenery in my life.'

Nash laughed. 'We are ready.'

'Shall we use the servants' hall to put everything to-gether?' Caroline gestured to the room where they'd eaten breakfast.

'Excellent idea.' Nash filled his arms with bundles of greenery.

Elliot did the same.

As they walked by the kitchen, Caroline peered in. 'Are you ready to make our finery, Lucy?'

Lucy looked up from whatever it was she was making. 'Yes,' the girl said.

'Come to the servants' hall.' Caroline caught up to the others.

No sooner had they placed their bundles on the table, than they heard the back door open.

'Yo!' Clem, the stable worker, called.

Nash poked his head out of the doorway. 'We're here!'

Clem and Will joined them.

'We found a fairly good log, Major,' he said.

Nash nodded. 'Excellent.' He turned to Caroline. 'When shall we light the yule log?'

'After dinner?' she responded.

'After dinner it is.' Nash agreed. 'Come help us with the greenery.'

Lucy looked up at Caroline, her brow furrowed. 'Ma'am, what do we do?'

Of course. They wouldn't know how to make the deco-rations, never having any at the orphanage.

'I'll show you, but you can make them any way you like.' Caroline reached for some holly and pine.

She tied the cuttings together with ribbons, then ar-ranged the leaves and needles to best advantage. When she finished, she placed her creation on the sideboard, then added two more so the entire length of the edge of the sideboard was covered with green.

'You are decorating down here?' Molly looked aghast. 'No! The decorating was for the house, not down here.'

'The greenery should be where we can see it. It is for *you*,' Caroline explained. 'Because you were left here. You deserve something special.'

'Oh, no, ma'am,' Molly went on. 'They taught us at the orphanage that we must earn what we need through hard work. We are lucky to have these positions.'

Clem spoke up. 'Listen, girl, Lord and Lady Bolton always let the servants decorate and have a Christmas Ball of their own. They even come dance with us.' He scoffed. 'Not that we want that. Can't let your hair down then, y'know.' He suddenly seemed to notice that Nash and Caroline were there. 'No offence meant, ma'am.'

'None taken, Clem,' she replied.

'My family always had a servants' ball at Christmas,' Nash said.

'So did mine.' Caroline remembered Nash's Christmas balls. She remembered dancing with him. Her own parents delayed the servants' ball until after Twelfth Night. Their house had always been full of guests at Christmas which only meant extra work for the servants.

Lucy's eyes grew wide. 'Do you mean a ball with music and dancing and all? We learned dancing, but we never went to a ball.'

'Then we should have one here.' Nash turned to Caroline. 'We could have dancing, could we not, Caro?'

How considerate to defer to her. 'We could.' The servants deserved a happy Christmas like the ones at Nash's house.

'Could you play the pianoforte, Caro?' Nash asked. 'You may be our only source of music.'

'I would be delighted to play,' she responded.

'Let us do the ball tomorrow after dinner,' Nash said.

She nodded. 'Tomorrow.'

Clem and Will excused themselves to tend to the horses. 'We'll bring the yule log in after. Where should we bring it?'

'Bring it through the front door into the Marble Hall,' Nash said. 'We'll use that fireplace.' He and Caroline had decided on this.

'And you must come for dinner,' added Caroline. 'We'll light the log and the Christmas candle then.'

Nash grinned. 'There will be wassail.'

Clem laughed. 'We'll be there, then, Major.'

They decorated the servants' hall, the butler's room, the kitchen and even the scullery. The hall would be last and they would set up refreshments there and make it ready for the yule log.

Caroline sent the servants to decorate their own bedchambers and she gathered up some of the cuttings and ribbons in a basket and started for the stairs.

'Where are you going next?' Nash asked.

He had been so amiable and helpful. He'd kept them all smiling. He was like he used to be, like she remembered, and she continued her resolve to simply enjoy being with him.

'I thought to put some greens in the drawing room,' she replied. 'And then in our bedchambers.'

'I'll help you.' He pushed away from leaning on the back of a chair and took the basket from her arms.

He favoured his bad leg, she noticed, and she thought she'd do better carrying the basket, but she did not say anything.

When they reached the drawing room, he placed the basket on the table. 'I'll sit and watch,' he said, choosing one of the comfortable chairs.

Caroline arranged some pine and holly cuttings in a vase she'd left in the room earlier.

'They are enjoying themselves so far, do you not think?' Nash raised his wounded leg onto the stool.

'Oh, I think so!' she responded.

She credited it all to Nash. He filled the time with laughter.

She lined the mantel with spruce adorned with ribbons, acutely aware of the silence between them.

He broke it. 'That looks nice. Smells nice, too.'

He always broke the silence between them, she realised. It did her no credit to fail at making conversation with him, but there was too much to say.

Best to stick to the task at hand. 'I think it is enough.' She picked up the basket again. 'I'll do our bedchambers now.'

Nash rose and again took the basket. He hoped she had not noticed his gaze always drifting back to her. How familiar it felt to see her move so gracefully.

How had she become so comfortable creating the decorations and placing them in to best advantage? At her parents' estate the servants decorated for Christmas.

As they walked to the stairway, he wondered if she was tired. He'd heard her rise early.

'You know, you do not have to decorate my bedchamber,' he said as they climbed the stairs.

She glanced at him. 'Would you rather do it yourself?'

He almost laughed. 'Me? I'd make a muck of it.'

She laughed. 'I do not see how you could. You can manage to put cuttings in a vase. I brought one upstairs to use in your room.'

'That was thoughtful,' he said sincerely.

Her cheeks tinged pink. 'It was very little trouble, believe me. And it is no trouble for me to do it, if you wish.'

'I would be grateful.' It was baffling that she had been

willing to help him at all. Or to work so closely with the servants. He admired her for that.

He added, 'The scent of the pine and spruce reminds me of being out of doors. That pleases me.'

She smiled.

They reached her room.

'The vases are in here,' she said. 'I'll get the one for your room.'

She'd chosen a vase for his room?

Not only chosen it but found one that matched the chinoiserie wallpaper that had all but driven him mad during his illness. The green of the vase matched the climbing bamboo of the wallpaper, as well as being suited for holding pine and spruce and holly. It touched him that she'd gone to that much trouble for him.

'There,' she said as she placed the vase of greenery on his mantel, next to the clock that had moved so slowly when she'd quarantined him. She stepped back to survey her work. 'It is not much.'

He smiled at her. 'Caro, it is enough. You've done more than enough for everybody.' He gestured to a chair. 'Sit a moment and rest.'

She obliged him and he gratefully sat on the other chair and raised his leg.

She looked concerned. 'Is your leg paining you?'

He hated looking weak in her eyes. 'It is trifling.' He changed the subject. 'What's left of our plans?'

'We need to set up in the Marble Hall,' she responded. 'We should do that soon. We need to make the wassail...' She trailed off. 'Oh, and I have cloth and ribbons to hold the coins you will be giving them.'

'I appreciate that.' He didn't know about Clem and Will, but the orphans surely had never received a Christmas gift.

She gazed at him with something like admiration. 'I

think you are kind to give them gifts. I—I did not bring enough money with me to give them vails.' Her voice was full of regret.

'Do not worry over that, Caro,' he said. 'We will say the money came from both of us.'

She stared at him a long time before responding, her voice soft. 'Thank you, Nash. That would be very good of you.'

Caroline hurried to her room and shut the door behind her.

He did not know of the loss of her fortune. Nobody did. Except her man of business, that was. She'd not wanted anyone to know how dire her straits had become.

Caroline suspected the servants were too new to even know about vails. Whatever he gave would likely be more than they'd ever had in their pockets. Nash had always been generous.

She placed the basket of cuttings on the table and reached for the vase, jabbing one cutting after the other into the vase. The scent of pine filled her nostrils. Would she ever smell Christmas evergreens and not think of Nash?

All those years with Percy, she'd forced herself not to think of Nash. Occasionally a memory would arise unbidden, a flash of something they'd done together or merely a flash of his smile. She'd quickly remind herself then that Nash did not love her. He'd left her at the altar.

Now, though, it was like a dam had broken and she knew she'd remember every moment of being with him. Especially here, as the man he'd become.

She placed her vase of greenery on the mantel, like she'd placed his, then undid the laces of her dress. She'd laid out another dress to change into, a dress no more elegant than the one she'd been wearing, but at least it was different. After donning her dress, she looked through her portmanteau, hoping to find something that might adorn it, something fit for the lighting of the yule log.

She found a gold heart-shaped locket that had once belonged to her mother. It was of little value, not worth selling like her other jewellery.

She fastened it around her neck.

Chapter Nine

Nash steadied the ladder while Elliot hung the mistletoe from the hall's chandelier. It was the finishing touch on the preparations. Elliot, Clem and Will had already moved a table and chairs from other rooms to serve as their dinner table. Caroline created an arrangement of evergreens around the Christmas candle for the table's centre. Molly and Lucy filled every spare space in the room with the rest of the pine, spruce and holly, saving seven sprigs for the yule log lighting. They even moved the pianoforte into the space.

Caroline, Molly and Lucy brought food up from the kitchen. Bread and cheese. Jams and butter. Slices of beef. Gingerbread cakes. Dishes of nuts. Dried fruits. All on the table at once. The wassail bowl brimming with drink was encircled by glasses waiting to be filled.

Nash had to smile at the servants. They could hardly contain their excitement. He caught each of them pausing to gaze around the room, filled with greenery, food and anticipation. He remembered how excited Caroline and he were that one Christmas Eve at his parents' country house, waiting for the yule log to be brought in, but that was because they were together, was it not?

Caroline also watched them with pleasure kindred to his own, Nash believed, but she also seemed subdued, as if she'd been robbed of gaiety. He understood. War had stolen his gaiety, had it not?

They had all changed clothes, the servants wearing what Nash suspected were their finest churchgoing clothes. Caroline's dress was quite plain, though. Perhaps she did not want to outshine the maids. He wore his red uniform coat.

Clem appointed himself master of ceremonies for the night. The stableman insisted that he knew precisely how to conduct the evening. Nash glanced at Caroline to see if she approved. She did not seem to mind.

'Let us begin, everyone!' Clem called. 'Come here. I will tell you where to stand while Will and I bring in the log.'

He positioned them near the door. Molly, Elliot and Lucy on one side; Nash and Caroline on the other. Will waited at the doorway.

Clem handed them each a sprig of evergreen.

He then stood at the door, facing them. 'Will and I are about to bring in the yule log or, as we say here in Lincoln-shire, the gule block. The evergreen in your hands stands for the woes of the past. When Will and I pass you with the log, touch the log with your sprig of evergreen. This will ward off evil spirits. After we pass you by, follow us to the fireplace. Be sure to bring your sprig with you.'

He nodded to Will who opened the door. A huge log sat right outside the doorway. Will and Clem hoisted it on their shoulders and carried it inside the hall. Elliot closed the door behind them and hurried back to his place. As the log passed by them, Molly and Lucy solemnly touched their sprig of evergreen to the log. Elliot, next. If woes came from evil spirits, Nash was more than glad to ward them off. He tapped his sprig against the log. Caroline was last. Her expression was even more solemn than Molly and Lucy's. She carefully tapped her sprig against the log.

Clem and Will carried the log to the huge fireplace, the only fireplace in the house that would accommodate it. Like soldiers performing a drill, they took the log off their shoulders and placed it on the hearth which had been prepared with plenty of kindling.

Clem took a bottle of wine and poured it over the log, then he turned to his audience. 'This good wine will wash away evil spirits and protect the house from ghosts and goblins.'

Lucy gasped. 'Ghosts and goblins!'

Clem smiled at her. 'Do not fear. The yule log never fails to do its job.' He surveyed them all. 'Now, who is the youngest among us?'

Molly piped up. 'Lucy is.'

'Lucy girl, step up here,' he ordered.

The kitchen maid hesitated, but Molly gave her a little shove.

Clem told her. 'You are going to light the yule log.'

He lit a taper from a nearby candle and handed it to her.

Lucy crept closer to the fireplace, almost entering the hearth herself. She guided the flame of the taper to the kindling beneath the log. It quickly turned to flames.

Clem intoned, 'Protect this house from all evil.'

They all watched intently for the fire to catch on the log. When it did, there was an audible sound of relief.

He gestured with his head. 'Now take turns throwing your sprigs into the fire. If it catches fire, your woes are gone. Lucy first.'

One by one they threw their sprigs in the fire and watched the flames catch them. Caroline was last and again she paused a moment with eyes closed before throwing her sprig in the fire. It landed at the edge of the yule log and remained green. The others shouted encouragement, as if their words could make it catch fire, but Caroline looked ashen, Nash thought.

He took the brass fireplace poker from its rack and pushed Caroline's evergreen sprig a few inches. It instantly burst into flames.

'A little help cannot hurt.' He grinned.

Everyone laughed.

Except Caroline.

Nash returned the poker to the rack and turned back to everyone. 'Wassail, anyone?'

The wassail made them all merry and Caroline could not help but enjoy their communal dinner. She was amused by Clem assuming the role of host which he performed to perfection. And she loved that Nash did not seem to mind at all, although he'd been the logical one for the role. The barriers between servant, stable worker and aristocrat receded for the moment. How lovely they could simply enjoy each other's company.

They'd started dinner as the sky was turning to dusk, and the sun had set completely by the time they'd finished the gingerbread and sweetmeats. Clem proclaimed it was time to light the Christmas candle, the largest and fattest candle they could find in the house.

'Who will light it?' Molly asked.

Clem looked at Nash. 'The head of the household. The Major, I suppose it is.'

'I do not know if I am the head of *this* household,' he said affably. 'But I'll light it.'

'From the yule log,' Clem directed.

Nash carried a taper to the fireplace and lit it from the log. He carried it to the table and lit the Christmas candle.

'Now if it burns through the night until Christmas

morn, good luck will come to this house and all who are in it.' Clem lifted his glass and began to sing.

Here we come a wassailing
Among the leaves so green...

Will joined him in the chorus, then Molly sang a new stanza.

'Sing the chorus with me,' Molly said to Elliot and Lucy. 'We know this song.'

They all sang the chorus. They sang until no one could remember any more stanzas.

And they refilled their glasses with wassail after it was over.

Caroline moved over to the pianoforte and began playing first 'The Twelve Days of Christmas', then 'Bring a Torch', 'Jeanette Isabella', 'God Rest You Merry Gentlemen' and every Christmas song she could remember.

Their voices sounded beautiful, echoing through the hall, filling the space with happiness and good will, blending as if one. It was magical, as if everyone's woes had indeed burned up in the fire, as if they were all good friends of long standing—she and Nash could certainly claim a connection of long standing. Her heart felt near bursting whenever she gazed at him, so resplendent in his red coat, so admirable in his camaraderie.

When she had exhausted her repertoire, she placed her hands in her lap. 'Those are all I know.'

But without skipping a beat, Molly began another song a cappella, in her sweet, pure soprano.

Alas, my love, you do me wrong
To cast me off discourteously...

The room fell completely silent except for Molly's sweet, pure soprano voice singing 'Greensleeves'. It was such an old song, the lament of a young man cast off by the woman he loved. Lucy joined Molly for the second verse and, as the two young maids sang, Caroline felt the pain of rejection, as if the lyrics were her words and the emotions of the song hers as well. She could not make herself look at Nash; it was all she could do to hold herself together as the pain of what might have been washed over her.

The maids began the last verse but it was quickly taken over by a male voice. Nash's lovely baritone voice.

Nash sang.

Ah, Greensleeves, now farewell, adieu
To God I pray to prosper thee
For I am still thy lover true
Come once again and love me.

Molly and Lucy joined him in the final chorus.

And who but my lady Greensleeves?

The song ended, but its spell lasted several seconds before they all—that is, Elliot, Clem and Will—began clapping.

Nash gazed at Caroline. Was he seeing correctly? Were those tears on her cheeks? He'd thought her impassive expression had been a mere reflection of the lady of the song. It might have been written about Caroline, after all.

Finally Clem stood. 'It is time to end our party. Tomorrow, after all, is Christmas.'

Tomorrow would be Christmas dinner and their Christmas ball.

Caroline stood, quickly wiping her face with her fingers. 'Yes. We must tend to the dishes.'

'No.' Molly stopped her with a raised hand. 'You did all the music on the pianoforte. Lucy, Elliot and I will clean up.'

'Will and I need to see to the horses,' Clem said. 'Good night.'

'Thank you, Clem,' Nash called after him. 'You led us well.'

The stablemen waved farewell. The maids cleared the table and Elliot doused the candles in the chandelier.

'Good night, Major.' Elliot bowed. 'Good night, ma'am.'

'Good night, Elliot,' Caroline said.

He and Caroline were alone with only the light from the Christmas candle and the fireplace to illuminate the room. His emotions still churned from the song and from seeing her tears. The walls of the spacious room seemed to close in on him. What's more, she was standing directly beneath the mistletoe. Although like the lady in the song she was completely out of reach, completely absorbed in her own thoughts.

He interrupted them. 'Caro, would you do something for me?'

She looked at him as if surprised to see him still there. 'Of course,' she replied. 'What do you need?'

You, he wanted to say. 'Would you take a walk with me outside? I need to be outside.' It was a foolish request. Surely she'd refuse.

'I—I would like that, Nash.'

They found warm cloaks and sturdy boots and walked out the garden door. The snow had done enough melting to make the path to the fountain passable. The night was clear and the moonlight shimmered on the white snow making it easy to see the way. Nash welcomed the bracing air and the wide expanse of the garden. No walls here.

He offered his arm, and they walked in silence.

For once Caroline spoke first. 'What do you do after this?' she asked. 'Where will you be bound?'

'To London,' he responded. 'I have a chance for a position in the War Office. My regiment will disband so I need a position to keep my commission.'

'London is a very desirable place to be,' she responded, but her tone was flat, as if speaking only what was expected.

Nash did not want polite conversation. He was burning for more from her. The song had affected him, as it affected her. He had to know. Once and for all he had to know....

They were halfway to the fountain, before he gathered the courage to speak. 'Caro, I—I want you to know—this time with you—' Be coherent, you fool! 'This time with you has been very—pleasurable.'

Her step slowed and her voice was little more than a whisper. 'Has it?'

'It has,' he mumbled, but that was not what he burned to say.

Don't lose courage now, he scolded himself.

He stopped and held her by her shoulders so he could face her. 'Caro, I must know—I must ask—why? Why did you send me that letter?'

Her brows drew together. 'What letter?'

'The letter!' he repeated, exasperated. 'The letter telling me you were marrying Percy.'

She pulled out of his grasp. 'I never wrote you a letter, Nash. How could I? I did not know where you were.'

He removed his hat and rubbed a hand through his hair.

'You knew where I was. I was in London. At the Steven's Hotel.'

She shook her head. 'No, that was before.'

'Before?' His voice rose. 'Before what?'

'Before you left for Portugal!' she cried, turning away and striding back to the house.

He caught up to her. 'Wait, Caro. Why do you think I went to Portugal? I left because of the letter.'

'I did not write you a letter!' she insisted. 'I never wrote to you at all. Ever. When you left me at the altar, I never wanted to see you again. I still do not!' She strode away again.

He called after her. 'But—but you cried off. You cancelled the wedding.'

She stopped and gaped at him.

'You said in the letter that you were crying off, that you cancelled the wedding.' He swallowed against the bitter memory. 'You said you preferred to marry Percy.'

Her mouth dropped open. 'Percy,' she breathed. She walked back to him. 'I was waiting for you at the altar. Our witnesses were there. My parents. The clergyman. We were all waiting. Then Percy came in, all distraught, to tell me you were not coming. You did not want to marry me after all. You wanted to join a regiment bound for Portugal and the war. You wanted the glory, he said. Not me.'

Nash felt the blood drain from his face. 'You were there? At the church? You thought I—?' He squinted and shook his head. 'But the letter was in a feminine hand. Yours. Percy said you asked him to deliver it personally.'

'It was not my writing, because I did not write it.' She paced in front of him. 'If Sybella were here, she could tell you that I believed to the day of our wedding that you wanted to marry me.'

He let it all painfully sink in. 'Percy did this. Percy.' It seemed so clear now. 'I believed him. We'd been friends since school. I believed him. He did this to us.'

Her voice turned scathing. 'He was, oh, so kind to me—after your absence. So understanding. So attentive. So concerned. So *devoted*. He insisted the only way to make the gossip stop was to marry. So much happened in so short a time. My mother got sick, then my father. They died and I was alone. He convinced me—' She broke off as if choking on her words. 'I wondered later if he'd killed them. Poisoned them or something. It seemed far-fetched—until he tried to kill me.'

Nash put his arms around her. 'Caro. Caro. Forgive me. I believed the letter. I believed Percy. And I never heard any of this.'

All these years he'd fought to forget her. He'd thrown himself into battle, never caring if he lived or died. Because life lost its meaning when he lost her. Had Percy counted on that as well? That Nash would die in battle?

The wind picked up, swirling crystals of snow around them. Caroline shivered and Nash held her tighter.

'We should go back in,' he said. 'It is getting colder.'

They walked back shoulder to shoulder, but not touching. Thoughts of how Percy had tricked them burned through his mind.

'Caro,' he said. 'I would never have left you at the altar. Did you not know that? I would never have hurt you that way.'

She did not answer for a moment. 'Did you not know I would never have written you such a letter? Did you not know my love was constant?'

No, Percy had convinced him that, as a younger son of scant means, he was unworthy of her. Percy was a baronet. He could give her a title, entrée into society.

What fools they'd both been. Rather, what fools Percy had made of them both.

They walked back to the house and left their boots and wet cloaks in the hall to dry. The black and white marble floor was cold under his stockinged feet. The Christmas candle still burned brightly lighting their way. The yule log hissed and popped and glowed as well.

Nash walked over to the fireplace and poked at the log. It burned slowly, just as expected. Had the Christmas legend come true? Had their previous woes truly gone up in smoke? Nothing worse could happen to them, could it? Nothing had been worse than believing she'd stopped loving him. He'd been wrong, though, all these years. She had loved him. She'd been there at the church to marry him.

But could she ever love him again?

Chapter Ten

Caroline watched Nash silhouetted against the light from the fireplace. Percy tricked him into leaving her. Percy had devastated every aspect of her life. He'd even wanted her dead.

But he hadn't killed her, had he? He'd beaten her down until she thought the best she could do was simply survive. She'd do more than survive even now, she vowed. She'd find a way to thrive again, even if thriving meant being the best beggar on the street.

Nash *had* loved her. That changed everything.

He walked back to her.

'Do you see where you are standing?' He pointed above her.

She glanced up. She was beneath the mistletoe.

He smiled. 'Do you remember standing under the mistletoe at my parents' Christmas ball?'

How could she forget? She'd been so happy then. 'I do remember.'

'I kissed you,'

She looked up at him, her eyes glittering. 'As I recall, it was not much of a kiss.'

He laughed. 'Well, I do believe it was my very first one.'

They had been so young.

He moved closer, close enough to touch her. 'Perhaps I need more practice.'

Her body flared into awareness of him, so close. His scent filled her nostrils, all man and fresh air and woody smoke. He leaned down, his lips an inch from hers. He hesitated, giving her the choice. She could step away if she wished. Nash always gave her a choice. When had Percy done so?

Percy. She would not think of him. No longer would he come between her and Nash. Ever.

She closed the distance, touching her lips to his. It was akin to her evergreen sprig suddenly bursting into flames. She wrapped her arms around his neck and deepened the kiss.

His arms encircled her and pressed her against him. He kissed her lips, her cheek, the tender skin beneath her ear. 'Caro, Caro,' he murmured. 'I yearned for this. I am sorry. So sorry.'

Her body ached for him. When younger, she hadn't known what that aching meant, but she knew now. Not that she'd ever ached for Percy, but Percy taught her about carnal love. What harm could it do to make love with Nash now? She was a widow. Widows could do such things.

And who knew what the future would bring? This might be her only chance to know what it was to make love with Nash. If tonight was all she could have, she'd very well enjoy it.

'Take me to your bed, Nash,' she managed between his kisses.

Nash pulled away, far enough to peruse her. 'Do you mean this?'

'I—I do mean it.' She looked suddenly uncertain. 'But only if you wish it.'

'Wish it?' He laughed again. 'Caro, I can barely restrain myself.'

He'd been drawn to her from his first sight of her on his sick bed, but he'd talked himself out of giving that attraction too much credit. Merely old memories, he'd called it. But, here, holding her in his arms, his body burned hotter for her than the yule fire.

'You must be certain about it, Caro.' Surely it was too soon. They'd only now learned the truth about what happened to them.

She flung her arms around him again and held him as tightly as he'd just held her. 'I am certain, Nash.'

He wanted her, too. Desperately. Too strongly to resist. 'Well, then.'

He scooped her up into his arms and carried her across the room to the stairway.

'You are not going to carry me the whole way,' she protested.

'Why not?' he asked.

'Because of your leg. It is too much, Nash.'

His leg was already paining him, though he hated admitting it.

'Besides,' she went on, 'we need a candle to light our way.'

Unlike most country houses Bolton House's staircase was in a smaller hall to the east of the main hall where they'd had their yule log celebration. The light from the Marble Hall barely reached to the bottom steps of the staircase.

He let her down. 'A moment.' He went back to the hall and returned with a lighted candle.

With their hands clasped, they walked up the stairs together and continued down the guest room hallway.

'Your room or mine?' he asked.

'Mine,' she said.

Once inside the room, he placed the candle on a table and took her in his arms again possessing her mouth with his kiss. Was it possible he was here with Caroline? He'd not dared to dream of holding her, kissing her, since the day that letter shattered his life.

When he released her, she unbuttoned his red coat and eased it off his shoulders and hung it over a chair. She pulled off his shirt next and for a moment rested her hands on his chest. He thought he would burst from wanting her.

Instead, he gently turned her around and untied the laces of her dress. She let it fall to the floor before picking it up again and draping it over another chair. Then she faced him again. Her stays tied in the front. She watched his face as he untied its strings and loosened it until it too fell to the floor.

She stepped out of the pool of cloth at her feet, and he scooped her in his arms again and carried her to the bed. Placing her on it, he asked her again, 'Are you sure, Caro? What of the risks?'

'Of getting with child?' She averted her gaze. 'There is no risk. I cannot conceive.'

A pang of sadness for her stopped him, but she reached for the buttons of his trousers and undid them.

Had she done this for Percy? he wondered, then hated himself for even thinking of the scoundrel. A jealous part of him, a remnant of his belief in the letter, hated that she'd lain with Percy. That part of him wanted to grill her about every aspect of it, but the bigger part of him simply wanted to love her.

His trousers, drawers and stockings were tossed aside. He climbed onto the bed. She removed her shift.

His gaze flickered over her naked body. 'Caro, you are beautiful,' he breathed.

* * *

His compliment was like a jab to Caroline's heart. How many times has she been told she was anything but beautiful?

He glanced up at her face, looking puzzled. 'Do you not believe me? That you are beautiful?'

She moved farther away. 'I know I am not. I am too thin. Too plain. Too—'

He touched his finger to her lips. 'To me you are beautiful,' he whispered. 'You have always been beautiful.'

'The years have not been kind to me,' she protested.

'More of Percy's lies, I suspect,' he shot back. 'But he is gone, and he will never hurt us again.'

She was not sure of that. His profligacy had impoverished her, and his words still echoed in her head. And then there was the memory of the day he died.

She covered herself with the bed linens.

'Look at me,' he insisted, sweeping his hand down his torso. 'The years have not been kind to me either. I am scarred.'

She looked at him. 'But you are magnificent!'

He gave a surprised laugh, but quickly sobered. He gently pulled the bed linen from her hands. 'And you are beautiful.'

He moved to her side and held her face. He kissed her again. His words, his touch, were like a soothing balm.

Give yourself to this moment, she reminded herself again.

Gently he stroked her skin. Her cheek. Her neck. He drew a finger down her breast, the touch so soft she was surprised at her body's response. As he stroked, her muscles turned to butter. She gazed at him. How dear his face was, so much like when they were young, but even more handsome. And his expression was loving. Reverent. It made her feel a little like she'd been before…

'Are you ready, Caro?' he murmured.

Ready? He was asking? Again he gave her a choice. He always gave her a choice.

Suddenly she knew. 'I am ready, Nash.'

'Good,' he groaned. 'Because I am more than ready.'

He rose over her and entered her slowly, carefully, as if she might break otherwise. She knew very well she would not break. She'd not broken before, hard as Percy tried.

She braced for the pain, but, to her surprise, there was none. No need to grit her teeth, only a sweet, delicious pleasure. And connection, a connection she'd never felt before.

'Oh, Caro.' His breath tickled her ear.

He moved faster and the pleasure increased. Caroline was seized with sensations she'd never experienced before. A need that grew more and more intense, until he cried out and the pleasure exploded inside her, waves and waves of pleasure. Of connection.

Her limbs turned to butter once more and he seemed to melt on top of her.

He quickly slid off to her side. She turned to face him, not wanting that feeling of connection to end. He smiled at her a lazy, peaceful sort of smile.

She thought she ought to say something. Thank you seemed inadequate, and no other words came to her.

He kissed her cheek. 'This was a perfect day, Caro. And the perfect end to a perfect day.'

The clock on the mantel struck the hour. Caroline counted the chimes. One. Two, Three… Ten. Eleven. Twelve.

Caroline smiled back. 'Happy Christmas.'

The next morning Nash woke from blessed uninterrupted sleep with Caroline at his side. He stayed next to her watching her peaceful face as she slept. She looked more like the girl he'd known than at any time these last few days. She was still in there somewhere, that joyful young Caroline who'd never had a care in the world.

Someday he'd ask her to tell him about her life with Percy, but not today. Today was Christmas and a day for celebration. The roads might be too treacherous to make their way to church services, but Nash decided he'd steal a few moments in the Boltons' chapel, rarely used these days according to his friend. Nash needed to say a prayer of thanks for bringing Caroline back to him.

Caroline's eyes flickered open, and she stared in wonder at him before breaking into a smile. 'I did not know you were real at first.'

He took her in his arms. 'Yes. We are both real.'

They made sweet love again.

Nash had been used to a soldier's kind of love, a furtive coupling with a willing woman, the act meaning nothing more to each of them than a momentary respite from life's trials. With Caroline the lovemaking was something else entirely. Instead of making him wish to forget, making love to her made him want to live on, to become a better man, to please her all his days. She'd *loved* him. She'd *not* chosen another. She'd loved *him*.

As he reluctantly left her and gathered his clothes to take to his own room, the aura from the lovemaking cleared a little. She'd wanted to marry him back then as planned, but he did not know at all about what she would want now. He knew he never wanted to leave her side, but perhaps she had other plans. Perhaps she preferred the freedom of being a widow.

Perhaps he ought not to presume anything, but simply see how things were between them as the days went on. That is what he would do, starting with enjoying this

Christmas Day and making certain that the three servants enjoyed it. And Caroline. Especially Caroline.

He washed and dressed and, before he left the room, placed in his pocket the cloth purses of coins he'd fixed for the servants and stablemen.

He knocked at Caroline's door.

'Come in.' She smiled when seeing him. 'I am ready.'

She wore the same dress as the day before, but she could have worn a rag and he'd have thought her lovely in it.

Nash loved that they were so easy with each other this morning. 'Shall we give the coins at breakfast?'

They told the servants they would eat breakfast in the servants' hall.

They walked side by side to the stairs.

Caroline started down first. She looked over her shoulder. 'I was thinking we should take some time to gather in the chapel. To honour Christmas, you know, since we cannot attend services.'

Nash grinned. 'You must stop reading my thoughts, Caro. I had the same idea.'

She smiled back. 'That used to happen when we were children, did it not?'

Yes, they had always been likeminded.

They reached the hall, the scene of their merriment the night before.

Caroline hurried over to the table where the Christmas candle had been lit. 'Look, the candle still burns!'

It was little more than a pool of wax, but the flame, tiny now, still burned.

'We shall have a year of good fortune,' Nash said. Not misfortune, like the year past.

The flame flickered a little, then went out, leaving only a thin line of smoke that disappeared quickly.

Caroline looked up at him. 'At least we can tell the others the flame lasted until Christmas Day.'

'Indeed we can.' Nash glanced at the fireplace as they turned away from the table. 'And that the yule log still burns.'

They passed beneath the mistletoe, but Nash stopped her. He pointed up. 'My good fortune has already begun.'

He kissed her. Not shyly as he'd done when a youth, not tentatively as he'd first kissed her last night. He kissed her as if she were the most precious treasure a man could hold.

They continued on to the kitchen where Elliot and the maids were busy with the day's preparations. The planned highlight of the day was to be the dinner followed by their makeshift ball. The three servants' happiness filled the room as completely as the aroma of baking bread.

'Happy Christmas,' Nash said as they entered.

'Happy Christmas!' the three responded all at once.

'Take a rest for a moment,' Caroline said. 'Come have a cup of tea with us while we eat breakfast.' Breakfast this morning was simply porridge and tea.

Lucy spooned out bowls of porridge from a pot on the fire and placed them on a tray. 'The bread is almost ready to come out of the oven. I cannot rest until then.'

'Come after it's out of the oven, then,' Caroline said. 'I'm certain we won't be finished.'

Elliot carried the tray of porridge to the servants' hall and Molly carried the pot of tea, sugar and milk. If they noticed the wrapped packages in Nash's and Caroline's hands, they did not show it. The bowls, spoons, cups and saucers were the plain dishes the servants used. There was no need to use the fine china, although that was precisely what they would do at dinner. Dinner was to be special in every way they could make it so.

As Nash and Caroline ate their porridge, Elliot and

Molly chattered on about the night before, all the wonderful things that they'd all shared.

'We did not know you had such a beautiful singing voice, Molly,' Nash said.

'Nor you, sir,' she responded shyly.

'Nor Clem,' Elliot added.

They all laughed.

Lucy came in wiping her hands on her apron. Caroline poured the tea for them all and it did not seem strange at all. The camaraderie they'd shared in their isolation made them equals for the moment.

Nash took a sip of tea before speaking. 'At our houses the children always received gifts on Christmas or on St Nicholas Day. Or both. You were not so lucky, but Caro—' he used his name for her without thinking '—Caro and I decided that you should have gifts this Christmas.'

He handed them each a cloth purse.

Elliot untied the ribbon. 'Major!' He spilled the coins into his palm.

Molly and Lucy carefully untied the ribbons on theirs as well. 'Oh!' they each exclaimed.

'I never had so much money in my life,' cried Lucy.

'Find a safe place to keep them,' Nash warned. 'When the snow melts and you can get to the village, you can purchase whatever you like.'

Their repeated thanks went on with no end in sight until Caroline spoke. 'Are things secure in the kitchen so we can all spend a few minutes in the Chapel? It is Christmas.'

'We attended services every Christmas,' Molly said.

There was a lot for them all to be thankful for, Nash thought.

Chapter Eleven

After their quiet moments of prayer in the chapel. Elliot and Nash handled various chores within the house, including tending to the fireplaces in the rooms they used and replenishing candles wherever needed. Caroline and the maids spent the rest of Christmas morning seeing to the food for dinner, especially the goose to be roasted.

Nash was never far from Caroline's mind, nor the love-making they had shared. Would he want to share her bed again?

As they worked, Molly and Lucy talked about the ball.

'We do not know many dances,' Lucy said.

'That should not pose a problem,' Caroline responded. 'Tell me what dances you would like and I'll look for the music for them. '

'I should like to dance the waltz,' sighed Molly.

'I am certain Lady Bolton has music for waltzes.' Caroline might even manage playing one by heart.

'Molly, you are talking nonsense.' Lucy broke in. 'We do not know how to dance the waltz,'

'I should still like to dance it,' protested Molly.

'And I would like to wear a proper ball gown,' Lucy shot back.

Molly's voice turned dreamy. 'A proper ball gown.' She sighed again. She turned to Caroline. 'What colour is your ball gown, ma'am?'

'Goodness. I did not bring a ball gown.' Caroline had sold all of hers on Petticoat Lane.

She continued to stir the soup and Molly to peel the potatoes.

'Ma'am?' Molly put her knife down.

'Yes?'

A mischievous look came into Molly's eye. 'I know where Lady Bolton stores her old gowns. We could find one of hers for you to wear.'

For Nash to see her in a pretty dress, even an out of fashion one? How could Caroline resist?

A few minutes later she and Molly were up in the attic, looking through the trunk where Sybella stored old gowns. Beautiful gowns in pale colours. Pink and yellow and blue and violet. Why should only Caroline have the pleasure of wearing something so pretty?

'We are going to select dresses for you and Lucy, as well,' she told Molly.

Molly's eyes brightened even as she protested, 'Oh, ma'am. We couldn't.'

'Of course you can!' Carolyn pulled out dress after dress until they found three perfect ones. 'They might need a little altering, but I can do that while you and Lucy finish cooking.'

This makeshift ball was going to be as proper a one as Carolyn could make it for Molly and Lucy.

And for herself.

By four o'clock they were sitting down to the Christmas dinner, having brought all the dishes to the table in the Marble Hall for convenience's sake, except the plum pudding which would make its entrance last.

Caroline surveyed their fare as Elliot served the soup. The goose was roasted to a perfect golden brown, as were the potatoes cooked in its juices. The Brussels sprouts, squash and carrots added colour and the mince pies made it look like Christmas. They'd even managed a jelly, although it was listing to one side.

Nash had raided the wine cellar, choosing well. He'd brought up a bottle of whisky for Clem and Will, who were quite happy with the gift of coins as well. Everyone was jovial and, after the busy preparations, everyone came to the meal with big appetites.

Caroline, Molly and Lucy had not changed into the dresses they'd found in the attic. They were not the sort of dresses to prepare food in and they were working on the meal right up to the point of serving it.

They served the meal on a pretty set of china and crystal, although prudently did not select Sybella's best china and crystal. Lucy, who took the meal as a personal reflection on her worth, looked by turns apprehensive and gratified as she watched the others taste the food and declare it delicious.

Most of the talk was of the food and all they'd done to prepare it, but Clem spoke up in a lull of the food's praises. 'There was a goodly amount of melting today.' It had been a sunny day with clear blue skies. 'Will and I went out to see how the roads fared. I suspect we'll see traffic on the roads tomorrow. They look passable to me.'

Caroline frowned. This little world they'd created out of necessity could not last, not if the greater world could again travel to its doors. She hoped they'd at least have until Twelfth Night.

Nash looked equally dismayed. 'One of you should get a

message to Lord and Lady Bolton. They should know there was never any typhus and no illness of any kind at present.'

'Aye, thought so myself,' said Clem. 'You write the note, Major, and I'll deliver it tomorrow.'

There were sad faces all around the table.

'I have had the best time. I will be sad when the others come back,' Lucy blurted out. It was what they all were thinking.

Caroline gave her an understanding smile. 'We will be certain to tell Lord and Lady Bolton how well you, Molly and Elliot did.' She turned to the stablemen. 'And how helpful you both were, Clem and Will. We cannot thank you enough.'

'Here, here, we should not become sad.' Nash lifted his wine glass. 'Here's to the rest of the evening and to hoping they do not travel back right away.'

'I'll drink to that,' Clem said.

And when that toast was finished, Nash asked, 'Is it about time for the Christmas pudding?'

'I'll drink to that, too.' Clem lifted his glass again.

They all helped clear the table, taking the dishes down to the kitchen and the scullery. Nash was elected to bring in the Christmas pudding after the others were seated again. The servants had never eaten Christmas pudding, so it fell to Nash to pour the brandy over it, set it aflame and bring it to the table to the sounds of oohs and ahhs.

They managed to eat the entire amount and, after they were done, the ladies sent the men down to the kitchen to start washing the dishes and putting things away.

'We must get ready for the ball,' Caroline told them.

Nash, Elliot, Clem and Will had removed their coats and rolled up their shirtsleeves to tackle washing the dishes. It was not easy work, dipping hands in hot, soapy water and rinsing in clean hot water. They'd done a fairly decent job of cleaning up from the meal when they went back up to the Marble Hall.

Nash poured each of them glasses of brandy to sip while they waited for the ladies to arrive. Nash's only complaint about the near-perfect day was that he and Caroline had no time alone. Still, his heart gladdened to see her working beside Molly and Lucy, thinking always of them. She'd not shirked from any of the hard work, she, who had never had to lift a finger as a girl.

He hoped Bolton and his wife would stay with her parents until Twelfth Night. It made sense they would. He and Caroline needed to learn to be friends again and, he hoped, learn to love each other again. As much as he cherished it, their lovemaking had more to do with the past than right now. They had to become acquainted with who they were right now.

He heard the ladies' voices coming down the stairs in the little Marble Hall.

'Are you ready for us?' he heard Caroline call.

Clem downed the rest of his brandy. Will and Elliot turned towards the doorway of the little hall. Nash rose from his chair and the others followed his example.

Lucy was the first to appear. She looked lovely in a pale yellow dress that seemed to make her brown skin glow. Her hair was pulled up high on her head, tied with a ribbon and curled into a mass of ringlets. She walked to the centre of the hall and curtsied to them. Then came Molly, equally resplendent in a pale blue dress that matched her eyes. Her hair was also atop her head, secured with a ribbon, but her curls were looser, longer, and moved as she walked.

'Where did they get those dresses?' Elliot asked, awe-struck.

But Nash had turned his gaze to the doorway, waiting for Caroline. No grand entrance for her. She slipped into the room and stood behind the maids. The maids wore dresses with gauze overskirts. They looked like society misses making their come-outs. Caroline, on the other hand, wore a gown of gold silk, simply trimmed with matching lace. She was elegance personified.

'Gentlemen,' she said. 'You must take turns partnering with these two fine ladies. The first dance will be a country dance.'

'I must pass,' Nash said. 'The dancing is too lively for my leg.'

Will, quiet Will, stepped forward. 'I'll dance with Miss Lucy. If she will have me.'

Lucy giggled. 'I'll dance with you, Will.'

Elliot walked up to Molly. 'May I have this dance?'

Molly nodded.

Caroline began to play the pianoforte.

After the country dance, they danced a jig, then a quadrille.

'Do you not want to dance?' Nash asked Clem.

Clem shook his head. 'Never learned and do not want to.'

Clem and Nash sat. Clem watched the dancers; Nash watched Caroline.

The two couples did not seem inclined to change partners, but they did need a rest after the three sets. They had punch and dried fruits and nuts and then had Caroline start to play all over again.

When resting again, Molly asked, 'Will you play a waltz? I would like to hear the music for one.'

'Of course.' Caroline played 'The Sussex Waltz'.

'It is slower,' Molly said.

'It is a very different sort of dance,' Caroline explained, playing the tune again.

Nash stood. 'We could show them, Caro.'

Her fingers stopped pressing the piano keys. 'We need music.'

Clem piped up. 'Play the tune one more time. I think I can sing it.'

She went through it once more and, when finished, Clem vocalised the tune without words. Nash walked over to her and extended his hand. She put her hand in his and let him lead her to their dance floor.

They started by holding hands and marching a few steps before facing each other and holding each other with their right hands to the other's waist. They twirled in a circle while also circling the floor. Together they raised their left hands and clasped them above their heads, still twirling. Then Nash placed his hands on her waist and Caroline moved hers to his shoulders and they were closer than ever, looking into each other's eyes. Nash forgot that the others were mimicking their steps or that it was not the pianoforte, but Clem making the music. All he could see was Caroline; all he could feel was her hands touching him.

Then Clem stopped singing and, even so, it took a moment to break the spell. Molly and Lucy laughed a little, and all the couples stepped away from each other.

Caroline seemed to collect herself. 'Do you want me to play more?'

'No.' Molly gazed up at Elliot. 'We had better stop now. It is late.'

'Don't move!' Clem warned.

Molly and Elliot looked at him with alarm.

He pointed upwards. 'You are under the mistletoe. You have to kiss her.'

Elliot gave her a light peck on her mouth, his face turning a bright red.

Nash leaned over to Caroline's ear. 'Who do they remind you of?'

She smiled at him.

The ball was over. Christmas was over. It was a day none of them would soon forget, Nash was certain. He would not forget it.

Everyone said their good nights and conveyed their gratitude for the gifts, the coin and the special days. A moment later Nash and Caroline were alone in the hall.

He turned to her and took her hand in his. 'It was a fine day, was it not?'

She looked into his eyes and nodded.

He picked up a candle and they walked to the stairs, still holding hands. They climbed the stairs to their floor and entered the guest room hallway. What to say to her? Simply ask to share her bed again this night?

They lingered at her door.

'Why do I feel this is some sort of ending?' she said in a quiet voice.

'Not the end of our night?' he asked. 'I—I have no wish to part from you.'

She touched his face. 'Nor I, you. Do—do you wish to come in my room?'

He grasped her hand and kissed her palm. 'Yes.'

'Will—will you make love with me tonight, like we did last night?' Her expression appeared uncertain of his answer.

'If you wish it,' he murmured.

They entered her room and he placed the candle on the table as he'd done before. He unbuttoned his red coat as he pulled off her gloves. He shrugged out of his coat and hung it over the same chair.

He gazed at her. The candlelight seemed to illuminate the gold of her dress. 'You look so very beautiful, Caro.' He moved closer, close enough to undo the buttons on the back of the dress.

'Take care with it,' she said. 'I have to put it back.'

'Back?' He helped her pull it over her head.

'It is Sybella's,' she responded. 'All the dresses are Sybella's.'

Nash did not know why, but that the dresses were Sybella's felt like a bad omen. No, probably a mere fear that a near-perfect day must have something to ruin it.

Their lovemaking that night was near perfect as well. What could ruin it? As he drifted off to sleep with Caroline in his arms, the doubt still nagged at him.

Something would go wrong.

Chapter Twelve

The next morning, Nash again woke in Caroline's arms and again they made love. They ate breakfast in the drawing room, returning to their proper roles. After breakfast Nash wrote a note to Bolton and sent Clem to deliver it.

They spent the morning putting everything back in its rightful place, no more table in the Marble Hall, no more yule log. It had burned itself out. The celebration was over.

Nash spent much time with Caroline. They took a walk when the midday sun was high in the sky, warming the air and clearing the paths. He needed to walk. For his leg. For the freedom of it.

Nash still intended to ask Caroline about her marriage to Percy, but the time still did not seem right. They needed to become used to each other again, like when they'd been young. He figured he had until Twelfth Night, eleven days away. Caroline asked him about the army, about his time in Portugal, Spain and France. About Waterloo.

She did not ask about the position at the War Office, though. Every day he delayed travelling back to London increased the chances of another officer earning the job, but staying with Caroline was more important. Staying with Caroline was like returning to life. Something had

nearly died in Nash after Percy gave him that damned letter. He'd certainly buried it so deep it had little chance to
return to life, but she was here, and Nash had the chance
to live again.

So he savoured this day with her. No demands. No agenda.
Not even celebrations to plan. They merely had time to be
together, to sleep side by side, to make love, to return to the
days of their youth.

The next day promised to be more of the same. Another
day with Caroline, another return to life. They slept late
and took their time dressing for breakfast. Afterwards they
went on another walk.

Returning from the walk, they approached the front of
the house and heard a distinctive sound.

'Carriages,' Nash said. 'Coming up the drive.' He could
just see them in the distance.

'Sybella and Bolton? Coming back?' Caroline sounded
as dismayed as Nash felt. 'Why are they coming back so
soon?'

They'd know in a moment. One thing certain, his and
Caroline's idyll was at an end.

Caroline and Nash hurried up the steps to the front door
and rushed inside. They had just enough time to rid themselves of their cloaks and boots and to warn Elliot, Molly
and Lucy that they believed Lord and Lady Bolton and
their entourage were returning. The three servants greeted
this news with the same disappointment and dread as she
and Nash had done.

'Do not worry,' she told them. 'You performed admirably
these few days. We will say so to Lord and Lady Bolton.'

Nash gestured to them. 'Elliot and Molly, best you be
in the hall ready to attend them.'

They all hurried back to the hall and watched the carriages approach.

With each turn of the carriage wheels Caroline's spirits sank lower. This magic interlude with Nash, this very special Christmas, was ending. She'd cherished these days with him. And these nights. She'd hoped there would be more of them.

The first carriage stopped in front of the steps. Elliot hurried down to assist the passengers. Bolton emerged first, then Sybella, then the nurse carrying Sybella's baby and a nanny holding their son's hand.

Sybella burst into the hall and, spying Caroline, rushed over to embrace her. 'Oh, Caroline! We are back! It is so good to see you. I am so sorry to have left you, but we were told we *must* by the doctor—that charlatan!' She leaned to Caroline's ear. 'Has it been dreadful?'

Caroline's emotions towards her friend were mixed. Sybella and her husband had abandoned them, after all. 'It was not dreadful.'

Bolton was shaking Nash's hand. 'So you are well! What a bungle!'

Sybella whispered in Caroline's ear again, 'Nash was supposed to be gone.'

'Do not fret. We have—' How was Caroline to put it? 'We have done well, under the circumstances.' Better than she could have dreamed, in fact.

'Oh?' Sybella's brows rose. 'You must tell me everything.'

Their little boy toddled over to pull on his mother's skirts. 'Mama! Mama!'

Sybella leaned down. 'What is it, Luke? I am talking to my friend!'

'Friend! Friend!' the little boy cried out, repeating the word over and over as he ran around the hall, nearly tripping the footmen who were bringing in boxes and bags from the carriage. Bolton shouted at him to stop at once.

The baby started to wail, then.

'For goodness sake,' cried Sybella. 'Take the children to the nursery at once. No wonder my mother wanted us to leave.'

The nurse and nanny took their charges away quickly, their cries fading as they ascended the stairs.

Sybella removed her cloak, gloves and hat, handing them to Elliot. She turned to him. 'Bring us some tea, would you? I am in great need of tea.'

Caroline said, 'We've been using the red drawing room, next to the saloon. It will have a fire.'

'That room?' Sybella sounded less than pleased. 'Very well. It will do.'

Dinner was served in the breakfast room, a room they had not used before. They ate late, perhaps because the cook and some of her kitchen maids arrived late in the day. Caroline wondered how Lucy fared when the cook returned. She tried to tell Sybella how well the three servants had performed, but Sybella hardly seemed to attend.

Bolton simply said, 'They'll be rewarded.'

Shortly after dinner, when they retired to the drawing room for tea, Sybella stifled a yawn. 'Do forgive me. I am so very tired. Travel always is so fatiguing.'

'Then we must be abed.' Bolton rose. 'Come, my dear, our guests will not mind if we say good night now.'

Sybella tossed a significant glance towards Nash and mouthed to Caroline, *Do you want me to stay?*

Caroline shook her head.

They left and Caroline and Nash were alone for the first time since the Boltons arrived. Then the butler entered with a footman to remove the tea things and to enquire if Nash needed a valet and if Caroline needed a maid.

They both declined.

When the butler and footman left, Nash moved from his chair to sit next to her on a settee. 'This is not what I wanted, Caro.'

It was not what she wanted either. 'It changes things.'

'Are you obligated to stay for this visit?' he asked.

'Sybella was kind enough to invite me. I cannot leave the moment she's arrived.' And she, of course, had nowhere else to go.

Nash set his jaw. 'Then I will stay too if they will have me.'

'We cannot really be alone here, Nash.' Not with servants coming and going. 'Not at night.'

'I understand. But I still want to stay.' He took her hands in his and looked directly in her eyes. 'I want to be with you, Caro. I want—I hope—we can rekindle what we once had between us.' He squeezed her hands. 'I love you, Caro. I have always loved you.'

She wanted to tell him she loved him back, that she'd always loved him, but she could not form the words. Instead, she withdrew. She was so well practised in withdrawing—because of Percy.

Caroline pulled her hands from Nash's. 'I—I need time, Nash.' Time to believe their love could work.

'I will stay. We will take our time. Bolton will understand.' He stood and extended his hand. 'Shall I escort you to your room?

They walked through the house together as they had the past three nights, except this time they passed a footman in the Marble Hall and a maid on the second floor.

'Good night, Caro,' he whispered. The guest room hallway was empty. He took her into his arms and gently kissed her.

Her body, now so attuned to him, flared into desire, but she had to dampen the flames.

'Good night,' she said, touching her lips to his one more time.

Caroline slept fitfully, nightmares of Percy returning. She dreamed of standing at the altar in her beautiful dress, waiting for Nash. Waiting. Waiting. Until Percy enters and laughs at her, like some deranged demon.

By dawn she fell asleep, only to be woken by a maid putting more coal on her fire. When the maid left, she heard Nash's voice in the hall telling the girl good morning. Hearing his voice relaxed her and she fell back to sleep, waking much later than she was accustomed to.

She dressed hurriedly and made her way to the breakfast room. How she wished she could simply go all the way down to the kitchen and find Lucy and Molly there to greet her.

As she approached the door, she heard Sybella talking to her husband.

'Do not tell me they are together?' Sybella cried.

'That is what Nash said, or rather, he said he wanted to marry her and take her back to London.'

'Oh, my goodness, he cannot!' Sybella's voice rose. 'Much as I love her, she will ruin him!'

'I know,' Bolton responded. 'I tried to tell him her reputation is unsalvageable. Bathurst would never allow him to join the War Office if so.' Lord Bathurst was the Secretary of State for War and the Colonies.

Sybella gave an audible sigh. 'No one in society will ever forgive her for killing Percy, accident or not. I feel so very sorry for her, but her reputation is in a shambles.'

This was her friend? Talking about her?

Caroline stepped into the room.

'Caroline!' Sybella turned red.

'Is it true?' she asked.

'Is what true?' Bolton asked.

'That a connection with me will ruin Nash's chances at the War Office?' she said. 'Is it true?'

Bolton gave her a direct look. 'You know it is, Caroline.'

Sybella looked at her with sympathy. 'He really must marry someone with money.'

Caroline nodded and turned away. She would ruin Nash's life as surely as Percy had ruined hers.

She returned to her bedchamber and packed her things. Her portmanteau carried enough for her to get by. Sybella could ship her trunk when she settled. Somewhere. She'd slip out of the house and make her way to the stables. All she needed was for Clem or Will to take her to the village where she could catch the next coach and disappear.

Before she left, though, she took a sprig of spruce from the vase and tucked it in her portmanteau.

To remember a magic Christmas.

Chapter Thirteen

Nash searched for Caroline, an uneasy feeling growing inside him when he could not find her. He looked in her room again. Besides her trunk in the corner, all signs of her were gone. He grew alarmed.

He descended the servants' stairs and startled several of the servants, looking for Molly and Lucy. They had not seen Caroline at all.

He disturbed Bolton and Sybella, who were dozing in the drawing room. 'Have you seen Caroline? I cannot find her anywhere.'

'No-o-o…' responded Bolton, stretching out the word. 'We have not seen her since breakfast.' He exchanged a glance with his wife.

Nash looked from one to the other. 'You know something. Tell me.'

'It is just that she overheard us talking at breakfast—' Sybella bit her lip.

'Talking about you, Nash,' his friend finished for her. 'What you and I discussed this morning. How she will ruin you if you remain connected to her. How Bathurst will not have you at the War Office—'

Nash had confided some in Bolton when they'd gone

for an early morning ride. Bolton had torn into him about Caroline's reputation.

Nash's hand curled into a fist. 'She heard that?'

'She did.' Sybella looked close to tears by now although she'd obviously not been concerned enough to seek out Caroline prior to her nap. 'She must be in her room,' Sybella said helpfully. 'Did you knock on her door?'

'Of course I looked in her room,' he snapped. 'There was nothing there of hers except a packed trunk.'

'You don't think she left!' Sybella protested.

'If she did, let her go,' Bolton urged. 'Do not ruin your life, man.'

Nash strode out of the room. He'd almost ruined his life once. He had no wish to do it again.

He entered the Marble Hall where Elliot was attending the door.

'Have you seen Caroline?' he asked, forgetting to use her formal name.

'No, sir.' Elliot looked at him with concern. 'Is something amiss, Major?'

Another footman walked through and heard this. 'Do you mean Lady Bolton's guest? I saw her leaving the house.'

'Did you see where she went?' Nash asked.

'No, sir,' the man said. 'I merely saw her walk out this door.'

Nash turned to Elliot. 'Can you bring me my topcoat?'

Elliot retrieved his topcoat in a flash and actually walked out the door with him. 'What is it, Major? Is Mrs Demain in trouble?'

'I fear she's left, Elliot,' Nash confided. 'And I must get her back.'

Elliot, coatless, walked with him to the stables where they almost immediately ran into Clem.

Clem threw up his hands immediately. 'She told me not to tell, but Will took her to the village. To the inn. She's taking a coach.'

'Help me saddle my horse,' Nash asked. 'I must go after her.'

In no time, he was galloping down the drive, hoping to reach the village in time.

Nash found Caroline in the public room of the inn, staring into a cup of tea, looking bleak and alone.

'Caro?' He spoke softly.

Surprise registered in her eyes, then warmth, then something like fear.

'What are you doing, Caro?' he asked.

She met his eye. 'I am leaving on the next coach. I will not ruin your life, Nash. I will not.'

He sat across from her. 'Do you think that a position in the War Office is more important to me than you?'

She gave him a resolved look. 'It was lovely seeing you again, Nash, but I want and need no attachments. You—you must not mistake a—a Christmas fling as anything else.'

Her words wounded, just as that letter wounded so many years ago. 'So, you decided to leave without telling anyone?'

She glanced away. 'It seemed best.'

He let the pain settle inside him where he'd stored his pain so many years ago. It seemed familiar. Almost comfortable.

But he watched her look so unaffected, so withdrawn, and he knew. 'Which is it, Caro? You leave because you do not wish to ruin my life, or you leave because you want no attachment?'

She did not answer.

He went on. 'I once believed a false letter and I hurt you and lost you. Why do I feel this is like the false letter? I do not believe you.'

Caroline's eyes stung with tears.

It was excruciating to sit across from him, to see his dear, dear face and hear his loving words and know she must give him up.

He spoke again in a firm tone. 'I *trust* that you love me and all I ask is for you to believe that I love you.'

Her misery increased. 'Oh, Nash. Love is not enough. Do you not see? You need money to live on. For food and shelter.' She could offer him nothing. 'I am impoverished now. I have no money, no home, no reputation—'

'Trust me, Caro,' he said. 'We will get by. No matter what. I cannot offer you anything like the life you led as a child, but I am not destitute, even without the War Office. We both proved we can lead a simpler life. I trust we can prosper together. Maybe not in riches, but in devotion. '

She wanted to believe this possible.

He leaned back. 'I will not give up this time, Caro. I will follow you. I'll be on whatever coach you take. I will not leave you this time.' He extended his hand across the table. 'What say you?'

It would mean a leap of faith to believe him now, to trust that their love for each other could weather any storm. Well, they'd made a happy Christmas from a snow storm that cut them off from the rest of the world, perhaps they could weather any other storm that came their way.

She lifted her hand from her lap and placed it in his. 'I wish to spend all my Christmases with you, Nash. I do not wish to part, so, yes, I will stay. With you.'

Epilogue

Theirs was a small farm in Suffolk, an almost forgotten piece of property in Nash's family, deeded to him after the death of an uncle. It became the perfect home for him and Caroline.

They married by special licence as soon as they were able and moved to the farmhouse. Elliot, Molly and Lucy, even Clem and Will, came with them, hired away from the Boltons even though Nash could not promise to match Bolton' wages right away.

By the following winter, the once severely neglected house was in order, and they once again prepared for Christmas. It was Christmas Eve and the men had gathered an abundance of greenery with which they planned to fill the whole house, not merely a room or two. Nash carried a bundle of greenery into their drawing room and spied Caroline whispering in a corner with Molly and Lucy.

Molly pushed her towards Nash. 'Tell him.' She and Lucy hurried away.

'Tell me what?' Nash put his bundle down on a table.

Caroline touched his cheek. 'News. Special news.'

She put her arms around his neck and looked into his eyes. 'I am certain—almost entirely certain—that I am with child.'

It took a moment to sink in. 'But you said—'

She nodded. 'I know. I know. But I was wrong.'

He gazed down at her beautiful face, then swept her in his arms and swung her around.

'I told you!' The joy burst out of him. 'I told you we would prosper!'

* * * * *

A PROPOSAL FOR THE PENNILESS LADY

Laura Martin

For Jack and George.
Your joy is the best thing about Christmas.

Dear Reader,

Christmas is one of my favorite times of year. I love the preparation and anticipation, and I find something quite magical about sitting beside a roaring fire while outside is cold and snowy. My absolute favorite thing about the festive period is getting to spend time with family, so when I was given the chance to write a Christmas story for this collection, I knew I wanted to incorporate the themes of coziness and family into the book.

A Proposal for the Penniless Lady is set in the small town of Battle in East Sussex. I grew up nearby in Hastings, on the south coast of England, and went to school in Battle. It is a beautiful town with a quaint high street dominated at one end by the impressive Battle Abbey. When I was younger, they always used to erect a huge tree outside Battle Abbey at Christmas, adorned with hundreds of lights. Even now when I think of Christmas one of the things I picture is that tree with the Abbey behind it. It meant when I was deciding on a setting for this book I could think of nowhere more perfect than Battle. I hope you enjoy a Regency Christmas somewhere so close to my heart.

Laura Martin

Chapter One

'I am sorry, Miss Partridge, the account is three months overdue. I cannot sell you anything more until the debt is paid,' Mrs Gillard said, not unkindly. She had lowered her voice, but there were plenty of other people in the small butcher's shop to hear her words.

Isobel felt her face flush, the heat flooding to her cheeks, and she wished in that moment for some great disaster to sweep her away from her embarrassment. Perhaps for the ground to crack and for her to fall into the chasm, or maybe for a giant hawk to swoop down and carry her away.

Nothing materialised. Instead she was forced to thank the butcher's wife and hurry out of the shop, head bowed low so she wouldn't have to see the mixture of pity and triumph in the villagers' eyes.

It was the third shop that had refused to serve her in the past month and they were fast running out of options. She would have to start travelling further afield, where the Partridge name still held some level of respect and people did not know the size of their crippling debts.

Pulling on her gloves roughly, she cursed under her breath as a seam unravelled and one of her fingers poked through the end. The material was thin, mended on many occasions, with more thread than original fabric left. It was another thing to add to her seemingly endless pile of clothes to be darned or patched.

Resolutely Isobel dipped her head against the icy wind and trudged through the snow.

The cold spell had started a week earlier with a thick layer of snow appearing overnight. For three days it had snowed, making the drifts two feet deep in some places and prompting the more whimsical of her companions to talk of a white Christmas. The last few days the skies had been clear, but the temperature meant the snow lingered and in busy areas was trodden down into a treacherous layer of ice.

Treading carefully, she made her way back along the busy high street, keeping her eyes lowered in the hope she wouldn't meet anyone she knew. Right now a kind word or warm gesture might make her let out deep, heart-wrenching sobs and she didn't want anyone to witness that.

For a moment she paused outside the brightly dressed window of the local draper's shop, the cottons and silks seeming to spill out of the drawers inside. It had been years since she had been fitted for a new dress, years since she had run such fine material through her fingers. Looking down at the drab brown skirt that poked out from underneath her cloak, she told herself to stop being so maudlin. Her situation was nowhere near as bad as thousands of others.

If her father could be persuaded to part with some of the remaining trinkets and furniture, they would have enough for a few more months of meat and she grew most of the other food they ate in their kitchen garden. They wouldn't starve and they had plenty of wood to keep them warm for winter.

Turning away, Isobel resolutely set her mind to the rest

of the jobs that needed doing that day. Brooding would not get the sheets washed or the chickens fed.

Thomas dismounted to lead his horse along the high street. It looked much changed from the last time he had walked along this road many years earlier. In general, he tried to avoid returning to his childhood home in Sussex. His mother still lived here, on her own now his father had passed away, but he preferred to send a carriage to bring her to his house twenty miles away rather than return here.

'Mr Williamson, is that you?' a portly man of around his age said, hurrying over. Thomas recognised him as the vicar of the pretty Norman church on the edge of the village. Reverend Smith had been a young man, fresh to the church, when Thomas had gone to seek his fortune ten years ago. Now he looked every one of his thirty years and a life of soft living had made him almost as wide as he was tall.

'Reverend, it is good to see you.'

'Your mother told me you were coming home. She has been eagerly awaiting your arrival.'

Thomas felt a sting of guilt that he had left it so long. His mother was ailing. She and his father had thought they would not be blessed with children until he had arrived, a surprise when his mother was almost forty. She was now in her seventy-first year and up until recently had been spritely and active, but the last six months her health had begun to wane and her movements slowed. Now her joints pained her and her eyesight was beginning to fade, although she would not let her ailments defeat her, keeping active in the village.

'I am on my way to see her now,' he said stiffly.

'I will not delay you then, Mr Williamson. Give your mother my regards.'

'I will. Thank you.'

Moving on, head bowed, he walked swiftly to try to avoid making eye contact with anyone else he knew. Ten years was a long time to be gone, but small places like Battle didn't change much in a decade. One or two people might leave, a couple of newcomers might arrive, but generally it was the same families in the same houses their father and grandfathers had grown up in.

The street was busy and a few times he had to wait for carts to pass through before he could move on. The shops on one side of the street were set higher than the other side, meaning there was a raised pavement on his right. He was standing in, leg pressed against the steps up to the raised pavement when an elderly woman slipped on one of the icy flagstones, sliding forward with a loud cry of surprise.

Conscious of the ice beneath his feet, he sprang forward, gripping hold of the woman in time to save her from a serious fall and possibly a broken bone or two.

'Thank you, sir,' she said, visibly shaken.

'Are you hurt?'

'No, just a little dazed,' the older woman said, patting him on the arm.

'Can I escort you somewhere?'

'That would be very kind, Mr...?'

'Mr Williamson.'

'Ah, you're Mrs Williamson's boy. She has been talking about your visit for weeks. I am Mrs Richards, a friend of your mother.' She motioned at a house set among the shops on the other side of the street. 'That is my front door— would you be so kind as to escort me over?'

'Of course, Mrs Richards.'

Carefully they picked their way over the ice in the road and Thomas waited until the elderly lady had stepped inside.

'You are most kind, Mr Williamson. Normally I would

invite you in, but it would be cruel of me to detain you when your mother is so eager to see you. Perhaps you might both call on me one day during your visit.'

'I will make sure we do.'

He bowed, waiting for the older woman to close the door before turning. It meant he was distracted, not looking where he was going, and as he turned he brushed against a young woman. It wasn't more than a light touch, but in these conditions, with the ice underfoot, Thomas worried he might unbalance the young woman and reached out to steady her arm. His hand connected with her coat and at the same time she turned towards him, her eyes lifting to meet his.

Thomas felt all the breath leave his lungs at once. It was as though he had been punched hard in the gut, the pain visceral and real.

'Thomas,' Isobel said, her brow creasing into a frown.

She still looked as beautiful as ever and, at first, he thought time must have stood still for her these past ten years. Then he began to see the minute differences. There were a few paper-thin creases around her eyes, although they retained their vitality, and her face had lost some of its roundness. Her cheekbones were a little more promi-nent and her hand as she placed it on his arm was as deli-cate as a little bird.

'Miss Partridge,' he managed to grunt, his voice low.

For a long moment neither of them moved—neither could do anything but look at the other.

'What are you doing here?' Isobel asked, her eyes searching his face. Once he had known every expres-sion, every nuance in her voice. He had known every-thing about Isobel, and it was a shock to realise how little those essential characteristics changed even in ten years. He could see the nervousness in her smile, the flicker of doubt in her eye. For a moment it was as if nothing had changed between them, even though in truth they were now worlds apart.

Quickly he released her arm, stepping back as if afraid she might burn him. He needed to put some physical distance between them. Despite all that had happened in the intervening years, still she could reduce him to a confused mess with one look.

With a surge of irritation he quickly regained his composure. Isobel Partridge had ruined his life once—he would not let her make him feel uncomfortable now.

'I am in Battle to visit my mother,' he said, gripping hold of Bombay's reins and going to sidestep around Isobel. She reached out again and placed a hand on his arm, seemingly unaffected by his presence, unlike he was by hers.

'Your mother is unwell?'

'No, growing frail only.' He shrugged her off again and took another step away. For once he did not care if he appeared rude. He needed to get away from Isobel, to stride off into the distance where hopefully there would be a little more air to breathe. Right now, he felt as though he were suffocating and his body beginning to shut down.

'She will be pleased to see you, I am sure. Are you staying for Christmas?'

Thomas regarded Isobel, wondering if she was really so unaffected by seeing him after all these years. She seemed calm, as if she were talking about the weather with a friendly neighbour, not conversing with the man whose heart she had shattered a decade earlier.

'I am. Please excuse me.' He bowed stiffly, moving away. It was rude, there was no other way to look at it, but Thomas didn't want to stand there pretending everything was normal between them. *This* was the very reason he had not returned to Battle for years.

'Thomas,' Isobel's voice called after him.

He contemplated ignoring her, but was aware of all the eyes watching them, some openly and some more covertly.

Slowly he spun. Now as he looked at her he could see the strain on her face, the almost imperceptible flicker at the edge of her eye.

'I hope you have a lovely Christmas,' she said quietly. 'Please give my regards to your mother.'

Now it was his turn to watch her walk away, taking her time as she picked her way through the snow and ice.

Chapter Two

'Isobel, where are you, girl?' The shout was accompanied by a loud thumping as her father banged the floor with his cane.

Taking a deep breath, Isobel summoned a smile and breezed into the study.

'At last. I've been calling for ages. Where is my tea, girl? It's past four o'clock.'

'I've been out seeing to the chickens, Father. I'll make tea next.'

Her father grumbled something under his breath that she was pleased she didn't hear.

'I couldn't get any meat from the butcher's,' she said, busying herself straightening a pile of books as she spoke. It was best not to look directly at her father when delivering bad news.

'Why not? Surely they didn't run out. It's their one job, to cut up the animals and sell the meat.'

'Our bill is too large, Father. They will not sell us any more until the debt is paid.'

Out of the corner of her eye she watched her father's face turn from pink to red as it always did when he was reminded of their struggles with money.

'Useless, cheating scoundrels. Where is their respect?

I am the Sixth Baron of Senlac. My family have a noble lineage all the way back to the Normans. What do the Gillards have? Bloody fingernails and a vermin-infested shop. I will not stand for it.' He struggled to his feet, leaning on the cane heavily and swaying from side to side. Her father was still mobile, still perfectly capable of walking without the cane.

Sometimes she placed the decanter of whisky on the other side of the room and then watched secretly as her father waited until he thought she was busy elsewhere, then hopped up from his chair and moved easily across the room to get his precious alcohol.

'Sit down, Father,' she said soothingly. 'Perhaps there is something we can sell to settle the debt with the Gillards.'

Her father let out a roar and began waving his cane around with displeasure. 'Don't you go giving those thieving heathens a single penny of my money.'

'It is their money, Father. We bought the goods…we ate the meat. We *do* need to pay for it.'

Grumbling under his breath, Lord Senlac thumped his stick on the ground a few more times, but settled back into the chair.

'I will make some tea and then talk to Mrs Hooper about what we might have for dinner.' Isobel paused, knowing she should tell her father about the encounter with Thomas in the village. Even though he barely left the house these days, he seemed to somehow obtain a near endless supply of village gossip. He would not be pleased to hear of Thomas Williamson's return from someone else.

For a moment she thought back to when they had collided, at the look of confusion quickly replaced by horror on Thomas's face. She hated that was still how she affected him all these years later, but she could understand it. Ten years ago, she had hurt him unforgivably. He had reached out and offered her the world and she had turned him down.

Isobel scoffed quietly, looking round her. She had been well and truly punished for her actions, but that didn't mean she felt any less guilty about how she had hurt him.

'I saw Mr Williamson in Battle,' she said, trying to make her tone nonchalant.

This made her father look up, eyes narrowing.

'What's he doing back?'

'I think he is home to visit his mother for Christmas,' Isobel said, moving so she wouldn't have to make eye contact with her father.

'Hmmm.'

She'd expected more of a reaction, certainly at least a low level of vitriol for the man her father had once forbade her to marry. Instead, the old man got a curious look on his face and began to stare out into the middle distance. Isobel exhaled slowly and then hurried from the room, mumbling she would fetch some tea.

Outside the study she paused, leaning to rest her head on the cold wood panelling. She was more shaken than she liked to admit by Thomas's appearance in the village. Of course, she knew it was a possibility, but in ten years she hadn't once known him to visit Battle. Whereas once she had been on edge every time she walked down the high street, for a long time she hadn't thought it likely he would appear.

'Enough,' she murmured. It wasn't as though she were going to see him again. No doubt he would spend a quiet Christmas with his mother and then disappear back to his grand life in London or wherever he was living nowadays.

'Something wrong, Miss Partridge?' Mrs Hooper, their elderly housekeeper, said as she shuffled round the corner. Senlac House had once been a grand and bustling house with near to twenty servants. Over the years the numbers had dwindled as the money situation had worsened, now leaving only Mrs Hooper. The housekeeper had been with the family since before Isobel was born and was now approaching sixty herself. She didn't have any family, anyone to take her in as her health and eyesight deteriorated, so here she stayed even though most months they couldn't afford to pay her.

'No, Mrs Hooper,' Isobel said, straightening up and rallying. Thomas was no longer her concern. He hadn't been her concern for an entire decade, not since she had made the worst mistake of her life.

'Isobel!' her father shouted from his study. 'Girl, get in here now.'

Taking a deep, steadying breath, Isobel plastered a smile on to her face and stepped back into the study.

'Yes, Father?'

'Get my coat and that damned contraption of a chair. We're going out.'

'Going out?' she said, incredulous.

'Yes, out, girl. Why am I having to repeat myself?'

'The snow is thick, Father, I doubt your chair will be able to make it in these conditions.'

'Nonsense. We'll get there. Come on, hurry up. The day is a wasting.'

Sometimes Isobel dreamed about standing up to her father, of turning to him and telling him exactly what she thought of him. There had been a few outbursts over the years when his rudeness and cruelty had become too much for her, but mostly she gritted her teeth and accepted the crotchety old man for what he was.

Never had he spared her a kind word and his thoughts were purely selfish, his schemes always plotting on how he could achieve what he needed for his own comfort.

Her friends often asked her why she stayed. Part of her wondered if she was a little cowed by her father's strong personality. She supposed perhaps that was part of it, but so was the promise she had made to her mother.

When Isobel was twelve her mother had found a growth in her breast. At first it had increased in size slowly, but after a while it seemed to take over her whole body, draining the life force out of the once vibrant woman. Her mother had known death was approaching and one day, when Isobel was sitting on the bed with her, tucked into the crook of her mother's arm, Lady Senlac had kissed her on the head and asked something of her.

'Look after your father,' Isobel's mother had said. *'He may be a man and a baron, but he is naive about many of the ways of the world.'*

Isobel would have promised her mother anything then and she had given her word solemnly. Now, sixteen years later, that promise felt like a prison sentence.

'Come on, hurry up,' her father chided her as Isobel helped him on with his coat.

'Where are we going?'

'Never you mind. I'll give you directions when we get out and about.' The old man sat himself down in the wheeled chair he had bought at great expense some years earlier when he claimed to be getting increasingly frail. He had sent to London to have it made specially and the bill when it came had made Isobel feel sick. The money they had spent on the chair could have fed them for at least a year, perhaps even two.

Outside the clouds were heavy and it looked as though there might be more snowfall before dark. Isobel nearly slipped on the step outside and had to grasp the wall to keep her balance.

'Take my chair out,' her father commanded.

Isobel eyed the ice beneath her feet.

'No,' she said, turning to her father. She felt a flutter of nerves inside as she always did when she stood up to him. Any open defiance and he would make her life hell for days.

'Don't be such a lazy layabout and take my chair out.'

'It is too dangerous,' Isobel said. 'The ice is thick and the chair will get stuck in the snow.'

Her father hobbled with his cane over to the door and to her surprise grunted in agreement. She expected him to turn and start divesting himself of his coat and gloves, but instead he leaned a little heavier on his cane and then stepped out.

'Father, you haven't left the house for months—is now really the best time to push yourself?'

'You always say I should get up and about more. Well, now you're getting your wish,' he said, tottering on the step. 'I'll know who to blame if I fall and hurt myself,' he murmured, just loud enough for Isobel to hear.

His cane slipped on the ice and Isobel reached out to steady him. As much as it would serve him right to slip, she would never wish injury on her father.

'Give me your arm, girl,' he barked and Isobel stepped closer, wincing as her father put most of his weight on her proffered arm.

The first few steps were the worst as they found an awkward equilibrium, but by the time they reached the road they were making slow but steady progress. Isobel just hoped her father wasn't planning on walking to the other end of the village.

Thomas pressed his mother to sit down, taking the kettle from her and pouring the steaming water into two cups. They were in the cosy kitchen of the cottage where

Thomas had grown up. Being there transported him back to childhood, to happy memories of days spent playing with friends and then evening wrapped in the warmth of his parent's love. The cottage hadn't changed much, although over the last few years Thomas had ensured the old building was kept draught free and in good repair.

'It is so good to have you here, my darling boy,' his mother said, beaming up at him.

Thomas felt a stab of guilt. He should have visited more, especially since his father's death. His mother was well established in the village, she had a close group of friends and volunteered for several charitable positions. Never once had she expressed any discontent, but still Thomas sensed she would love to see him more.

'You know you are welcome to come and stay with me whenever you wish,' Thomas said as he handed his mother her cup of tea. 'Or there is a beautiful little cottage tucked into the corner of my estate. If you wish, I could help you move in there.'

His mother smiled indulgently. 'You do not want your mother interrupting the life you have built for yourself, not when I am hopeful one day soon you will find a young lady to marry and start a family with.'

Thomas sat down silently, ignoring the last comment. He knew his mother only wanted to see him happy and for her the way to happiness had been through a good marriage to a kind man and having a family. Once he had thought he wanted the same, once he had believed finding love and sharing his life with someone was all he wanted, but for years now he had been disillusioned.

His mind flicked to the meeting with Isobel Partridge in the high street. She had been the reason he had stayed away all these years. Ten years earlier she had convinced him she loved him and then broken his heart so completely he had wondered if he would ever heal. The encounter today had rocked him, but he realised in a way it was a relief to have it over with. Now perhaps he could visit Battle more often, not always afraid he might run into the woman who had refused him. If he did encounter her, he would merely incline his head politely and move on.

For an instant his treacherous heart squeezed in his chest when he remembered how thin Isobel had looked, how pale and cold her face had seemed, but her circumstances were none of his concern. It was no secret the Partridges had fallen on hard times. Isobel's father, once so haughty and arrogant, was barely managing to stay out of debtors' prison. Of course, it would mean Isobel did not enjoy the life she once had.

Pushing all thoughts of Isobel Partridge from his mind, he took a sip of tea and allowed the hot liquid to warm him. For the next week he would be the dutiful son and then he could escape Battle once again and return to the life he had built for himself after Isobel had broken his heart all those years ago.

Chapter Three

'No,' Isobel said resolutely, planting her feet firmly in the snow at the edge of the path.

Her father turned to her, face red and dripping with sweat from the effort of walking the four hundred yards across the ice and snow and she recoiled as he snarled at her, 'Either you knock on that door, or you will have to carry me back.'

Isobel still could not move. The cottage was old with heavy dark beams and a thatched roof. In the spring and summer it was pretty, with roses growing by the door and a garden full of brightly coloured flowers, but now the garden looked bleak. It wasn't the building that was making her recoil though, it was the knowledge of who was inside.

'Fine, I'll do it,' her father said, staggering up the path. He was close to collapse, Isobel could see that, but it was his own fault for insisting he take his first walk outdoors in months in such conditions.

He thumped on the door, leaning heavily on the wood until it began to open. Isobel darted forward to catch his arm, worried he might fall, but he brushed her off. It meant she was tottering backwards as the door opened and all too familiar green eyes looked out at her.

'You,' Thomas barked.

Isobel saw movement behind him and then the soft, kind face of Mrs Williamson looking past her son's shoulder.

'What a pleasant surprise,' she said, beaming as she wriggled her way past Thomas in the narrow hallway. 'Lord Senlac, are you unwell?'

Isobel saw her father bristle and was shocked when he laughed jovially instead of snapping at the woman.

'This snow is a bit hard on the old joints,' he said, even summoning a smile. 'My daughter and I were out enjoying the afternoon air, but the walk got a little much for me. I remembered you lived here and hoped we might impose on your hospitality for a few minutes.'

'Of course, Lord Senlac,' Mrs Williamson said, motioning for them to come in. 'It is lovely to see you, Miss Partridge.'

Isobel couldn't move for a moment, but her father quickly disappeared inside the house after Mrs Williamson. Reluctantly Isobel stepped forward, but Thomas filled the doorway, barring her way.

'What are you doing?' he said, his voice cold.

Isobel felt her body stiffen. It hurt to know Thomas disliked her so much he could not even summon a civil tone, but it was all her own fault.

'My father insisted,' she murmured.

'Ah, yes, and we all know what happens when the mighty Lord Senlac decrees something.'

'I can wait outside if you would prefer,' Isobel said, raising her eyes to meet his. She would be sorry for ever that she'd destroyed the love that they had once shared, but there was no need for him to treat her like this. She took a step back to show him she was not bluffing.

He regarded her for a long moment and then fell back, motioning for her to pass.

The hallway in the cottage was small and Isobel couldn't

help but brush against him as she entered. She felt him stiffen at her touch and for a moment she glanced up at him. Thankfully it was dark and she couldn't see the expression on his face. It would be too much to see his hatred of her so close up.

Following the sound of voices, Isobel stepped through the hall into a bright and cheerful kitchen. It was scrubbed so all the surfaces were shiny and kept meticulously tidy, yet despite that it was one of the most inviting rooms Isobel had ever been in.

'Have a seat, Miss Partridge,' Mrs Williamson said, motioning to one of the chairs by the table. Her father already occupied the other one. 'Thomas, perhaps you could fetch a couple of chairs from the parlour. I am sorry to keep you in here, but it is the warmest room in the house and you look like you could do with the heat from the fire.'

The kitchen felt wonderfully familiar and Isobel felt a wave of nostalgia pass over her. When she had been young, she and Thomas were the best of friends. They'd spent summer days playing in the fields at the edge of the village and as dusk fell, they would return here to eat freshly baked biscuits and drink warm milk before Isobel would reluctantly run home.

Perching uneasily on the chair next to her father, Isobel looked across at the old man. She didn't know what he was planning or why he had insisted they visit the Williamsons today, but she was certain there was nothing altruistic in his intentions.

'Here, a lovely warming cup of tea,' Mrs Williamson said, setting a steaming cup in front of Isobel. 'My, you are a beauty, aren't you, Miss Partridge? Don't you agree, Thomas? Miss Partridge grows more stunning each time I see her.'

Isobel felt her cheeks flush and couldn't help but glance

at Thomas, who was leaning against the doorframe frowning at her.

'I am glad of the opportunity to speak to you,' Lord Senlac said, none of his usual cantankerousness in his demeanour. 'I heard you were visiting, Mr Williamson, and I wanted to invite you both for dinner one day during your stay.'

Isobel blanched. It was a terrible idea. A few minutes of sharing a cup of tea was painful enough, but a whole dinner would be beyond terrible. Her father also seemed to have forgotten the butchers were refusing to sell them anything until their debts were settled. It would be a fine dinner party if all Isobel could serve was a vegetable stew and some hard bread.

'No, thank you.' Thomas said quickly, not offering any more explanation.

'I think we will have time, Thomas dear,' Mrs Williamson said softly.'You are here for a week after all.'

They were saved from further argument by a deep rumble coming from above them, followed by an almighty crash.

Thomas moved immediately, darting from his position in the doorway and disappearing into the darkness. Even though it wasn't her house Isobel's instinct was to follow him. She dashed into the interior of the house, running in Thomas's footsteps, and almost barrelling into the back of him when he stopped abruptly at the top of the stairs.

'What's happened?'

Thomas was tall and broad and Isobel had to stand on tiptoe to see over his shoulders, but even when she could see the scene in front of her didn't seem to make any sense.

'The roof has come down,' he said eventually, taking a step forward, but unable to go much further as his way was blocked by a haphazard mass of splintered wood, thatch and snow.

Isobel reached out instinctively and placed her hand on his arm, thinking of nothing but wanting to comfort him. Immediately he shrugged her off and turned abruptly.

'This is not a circus, Miss Partridge. My mother's misfortune is not for you to gape at.'

'I was not gaping.'

'What are you doing here?' She saw the fire in his eyes, the barely concealed contempt.

She exhaled slowly and then turned without answering him. It took her by surprise when he reached out and caught her by the arm, spinning her back to face him.

'I asked you a question.'

Isobel sighed. 'Not one you care to hear the answer to, I think. Whatever I say you will think the worst of me. I think it best my father and I get out of your way.'

He let go of her arm and, with tears pricking her eyes, Isobel ran down the stairs, almost bumping into Mrs Williamson.

'What has happened?'

'It looks as though the weight of the snow has brought part of the roof down.'

'Oh, my.'

Isobel placed a reassuring hand on the older woman's arm. 'I am so sorry,' she said softly. 'I am sure it is something that can be fixed.'

She led Mrs Williamson back into the kitchen and settled her into a chair, bringing across the woman's now lukewarm cup of tea and pressing it into her hands.

'You can't stay here,' Thomas said as he reappeared back in the kitchen. 'The whole roof in the bedroom is unstable. Thank the lord you weren't in bed when it happened.' He shook his head. 'I had no idea the beams had rotted.'

'It is not your fault, my dear,' Mrs Williamson said.

'If only I had brought the carriage, we could set off to

Tunbridge Wells straight away and I could oversee the repairs from there.'

'The roads are treacherous,' Lord Senlac said and Isobel thought she saw a hint of glee in his eyes. He always did like a disaster to revel in.

'Lord Senlac is right. I do not want you riding in this weather.'

'We can try the King's Head, I suppose, but it is likely to be busy with Christmas fast approaching. When I took Bombay to be stabled there the stable boy said they were almost full.'

'You must stay with us, of course,' Lord Senlac declared.

Three pairs of startled eyes whipped round to look at the Baron.

'We couldn't inconvenience you,' Mrs Williamson said.

'Father, surely...' Isobel began.

'No,' Thomas said.

'I insist. What other choice do you have? Your carriage is twenty miles away, the roads too icy for even a messenger on horseback to pass to take a message to send it. The inn is likely to be full, you said so yourself.'

'Perhaps one of your friends?' Thomas asked his mother.

'My friends are widows, Thomas, respectable, but none of them has large houses with rooms to spare.'

'Then it is settled,' Lord Senlac said, clapping his hands together. 'You will stay with us. Isobel and I will return now and tell Mrs Hooper to prepare two of our best rooms. You gather what you need and follow on when you are ready.'

He stood, tottering a little, and Isobel moved to his side. He brushed her off and instead walked with his cane tapping through the hall.

In shock Isobel followed, pausing when she reached the door, turning to find Thomas immediately behind her.

'I do not know what scheme this is,' he said, leaning in so his lips almost brushed her ear, 'but do not think I am foolish enough to be taken in by it.'

Isobel felt a shiver run through her body. So many nights she had lain awake and imagined Thomas leaning in close to her these last ten years, but always in her mind the words were sweet like honey. Rallying after a moment, she straightened.

'You are deluded Mr Williamson. Ask yourself how I could have influenced your mother's roof falling in.'

The momentary look of uncertainty set off a ripple of satisfaction within her and she resolved to keep out of his way as much as possible. Perhaps he would find some other solution, some way that meant he did not have to come to stay at Senlac House.

Chapter Four

There was no other solution: they would have to stay in Senlac House for at least a few days. It was snowing again, making the roads even more treacherous, and Thomas had enquired at the King's Head only to find all their rooms were full for the next few days.

Exhaling slowly, he told himself to accept his fate and threw himself on to the bed. The room he had been given once would have been grand. The walls were all dark panelling and ancient tapestries, the bed a huge mahogany creation with four ornately carved posts in the corners and a canopy over the top. Everything looked worn, though, as though it had reached its peak a few decades earlier and had been left to decline and crumble ever since.

Of course, he had known Isobel's family were struggling a little. His mother kept him informed, even though each time she mentioned Isobel or the Partridges he told her sternly he did not care. Even without the steady flow of village gossip from his mother, it would be hard not to be aware of Lord Senlac's troubles. He owed money all over the county and only a few old but influential friends stood between him and debtors' prison.

There was a soft knock on the door and he called out

to come in, expecting a maid, but instead it was Isobel, standing with her arms wrapped around his trunk, struggling with the weight of it.

'Here are your things,' she said, stepping into the room, almost tripping on the edge of the rug where she couldn't see her feet. He reached out to steady her and to take the trunk from her. 'Dinner is at seven. Is there anything I can get you before then?'

He frowned, taking in the worn skirt and the thin apron over the top. If he did not know her, he would assume she was the maid of a poor household.

'A drink,' he said, feeling a little uncomfortable at having Isobel serve him. Once their relationship had been very different and their circumstances reversed, but when they had been young Isobel had been careful not to let him feel inferior. Not until the day she had refused him.

'Of course—what would you like?'

'You're going to make it?'

He saw her shift a little and straighten her back and wondered how she had survived these last few years having everything she had grown up to expect chipped away. Once she had been the wealthiest young woman in the neighbourhood, the one with the best prospects, the biggest house, a carriage and six horses. Now she was reduced to running around after her guests like a serving maid.

Thomas had never shirked from hard work. His parents had lived modest lives and he had grown up helping with anything that needed doing and taking on odd jobs for other people to earn a little money. Only once he had left Battle did he start to make his money, turning a moderately successful business into a booming empire in the space of a few years.

'Yes,' she said curtly, giving him a challenging look.

'Then I will accompany you.'

'There is no need.'

In truth, he was intrigued to see what sort of life Isobel led. Ten years earlier she had tearfully refused his offer of marriage because her father had forbidden it. He always assumed it was so Isobel could make a better match, a match with a man of money to save the Partridge family from ruin and a status in society to match her own. It was curious that she hadn't ever married and, despite telling himself he no longer cared, he was eager to know what had gone wrong.

Without another word she spun on her heels and hurried downstairs, descending into the depths of the basement where the kitchen was located. It was tidy but sparse, with a few pots and pans hanging from the hooks on the wall and some plates on a dresser in the corner.

'Something smells good,' he said, taking in a deep in-halation of whatever was bubbling in the pot on the stove.

There was a flicker of a smile on Isobel's face, gone as quickly as it appeared, and he wondered if she had taken on the role of cook, too.

'Tea?' she asked, 'Or something stronger?'

'Tea will be fine.'

She set about putting the kettle to boil and fetching the teapot while he explored the kitchen and larder. He grabbed the jug of milk stored in the coolness and brought it out, stunned to see how little food there was in the pantry.

At home he left the running of his household to his very efficient housekeeper, Mrs Falmouth. She ensured the kitchen was stocked with everything the cook might need and his larder was a delight of different delicacies from around the world. There were spices and sugars and huge canisters full of tea and coffee. Very different to the sparseness of Isobel's pantry.

As he poured the milk into the cups he saw movement

outside the high window, something that had also caught Isobel's eye.

The kitchen was in the basement, but not entirely underground, with natural light let in through high windows that looked on to the garden beyond the house.

'No,' Isobel shouted suddenly, dropping the cup she was moving with a clatter into the saucer. Her face pale, she darted past him, disappearing up the stairs and within seconds he heard a door opening to the outside. Startled by the sudden movement, he dashed after her, catching up with her in the garden where she had pulled up short.

At first he didn't see what had made her turn so pale. The garden was different from how he remembered it. Gone were the cultivated beds of flowers and instead in their place were rows of neatly planted vegetables. Even in the thick snow he could see where the Partridges grew their beans, root vegetables and fresh herbs. The next part of the garden was taken up with a fenced enclosure where the chickens were kept. It was this Isobel was staring at with horror.

The chickens were squawking loudly, strutting about, but there was an air of panic about the birds. Movement caught his eye and he saw a puff of feathers emerging from the rickety hen house in one corner.

Isobel leapt over the fence, lifting her skirts and running over to the wooden structure. He saw her hesitate for a second and then lift the roof off. The sound that emerged from her throat was a strangled cry and it cut straight through him.

Quickly he jumped over the fence to join her and as he approached there was a flash of rust red as a fox darted out. He watched as it made for a rickety section of fence and squeezed under the slats, disappearing into the garden.

There was a scene of devastation in the hen house.

Blood was mixed with feathers and in the middle lay the limp body of a fat hen. Next to him he heard Isobel let out a sob and he turned to see her wiping a tear from her cheek. Carefully, almost reverently, she reached in and lifted the mauled body of the hen.

'Let me do that,' Thomas said quietly, taking the dead chicken from her hands. She handed it over without protest, turning her face away as she struggled to regain her composure.

Thomas was struck by a memory of when they had been eleven or twelve and playing in the woods at the edge of the village. They had come across a wounded rabbit, alive but barely so, whimpering in distress. It had a bloody and broken leg and a huge gash on its abdomen, injuries there was no way it could ever survive.

Isobel had wept for the rabbit then, begging him to help the animal, even though they both knew the kindest thing would be to break its neck and end its suffering. Thomas had taken it away, planning on doing just that, but the rabbit had died as he moved somewhere quiet.

Isobel had been withdrawn for days after that and he could tell she was thinking about the poor creature. It was the same look she had now.

'Damn fox,' she said, regaining some of her colour.

'Has it bothered them before?'

'I caught it sniffing round a few nights ago, but at nighttime I lock everything up and it can't get in. I never thought it would be so brave as to approach during the day.'

'The fence needs mending and strengthening.'

'I know,' she said wearily and it struck him that Isobel probably looked after all of this as well. No wonder she looked pale and drawn. He felt a flicker of sympathy for her and quickly tried to push it away. She had made her choices ten years ago— he shouldn't feel bad for her having to live with the consequences.

Suddenly she sagged, clutching at the closest fence post and leaning on it heavily. Her face was pale and for a moment he thought she might swoon. He moved without thinking, propping his shoulder underneath her arm and taking her weight easily.

'We should get you inside, he said, wishing his hands were not bloody from the bird. Then he could lift her over the fence and ensure she got back to the kitchen without injuring herself.

'I'm sorry, I will be fine in a moment.'

'It is a shock, there is nothing to apologise for.' It felt strange to be talking to Isobel again, but to address her so formally, as if they didn't know everything about one another. He supposed now though they didn't. Ten years was a long time and much had changed. He was no longer the same person and he doubted Isobel was either.

She staggered as she tried to lift her leg over the fence and Thomas made the decision to put the dead bird down, wiping his hands on his trousers and sweeping Isobel into his arms. She gave a little mutter of protest, but rested her head against his shoulder all the same.

As her body pressed against his Thomas felt a surge of memory and desire and comfort all at once. It was an unsettling feeling and he had to force himself to put one foot in front of the other, retracing their steps back to the kitchen.

Only once she was settled on a hard stool at the kitchen table did he step away, glad to put some distance between them.

Chapter Five

Isobel felt like a fool. She was not afraid of a little blood—that did not make her swoon like some women she knew—but standing in the chicken coop she *had* felt light-headed. It was only now as she sat in the kitchen that she realised she hadn't eaten anything all day. That wasn't an unusual occurrence, but she'd been out twice in the snow, battling the cold and the icy conditions and no doubt that had taken its toll.

She glanced over at Thomas where he stood a good four feet away. As soon as he had set her down, he had retreated, putting the solid wooden table between them as if afraid she might pounce on him.

Closing her eyes, she suppressed a grim smile at the thought. He couldn't make his contempt for her clearer if he tried. Not that she blamed him. Ten years ago, they had been completely and utterly in love. If anyone had asked, she would have said she would die for him, but then he had asked her to marry him, to take a chance on him and the opportunity he had been offered to go into business with a successful cloth merchant.

She'd wanted to more than anything else, but her father had found out and had forbidden her to ever have contact with Thomas again. Her first instinct had been to rail and push against the order, but then her father had fallen ill and she had remembered her promise to her mother to care for the old man. Isobel had turned down Thomas's proposal, even though she had loved him with all her heart, and she had regretted her decision every day since.

'Drink,' he ordered and then disappeared into the pantry. For a minute all she could hear was the rustling and clinking of paper and jars as he opened and looked inside everything. 'Where is all your food, Isobel?' he said, poking his head round the corner.

'In the pot.'

'That's dinner, but what about the rest?'

'There's some bread and cheese for Father's breakfast on the top shelf, don't touch that.'

'What about your breakfast?'

She shrugged.

Thomas came and sat next to her, his face grim.

'Tell me truthfully, what have you eaten today, Isobel?'

She couldn't meet his eye and shrugged. 'Nothing,' she said eventually.

'Nothing?'

'It's been a busy day.' She took a sip of the tea he had set before her, savouring the flavour.

'Do you have any servants?'

'Just Mrs Hooper.'

'Mrs Hooper? She must be seventy.'

'I think she is around sixty.'

He peered out the window and then seemed to make a decision. Striding off, she heard him calling for the old housekeeper and then there was a murmur of voices, the words she could not quite make out.

Coming back into the kitchen, he took a seat next to her, his expression grim.

'Isobel,' he said, his hands clasped together in front of him as if he were a vicar talking to a troubled parishioner. 'I cannot believe your father has so little money he cannot afford to give you anything for food.' He held up a hand. 'I know it is none of my concern, we are not friends any more, we lead completely separate lives, but I speak as anyone with a shred of humanity would. If you do not eat, you will fall ill.'

'I merely forgot this morning.'

He raised his eyebrows to show her he didn't believe her for one second.

'There are things we could sell,' Isobel said softly, 'Things we will sell. I have broached the subject with Father, but first he needs a little time to get used to the idea.'

'And until then you must starve?'

She stood, feeling her head spin slightly. 'You're right, it is none of your concern.'

She felt a wave of shame. Isobel was sensible enough to know her family's misfortune was not of her making, but she still sometimes felt guilt that she had not done more to ease it.

When she had been younger her father had talked of her saving the family, of restoring the Senlac fortune, by marrying well. It had been one of the main reasons he had objected to her romance with Thomas. Thomas had been ambitious but penniless at the time of the proposal.

After Thomas had left, she fallen into a deep despair and even as she had slowly pulled herself from it she had not been able to summon any enthusiasm for the suitors her father had pushed her way. As it was, their debts had caught up with them soon after and there had been no more talk of a London Season, no more fine gowns, or dances, no more invitations to dinner parties.

'Sit,' he said, his tone firm. 'You can scowl at me all

you like from down there, but do not make yourself swoon on my account.'

Isobel thought about defiance, but her head was spinning so she staggered back to the stool and slumped on to it, closing her eyes.

'Good. Don't even think about moving until Mrs Hooper gets back with some food.'

'Food?'

'Yes, food. Proper, hearty, filling food.'

'It is only a little over two hours until dinner.'

'Then you will at least have two meals today.' He left the room without a backward glance and Isobel felt a rush of mixed emotions. It was difficult seeing him again. Part of her wanted to throw her arms around him, to forget the intervening years had ever happened and kiss as she used to a decade earlier. The other part felt a deep regret and guilt, for she was aware how much she had hurt him with her betrayal.

She sat for a long time, drinking her tea, only occasionally getting up to stir the pot on the stove. It was a thick stew, seasoned with dried herbs from her garden and filled with root vegetables. She hoped the thickness of the sauce would disguise the fact there was no meat in the pot.

Mrs Hooper returned after half an hour with a basket filled to the brim. As she unpacked it Isobel's mouth began to water. Guiltily she cut herself a slice of crusty bread and spread a large knob of butter across it. It was delicious and she felt some of her vitality returning.

'What's Mr Williamson doing outside?' Mrs Hooper asked, peering out the high window, straining to see.

Isobel joined her, unable to see much given her height. Feeling revitalised, she left Mrs Hooper in the kitchen with instructions to watch the stew and went out into the garden.

Her heart squeezed as she realised what Thomas was

doing. Without being asked, without even a hint or any expectation, he had hunted down a hammer and some nails and was methodically fixing the fence around the chicken enclosure so no fox could get in underneath.

Isobel stood quietly, not saying a word for a moment, just watching. As Thomas straightened she moved silently towards him and, lifting herself up on tiptoes, kissed him on the cheek.

He spun to look at her, but she was already retreating, disappearing back inside the house without making a sound.

Thomas stood, hand on cheek, unsure if he was trying to hold on to the feel of her kiss or if he was wiping it away.

For ten long years, after he had got over the initial shock and heart-wrenching sorrow when Isobel had refused him, he had resolutely told himself he felt nothing towards the woman who had caused him so much pain. He had tried to push her entirely from his mind, leaving the room if a mutual acquaintance started speaking of her and reminding his family time and again his and Isobel's friendship was over. Over the years he thought he had done a good job of getting over Isobel, but with that one, gentle kiss it was as if the whole charade had come crashing down around him.

His heart thumped in his chest and his instinct was to stride after her, to hold her close to him and to kiss her until they both forgot they had been apart for a decade.

'Control yourself,' he murmured, trying to tell himself it was merely a visceral reaction. After having not seen Isobel for ten long years, it was only natural his body would remind him he had once loved her more than life itself.

Bending, he continued with his work, looking up with a frown when he heard the door opening again. If she was going to kiss him again, at least this time he would be prepared.

'You never could rest on your laurels,' his mother said, beaming at him. 'Even when you were little, even after a day of roaming the fields and woods with Isobel, you would return home and soon I would heard the tap-tap of you mending something. You always were very industrious.'

Thomas smiled, relaxing a little. It was true, he found it difficult to stay still when there was something that needed mending or fixing.

'I saw you and Isobel out here earlier, did something happen with the chickens?'

'A fox got it,' he said, motioning to the dead bird he still needed to dispose of.

'You carried her in. It is not like the Isobel I know to swoon.'

Thomas grunted, feeling his anger rise again at the fact her father was withholding the funds that allowed Isobel to eat more than one meal a day.

'She hasn't eaten all day,' he said quietly. 'Apparently she is waiting for her father to agree to sell some of their furniture, so they have a little money.'

'Ah. Poor girl.'

Thomas passed a hand over his brow, reminding himself it was acceptable to feel sympathy for her without it needing to signify anything more.

'It is surprising she never married,' Mrs Williamson said quietly and Thomas could see her watching him carefully.

'Hardly,' he barked, motioning to the house. 'Her father wants someone to share his misery now he's ruined everything he once had and he likes to have a servant he does not have to pay to do his bidding.'

'I wonder why she stays, though?'

Thomas bent back to his work so his mother would not see his expression. That hurt more than anything else. Isobel not only rejected him, but she chose a life of misery with her father over the life they had dreamed of together.

Mrs Williamson shook her head. 'I suppose she does not have many options, not after she refused the last of her suitors. Once a woman turns down enough men, she gets enough of a reputation that people stop asking.'

Turning to his mother in surprise, he raised an eyebrow. 'You never told me someone proposed?'

'You don't like talking about her.' She smiled and patted him on the arm. 'And she said no. There were three, I think, all wealthy and two had titles. One was old, one had an unfortunate face, but the last was a good prospect.'

Thomas remained silent, trying to work out why this information felt like it mattered to him.

'Well,' his mother said eventually, 'it is nice to see you two together again.'

'We're not together,' he said abruptly. 'We have been thrown into close proximity by difficult circumstances.

For a long time after his mother disappeared back inside the house Thomas considered the information she had given him. What he should do was push any thought of Isobel from his mind. This afternoon he had a job to do. Tomorrow would be taken up with organising someone to fix the roof of his mother's cottage and then there would only be a few more days until hopefully the snow cleared enough to allow him to retreat to home. He could survive that.

Chapter Six

'This is delicious, Miss Partridge,' Mrs Williamson said, smiling with all her grace and kindness across the table at Isobel. 'What talent you have.'

Isobel inclined her head graciously. Cooking was not one of her natural talents, but necessity had made her an expert over recent years. Mrs Hooper cooked some of the meals, but the housekeeper's hands were swollen and curled with arthritis and some days she could not hold a knife let alone prepare a full meal.

Slowly Isobel had taken over those duties and as their funds had dwindled, she had learned to make something filling and full of flavour with few ingredients.

'Tell me about your business, Mr Williamson,' Lord Senlac said from his position at the top of the table.

Isobel saw the cold dislike in Thomas's eyes as he regarded her father, but his answer was polite enough.

'I import fabric from all over the world and sell it to the drapers and dressmakers of London and the south of England.'

'I understand you've made quite the success of it.'

'I am pleased to say the business thrives.'

'Hear that, Isobel?' her father barked. 'Mr Williamson's business thrives.'

'I am pleased for you, Mr Williamson,' Isobel said, letting her eyes flick up to meet his for an instant only. Ever since she had found him mending the chicken enclosure earlier that afternoon, she had felt a pressure in her chest every time she looked at him. They had been friends for longer than they had been apart and it was hard to lose that friendship.

When Thomas had left Battle to seek his fortune, Isobel had been doubly bereft, losing the man she loved, but also her closest friend at the same time. It had been a lonely time for her, with no one to confide in.

Seeing him this afternoon quietly taking charge and doing something kind for her was a bittersweet reminder of why she had loved him so much. Thomas was kind and generous. In a life where her main influence was her father, it was wonderfully novel to have someone who didn't just think of his own gain, his own wants and needs.

'You're a successful man,' her father said, brandishing his spoon as if it were an extension of himself. 'Yet you are not married—why is that?'

Isobel's eyes widened and she felt her cheeks begin to burn.

Thomas didn't speak for a long moment, giving Lord Senlac an assessing stare, and then shrugged. 'I haven't found a woman I can trust.'

Lord Senlac let out a short bark of laughter and thumped the table.

'Now that's an honest answer. And you are a sensible man, Mr Williamson. I never remarried after my late wife passed. You get to a certain age and you can be sure all the women want you for is your title or your money.'

'Who would like dessert?' Isobel said, standing up abruptly and setting the cutlery clattering.

'Sit down, girl, we haven't finished. You want to find

yourself a woman like my Isobel here,' Lord Senlac said, grinning to show a full set of yellow teeth. 'Too old to have her pick of men, a woman like that is just *grateful* to be finally chosen. You get devotion and gratitude, like a master gets from his dog.'

She spun to leave the room, knowing she could not stop her father from saying these horrible things, but also aware she did not have to stand here and listen to them. He'd always been cruel, but these last few years he had become bitter, too, and it was as though any hint of kindness had shrivelled and blackened inside him.

Thomas moved quickly and caught her by the wrist, a subtle movement, but unmissable for everyone at the table.

'You insult your daughter, my lord,' he said curtly. 'I suggest you apologise.'

'She doesn't need my apology,' Lord Senlac said, leaning back in his chair, 'She knows I speak the truth. The suitors I arranged for you don't seem so bad now, do they, Isobel?'

Isobel wrenched her hand from Thomas's wrist and, with a disgusted look at her father, left the room, fleeing upstairs where he or his words could not follow her.

She didn't expect the footsteps that echoed after her own, or the hand that reached out to stop her bedroom door from shutting.

Slowly, wiping away the tears on her cheeks, she turned to face Thomas.

'What are you doing?'

'He shouldn't speak to you like that.'

Isobel looked away. Her father had always been cruel and most of the time she let his words slip over her, not ever affecting her enough to make her cry. Sometimes, though, when she felt at her most vulnerable, she couldn't help but wonder if what he said were true.

Thomas took a step towards her and gently placed his

hands on her upper arms, waiting until she looked at him to speak again.

'He shouldn't speak to you like that,' he repeated.

'I know. He is cruel, it is just how he is.'

'Why do you put up with it?'

Isobel recoiled a little, shocked by the question. 'I do not choose to be insulted by my father every day, to be treated like a worthless being. It is not something which is in my control.'

He was still holding her by the arms and Isobel felt the urge to step closer, to bury her face in his chest and inhale the scent she knew so well. More than anything she wanted Thomas to wrap his arms around her, to enfold her in his strength and the safety he could offer.

'I would not stay,' Thomas said quietly. 'If I were you, I would not stay and put up with that.'

Isobel snorted and turned away, breaking the connection between them.

'You think it is that easy for a woman, a near enough destitute woman, to strike out on her own?'

'It sounds like you had offers of marriage. Surely they would have provided better options than the one you are in now.'

Isobel searched his face and realised the true question he was seeking an answer to.

'Surely I was a better option than *that*,' he said quietly.

'It's not that simple.'

'I really think it is, Isobel. When you turned me down, I was upset, but I could sort of understand your motivations. You thought you could make a better match than the penniless son of a clerk. You are the daughter of a baron, after all, the exalted Partridge family. Yet in the last ten years you have chosen not to marry, but instead to stay here and be treated worse than a dog by a man who clearly does not care for you. Is that life truly better than the one you could have shared with me?'

'I was eighteen, Thomas, naive in the ways of the world. I made a mistake and I have been paying for that mistake every day since.'

She sighed and turned away, moving to the curtains, and pulling them shut, moving the sole candle in the room to the little bedside table. Thomas shouldn't be in here, but there was no one to cause any trouble. Mrs Williamson was hardly going to do anything to ruin her son's reputation and Isobel's own father couldn't get up the stairs without help to catch them.

He was silent for a long time and Isobel had to glance back to the entrance to the bedroom to check he hadn't left.

'A mistake?' he echoed eventually.

'Yes, a mistake.' She gave a sad little smile. 'I loved you more than anything in the world, but I was scared to leave everything I knew behind. I had my father telling me I would be a disappointment, that my purpose in life was to marry someone who could save our family from destitution. And I had the promise I made my mother to contend with—I promised her I would look after Father.'

She fingered the candlestick, wiping some solidified wax from the heavy base. 'I wish I had been braver, but I wasn't.'

For a long moment Thomas didn't speak, then without another word he turned and left the room. Isobel sighed. This reunion was never going to be easy. For her it was forcing her to think of the life she could have had with Thomas, the decade she could have spent with the man she loved rather than wallowing in misery here in Senlac House.

Chapter Seven

Thomas rose early despite not sleeping well. He didn't feel comfortable staying under Lord Senlac's roof and hadn't been able to relax enough to do more than doze off throughout the night. Isobel's words had haunted him too. *A mistake.*

When she had refused him ten years ago, he had been too heartbroken to fully take in her explanations, her words of entreaty. All he had heard was no. Now she was admitting she had been scared, worried about letting her family down, uncertain about what to do for the best.

It didn't matter, he told himself, it was all ancient history.

These past few years he had been confident he was over Isobel, over the heartbreak, but being here in Battle, seeing her again, brought a rush of emotions back.

'Enough,' he murmured to himself. Today he would put Isobel from his mind. There was plenty to arrange to get the roof of his mother's cottage fixed and he would occupy himself there for the day. The sky was clear for the first time in almost a week and perhaps, if he was lucky, some of the snow might begin to melt and their forced stay at Senlac House would soon be coming to an end.

Upstairs the house was quiet, but downstairs he paused

as he heard a soft voice singing. Immediately he knew it was Isobel, already up and working, no doubt. It was a curious situation here, a large crumbling mansion house with some grand but tattered furniture and no real money to maintain it.

Isobel played the role of housemaid and cook and housekeeper all at once and he acknowledged she must find it exhausting and that was before you even considered the burden of looking after her father.

For a moment he did nothing more than listen to her voice, trying to ignore the stabbing pain in his chest as the notes rose and fell. She'd always had a beautiful voice, but in the darkness of the downstairs rooms it sounded haunting. He was drawn to the sound, carried along as if bewitched, until he stood in the doorway to the kitchen.

Isobel broke off when she saw him, looking up with a sadness in her eyes that he hated to see. He wanted to go to her, to sweep her into his arms and brush away the desolation he saw there.

Thomas wondered if he would ever truly be over Isobel. He could pretend all he liked, assure his mother he never thought of the woman who had broken his heart, scoff at the idea of love if his friends ever raised the subject, but all the time the ghost of Isobel, of their relationship and everything they had shared, all the time he carried that with him.

'Good morning,' he said gruffly, wishing he had escaped out of the front door without her seeing him.

'Good morning.' She gave him a smile that didn't quite reach her eyes and he realised for the first time the strain it must be putting on her, having him back in her life.

'I didn't expect anyone else to be up.'

'I don't often sleep past six o'clock—there is so much to be done first thing in the morning.'

He could see she had been busy. Eggs were collected and sitting in a basket on the countertop and her hands were sticky with the dough she was kneading.

'I am planning on going to my mother's cottage this morning, to assess the damage. Hopefully I will be able to find someone who can do the work to repair it.'

'You'll want to speak to the Loweridge brothers.'

'Oh?'

'They are hard workers and there is not much they cannot fix. A few years back we had some repairs that urgently needed doing and they came highly recommended. I couldn't fault their work.'

'If they are that good, then I expect they will be busy.'

'No doubt, but if they cannot do it, you could try Mr Hemsby.'

Thomas paused before speaking, trying to work out if he would regret his next words before it became too late to take them back.

'I would like it if you came with me,' he said softly.

Isobel's eyes widened with surprise, her tongue darting out over her lips. He had the sudden urge to kiss her, to taste those soft, sweet lips of hers. It was an unexpected and unbidden thought and hastily he pushed it away.

'I would like to assist you in any way I can,' she said slowly, 'but I am needed here.'

'Nonsense. Your father can do without you for a few hours.'

'What about your mother—she will want breakfast when she rises?'

'My mother is perfectly capable of preparing anything she needs herself.'

Isobel looked horrified at the thought of a guest having to cater for themselves.

'But do not fear, she has not eaten breakfast for twenty years. She will make herself a cup of tea, nothing more.'

Isobel chewed on her lip.

'I was eager to get out this morning to collect some holly and mistletoe to decorate the house with for Christmas.'

'Then it is settled. We will inspect my mother's house, speak to the Loweridge brothers and then find you some festive greenery.'

Firmly he told himself he had asked her along merely to make his life easier. He had not resided in Battle for ten years. He did not know all the builders and labourers like Isobel did. It made sense to take someone with him who could advise on the best person to employ as well as where to find them.

The flush of pleasure he felt at spending some time with Isobel away from the oppressive house he quickly tried his hardest to suppress.

It felt good to get outside. These last few days Isobel had felt as though she were slowly suffocating in her father's presence and it was freeing to be away from the house.

'Take my arm, Isobel, the path is icy. I will not bite,' Thomas said, giving her a quick smile. He, too, had relaxed out here in the open, the crisp fresh air seeming to calm them both.

She slipped a gloved hand into the crook of his elbow and they silently fell into step beside one another.

'I think about you a lot,' Isobel said after a few minutes and couldn't help but laugh when she saw the horror on Thomas's face. 'Don't look so disturbed. All I mean is a lot of things remind me of you and I find myself wondering about your life.'

There was more to it than that, but she didn't want Thomas to go running off into the snow, never to tread the streets of Battle again.

'That tree there, for example,' Isobel said, pointing to a

great oak tree that stood at the end of their garden where their land met the road. 'I can remember, when I was eight or nine, we spent weeks sitting up in the branches, waiting for people to pass and then throwing acorns down.'

'Mr Kemp, the old blacksmith, thrashed me so hard I couldn't walk straight for a week,' Thomas said. He smiled ruefully at the memory and Isobel felt a flood of warmth pass through her. 'I was always getting thrashed when they caught us, whereas if I remember correctly you would be told to run home and stop associating with such an unruly troublemaker.'

'I would try to tell them it was all my idea...' She laughed. It had been a carefree time, those days when her mother was alive to provide a barrier between Isobel and her father's worst moods and Isobel had spent most of her days running wild with Thomas.

'Do you remember when we were setting paper boats to float in the stream and Peter Jarvis came bothering us as he often did? He fell in and soaked his new Sunday outfit and was so incensed he promised to make both our lives hell?'

Isobel nodded, able to picture the moment clearly.

'He was a brute, always following me home and pulling my hair or trying to scare me with some insect he had found.' She smiled ruefully. 'I know you have tried to put your time here in Battle from your mind, but I think of our childhood, of our time together, fondly. Those years I spent with you were the best anyone could hope for.'

Thomas regarded her hard for a second and then looked away, quickening his pace so she had to hurry to keep up.

'Have I upset you?'

'No,' he said shortly, but the smile was gone from his face and the frown back between his brows.

'I have. I am sorry.'

'I am not upset,' he said firmly.

Isobel slipped her arm out from his and paused for a second, waiting until he turned back to face her, then bent and scooped up some snow from the ground very deliberately. It was soft and fluffy in her hands, compressing perfectly into a little round ball.

'Isobel,' he said, a warning note in his voice.

'Yes, Thomas.'

'Whatever you plan on doing, think again.'

She raised her arm, taking her hand well back beyond her shoulder, and threw as hard as she could, the snowball striking him where his neck met his collar.

'Isobel Partridge you will stop that at once,' he said, shuddering as the snow seeped down under the collar of his coat.

Very slowly she bent again, scooping up another ball of snow.

'Don't even think about it.'

'Or what, Thomas?'

For a long moment he was silent and Isobel found herself holding her breath, knowing this was a pivotal moment for their relationship. Either he would stride away, refusing to be drawn into the frivolity of a snowball fight, or he would turn and face her.

She felt her heart soar as he turned and faced her, bending to scoop up the biggest handful of snow and shaping it into a ball.

'I am stronger than you, I am a better shot than you and I promise I will have no mercy whatsoever.'

Isobel threw her snowball, shrieking as Thomas let his loose at the same time. His hit her squarely in the chest, flattening against her coat, but easily brushed off. Hers glanced off his shoulder.

Thomas was moving forward now and she could see he had another snowball in his hand. She darted to the left, thankful of her sturdy boots as she picked her way as quickly as she could to find shelter behind one of the broad tree trunks that lined the road.

Thomas's next throw was a miss, smacking into the tree with a thud and drawing a curse from Thomas. Isobel gathered her next missile and leapt out from behind the tree, yelling in triumph as it hit him in the side of the head.

He stood there, shaking his head. 'That is it, Isobel. No more holding back. I'm going to pelt you with snowballs until you beg for mercy.'

Isobel fled back behind the tree to gather some more snow and press it into the firm ball, feeling a lightness inside she hadn't felt for a very long time.

With a loud battle cry she jumped out on to the road, only to find it empty. Too late she spun to find Thomas creeping up behind her, ready to attack at close range. Three snowballs in quick succession hit her, the final one glancing off her jaw, sending icy droplets down her neck and making her shudder. Isobel gasped and then without thinking ran at full speed at Thomas, planning on pressing the snowball in her hand into any exposed piece of skin.

Her body hit his and together they went tumbling down into the soft snow. Isobel was laughing so much she could hardly catch her breath and she felt a joy unlike anything she had experienced in the last few years. Her days of care-free pursuits, of anything other than duty and hardship, were long behind her, but right now, in this moment, she could pretend she was seventeen again and wildly happy.

She knew she should move, should lever her body off Thomas's. If anyone were to come upon them, they did not have the excuse of youth any longer. This sort of behaviour would not be put down to youthful foolishness, there would be real consequences.

For a moment Isobel allowed herself to imagine those consequences. Married to Thomas, a life away from Senlac House and her father, a household of her own, perhaps even a brood of children, all with Thomas's green eyes.

It was too much and Isobel quickly shifted. Over the years she had often thought of what she had missed out on. Of course, there had been other opportunities to be a wife, a mother, but she had not been able to push herself to take them. The truth was she had made a horrific mistake, refusing Thomas's proposal, and she had not been able to move past it and move on with her life. She had become stuck in this never-ending nightmare of her own making.

She felt Thomas catch her arm as she began to push herself up and she froze in place, her eyes meeting his. Perplexed, she thought she saw a flare of desire in them. Isobel knew that could never be.

Thomas was kind and generous and perhaps this short reunion might allow him to think of her more charitably, but she was aware he wouldn't be able to forgive her for breaking his heart and destroying what they had together. It was too much to ask even from a good man like Thomas.

After a moment she forced herself to look away and stood, slipping a little as she got up, but was able to find her balance after a few seconds. She reached out a hand to pull Thomas up, self-conscious when his body brushed against hers.

'That was irresponsible,' he murmured, but she could hear the smile in his voice even without looking at him.

'Irresponsible, but fun,' Isobel said.

'I cannot deny it.'

'I haven't had fun like that in ten years,' Isobel murmured, trying to disguise the sadness in her voice.

Chapter Eight

'Dazzle me,' Isobel said as they turned off the main road and into a small lane. 'Dazzle me with tales of your adventures. I have never left the borders of Sussex and I doubt I will now. I want to live vicariously through you.'

It was almost lunchtime and Thomas's stomach was rumbling given he hadn't had breakfast, but he didn't protest at the detour. The morning had been much less stressful than it could have been, and he had to acknowledge much of that was because Isobel was by his side.

Together they had assessed the damage at his mother's cottage and secured what they could from any further rain or snow. Then they had travelled to the Loweridge brothers' house and Isobel had proceeded to charm and cajole the two men into promising they would look at the roof first thing tomorrow morning, despite it being Christmas Eve.

Thomas could see how much the people in the village liked Isobel and he had got a sense of the way she had found a place for herself in the community as her home life had deteriorated. Everywhere they went someone called out a friendly greeting and she enquired after children or infirm relatives.

Now, with a plan for the repairs needed on his mother's cottage, all that remained to do this morning was to gather the holly and mistletoe Isobel wanted to decorate the house with.

'You want to hear of tigers prowling through the forests of India and tropical storms off the coast of Africa?'

'You've been to India and Africa?'

'Yes, although a few years ago now. The man who offered me a part of his business was elderly with no close relatives. He wanted someone who could travel and seek out new sources of fabrics that we could import. I was eager to get out of the country and told him I would go anywhere he wanted. I travelled to Africa, to the great dusty markets of the north, then sailed on round the Cape, travelling by boat to India. It was exactly what I needed.'

Isobel nodded solemnly. 'I am sorry,' she said quietly, her eyes filled with regret.

For a moment he didn't respond and then he nodded. He believed it now, believed that she regretted breaking his heart, believed that she hated the thought of hurting him. For years he had held on to this notion that he had never truly known her, that the Isobel he thought he knew was a fiction, something conjured up by his mind, for that woman wouldn't have broken his heart so completely.

Now he could see that Isobel had suffered in the years since they had last seen one another. She had turned down the offers from other suitors, condemned herself to a life of misery living with her father. He wondered if it was a punishment of sorts, a punishment to herself for making the wrong decision when she was a girl of eighteen.

It was one good thing that had come out of this eventful trip at least. Perhaps now he would be able to let go of some of the anger and bitterness he felt towards her. Perhaps now he might be able to move on. These last few years as his peers had married and started their families Thomas had been self-aware enough to realise he had been irretrievably changed by the heartbreak with Isobel. He wouldn't allow anyone close for fear they might hurt him as she had. It would be a relief to be able to let go of that, to move past it.

'I know.' He paused for a long moment, hating the sadness in her expression. Most of the morning she had been cheerful, able to shake the air of melancholy she had about her when around her father, but now she looked dejected again. 'Tell me where we are going?'

She brightened a little and gripped hold of his hand, the touch innocent and natural, but it sent a sharp bolt of desire ripping through him. Isobel was still beautiful, inside and out, and whenever she touched him, he had this overwhelming desire to forget everything that had happened between them and kiss her as if they were still in the first flush of youth.

'This way,' she said, walking through the snow as easily as if it were a meadow of spring flowers.

They followed the narrow lane for a few hundred feet and then branched off down a path that felt familiar to Thomas. The snow made everything look a little different, but when they came to a set of wooden steps leading down to a stream he knew exactly where they were.

The stream itself was frozen over, thick ice covering its surface, but they stuck to the path along its edge. They walked a little way along the banks of the stream before Isobel pointed out a healthy holly bush, thick with the green leaves and red berries.

From her basket she brought out a small knife and began snipping sprigs of the holly off, her fingers moving quickly but carefully. She placed the greenery in the basket, continuing until she had a good amount and then turned to a nearby tree with a look of grim determination on her face.

'Hold this,' she said, thrusting the knife and basket at him.

He took the basket with a frown, watching as she walked a few paces away.

'Isobel, what are you doing?'

'We have no money for presents this year and at the moment I think the only way we will have any meat on Christmas Day is if I kill one of my chickens. I cannot afford good candles or sweetmeats, but mistletoe is free, and I will have something that marks Christmas as special.'

Slowly he looked up, his heart sinking as he realised what she planned to do.

'You don't mean to climb up there?'

'It is just a little climb.'

'Isobel. The tree is covered in snow, the branches are slippery and it's ten feet up in the air.'

She gripped hold of a branch, 'But think how lovely my dining room will look decorated in holly and mistletoe.'

As she went to pull herself up Thomas placed the basket down and stepped forward and looped an arm around her waist.

'Don't,' he said softly, his lips close to her neck. From here he could smell her familiar scent, the mix of lavender and soap. It took him back ten years to when he had taken any opportunity to get close to Isobel.

Slowly she turned, his arms still wrapped around her waist. They were standing far too close, their bodies pressed against one another. Her chest was rising and falling rapidly, as if she were out of breath even though she hadn't begun to climb yet.

Without thinking of the consequences Thomas brushed his lips against hers, a feeling of triumph erupting inside him as he reclaimed what he had lost ten years ago. She tasted sweet and after a moment her body relaxed into his.

Pressing her back against the tree, Thomas kissed her as if there was no tomorrow. Part of him must have acknowledged that this kiss could never be repeated and he told himself that was the reason he never wanted it to end.

After a minute he pulled away, loving the dreamy, far-away look in Isobel's eyes. It took her a moment to focus on him and only then did he see the mix of shock and desire dawning in her expression.

She shifted a little, her hand reaching out for his, but that tiny movement was enough to jerk him out of his reverie, to break the spell. Regret crashed down and he hurriedly took a step back and then another.

'Thomas,' Isobel said, confusion in her voice.

'That shouldn't have happened,' he said gruffly. 'Go home.'

'Thomas…'

'Go home, Isobel. We will talk later.'

He needed some time to himself, needed to pull apart all the conflicting emotions he was feeling. More than anything he needed Isobel to get far away from him before they did something he regretted.

For a long moment she looked up at him, tears glistening in her eyes, then she gave a short, sharp nod and hurried off in the direction of Senlac House.

As she disappeared into the distance Thomas collapsed against the tree, flooded with relief. His body was wound tight, tension in every muscle. He hadn't meant to kiss her, but as she stood there, body pressed against his, he hadn't been able to resist. Then she had been so willing, so responsive in his arms.

Running a hand through his hair, he acknowledged how close he had been to taking things further. *That* would have been disastrous, something he could not have come back from. As it was a kiss was forgivable, perhaps even understandable given the history and the attraction that still simmered between them. A kiss he could apologise for and nothing else would have to change.

He waited for a long time in the snow, trying not to think of how right it had felt with Isobel in his arms, before following her footprints down the path to Senlac House.

Chapter Nine

'You're back,' the friendly voice of Mrs Williamson greeted her as Isobel hurried into the kitchen.

For a moment she was shocked to find someone else in her domain, but as the older woman bustled round her the shock turned into her desperately trying to hold in the tears.

Out in the snow she had felt her heart soar when Thomas kissed her. In those few seconds she had built up her hopes and dreams. Then, as he pulled away, it had all come crashing down. She had seen the undisguised panic in his eyes, the way he had sent her off because he couldn't bear to look at her. Not that she blamed him. She had broken his heart—of course he wouldn't be in a hurry to put it in jeopardy again.

'Sit down, dear, you must be ravenous. Thomas told me you are barely eating and I can see you are all skin and bone.'

Mrs Williamson took Isobel's coat from her and pressed her on to one of the stools next to the kitchen table. A delicious smell pervaded the kitchens and Isobel realised her mouth was watering.

'I know it is nearly lunchtime, but what if I make you a little breakfast first? It won't do you any harm to have two meals close together. We need to feed you up.'

'You really don't need to go to so much trouble, Mrs Williamson.'

'Nonsense, child, you need looking after.'

For the second time that morning tears pricked Isobel's eyes. It had been a long time since anyone had looked after her. Ever since her mother had died, she had been expected to run the house, to cook and clean and make all the difficult decisions as their finances worsened. She hadn't received a gift on a special occasion for years and she certainly hadn't had anyone telling her she needed looking after.

'You sit there and let me cook you some bacon.'

Isobel frowned. There hadn't been any bacon in the larder that morning.

'I went out to the butcher's,' Mrs Williamson said, seeing Isobel's expression. 'I noticed how little food you had here. I think you are struggling, aren't you, dear?'

Nodding, Isobel closed her eyes for a minute. It was so tempting to let all her worries spill out, but this was Thomas's mother, a woman who should hate her for all the heartache Isobel had piled on her son.

Mrs Williamson laid a hand on her shoulder and squeezed gently and Isobel felt a solidarity that she had never felt before.

'Money is tight,' she said softly. 'We have more to sell, but my father refuses to part with anything until things become truly dire.' She sighed, wishing she could take control of things properly.

'If I had my way, we would sell this house that is crumbling around us and find somewhere smaller, easier to upkeep, but he refuses. He says the Sixth Baron of Senlac should be housed in a manor house, not some decaying cottage hidden in the countryside.'

'You are in a difficult situation here, my dear,' Mrs Williamson acknowledged, 'watching your home and your health decline because your father is too stubborn to admit what he has lost. There are other options open to you,' she said quietly.

Isobel shook her head. 'Do not think I have not considered them. I have a distant cousin in Cornwall who has three young children. She offered me a position as their nanny a few months ago. I have friends, too, who would help me, at least to get started on my own.'

'Yet you cannot bring yourself to leave.'

'No.'

'Is there a reason, I wonder? Beyond filial loyalty.'

Isobel was quiet for a long time. 'You were acquainted with my mother, I think?'

'Yes. A wonderful woman. So generous and kind and always wanting to help others.'

'I loved her so much and when she fell ill, I thought my whole world was ending. She loved my father, even though she was often a victim of his moods as I am now. He was the one thing she seemed blind about, blind to his faults, blind to his cruelty.'

'That is often the way when we are in love.'

'She told me, when she knew she was dying, that she never had to worry about me, that I had a sensible head on my shoulders, but she worried about my father. She made me promise I would look after him, as she had done all those years.'

'Ah, I see,' Mrs Williamson said, moving to flip the bacon that was now sizzling in the pan.

'So, every time I get the courage to leave, every time I gather my things and make plans for the future that do not involve being servant to my father in a crumbling house, I remember my promise to my mother and I find my courage abandons me.'

Mrs Williamson quietly dished up the bacon and set the plate in front of Isobel and then took a seat next to her.

'Eat, dear, and listen carefully to what I have to say.'

Isobel took a bite of the bacon, closing her eyes for a second to savour the rich taste. They hadn't had bacon for months, with Isobel trying to draw out their funds by buying only the cheapest cuts of meat.

'One day, when you have children, you will understand the all-encompassing love a mother has for her children. It overshadows any other relationship and burns with a fierce intensity that never dulls.'

Isobel took another bite and nodded slowly. Her mother had loved her like that, investing every free moment in spending time with Isobel, of teaching her what she knew and exploring what she did not with Isobel by her side.

'That is why I *know* your mother never wanted you to have a life like this. She wouldn't want you to put aside your hopes and dreams to become an overworked, underfed servant to your father. She might have loved him, too, but if she were alive, she would not have tolerated him treating you in this way.' Mrs Williamson reached out and took Isobel's hand. 'It is not too late to reach for what you want from this life. Do it without any guilt or worry that you are letting anyone down.'

'If I leave him, he will die.'

'Unlikely,' Mrs Williamson said. 'I do not mean to be cruel, but men like your father always land on their feet. I expect he would trick someone else into taking care of him for a while. And if he doesn't, you don't have to cut all contact completely, just make the decision you are no longer going to waste your life doing nothing but allowing him to use you.'

She smiled reassuringly. 'It is your choice, of course,

but I want you to know that no mother wants her child to be trapped in a life like yours. It will slowly kill you.'

Isobel couldn't find the words to speak, realising that on many points Mrs Williamson spoke the truth. Her mother had loved her more than anything else. When she had extracted the promise from Isobel to look after her father, it would have been without knowing exactly how much care that would entail.

'Now, I have things to do. I will leave you to think, but do not wait too long as opportunities are sometimes fleeting.'

Thomas had found the wood pile and was at that moment attacking a heavy log with relish, enjoying the burn in his arms as he swung the small axe to split the log in two. There was already a small pile of split logs beside him, but he couldn't see himself stopping soon.

The kiss had been a foolish moment, one he might live to regret. Despite everything Isobel had put him through he didn't want to hurt her. He wasn't a cruel man, and he could see her life was far from ideal—he never wanted to make it any worse.

It had been foolish, but unavoidable, and this was from a man who prided himself on his self-control. In that moment by the frozen stream, he had been unable to stop himself from kissing her. Desire and attraction and an overwhelming primal urge had mixed together and he had wanted to forget the pain she had put him through and the interceding years of loneliness.

As their lips had met, for one wonderful moment Thomas had wondered if this might be the answer to his happiness. Perhaps forgiveness and striving for a future with Isobel was what he needed to be happy.

Ruefully he shook his head. Nothing was as simple as that.

'Working hard, I see,' his mother said as she stepped out into the cold, rubbing her hands together.

'Don't get a chill, Mother,' he said, swinging the axe at the wood.

'How was your trip into the village earlier?'

'Successful,' he said succinctly, trying not to think of the kiss at the end. 'Work should begin on your roof tomorrow and we moved anything from the bedroom that could get wet and spoil when exposed to the elements.'

'You took Miss Partridge with you.'

'Yes.'

'That is good. I think you needed to spend some time together.'

He gave his mother a long assessing look and then swung the axe again.

'Ten years is a long time to hold on to all that hurt,' she continued.

Thomas picked up another piece of wood and set it on the block.

'Perhaps this is the push you need to let go of your anger and move on.'

Thomas didn't say anything, although his mother's words certainly permeated his mind.

'Unless you don't want to move on,' Mrs Williamson said quietly. 'She is a lovely girl. You have both grown up a lot—perhaps ten years ago wasn't the right time, but now is.'

'How could I ever trust her?' he said quietly. Over the past decade he'd spent long spells away from home, often out of the country, but each time he came back his mother looked at him and seemed to be able to fathom his deepest thoughts. When he was honest with himself, he knew he hadn't married, hadn't even allowed any woman to get close, these past ten years, because he still loved Isobel. Even after everything she had done, even after the rejection.

Yet he couldn't simply pull her back into his arms. He could never trust her. Ten years ago he wasn't good enough for her or her family when he was an honest, hardworking but poor man. Now he had made his fortune, a fortune that could easily prop up the failing Senlac dynasty, it was clear in the way Lord Senlac welcomed him that he was interested in him only for the money he could provide should Thomas marry Isobel.

Isobel was not shallow, but she had put her family's needs above her own before so he knew she could again. If he proposed to her, if he gave in to the desire and yearning that flooded him every time he saw her, he would always be wondering if she truly cared or if she had agreed to marry him because of his fortune.

'She was young ten years ago, barely more than a child,' Mrs Williamson said, 'Do not judge her now on the girl she was then.' His mother reached out and placed a hand on his arm. 'I cannot tell you what to do, Thomas, that is for you to work out, but I want you to fully consider every option. Do not make a decision in anger and then regret it for the rest of your life.'

He thought of the regret he saw on Isobel's face when she looked him, hastily hidden. He did believe she was aware she had made a poor decision, but he couldn't be sure she wouldn't repeat it again.

As silently as she had arrived his mother left as Thomas swung the axe again. His fingers were going numb and soon he would have to return inside or risk an injury, but for a little longer he enjoyed the biting cold as the wind whipped at him.

Chapter Ten

It was late and the house was quiet as Isobel padded through the downstairs rooms. She carried a candle with her even though she was familiar with every step, every creaky floorboard, every uneven surface. She paused outside the library, letting out a low sigh, trying to make some of the tension she had been carrying around all day ebb and disappear from her shoulders. These few minutes before bed were sometimes the only time she got to sit and relax after a busy day.

Inside the library she set the candle down on a small table, well away from the books. She didn't need it near the bookshelves. Long ago she had learned where each of the precious volumes were kept. Three years earlier her father had burst into the library with a bookseller, pillaging it for the more precious and expensive tomes. He'd gone away with over three-quarters of the collection and Isobel had sobbed for days.

These books had been her only escape from the drudgery of her day-to-day life and to lose so many at once had been difficult. Ever since she had lived in fear that her father would arrange for the bookseller to return, to come and strip the rest of the books from the shelves, not because of any monetary value, but for the simple fact that she found pleasure here.

Thankfully that day had not come yet, but Isobel was careful only to visit the half-empty library when her father was safely ensconced in his room, snoring away.

Running her fingers over the books she selected a slim volume, a tale of one man's voyage to Africa and his quest for gold in the dusty interior. It was one of her favourites, simply written but evocative all the same. She pulled it from the shelves and turned to pick up her candle. Tonight she would read in bed for a few minutes.

As she made her way towards the door of the library she heard quick footsteps and let out a small cry of surprise as the door opened wider and a shadow fell into the room.

'You're up late,' Thomas said as he frowned at her.

Isobel resisted the urge to cover her body with her arms. She was properly attired to be walking around her own house at night-time, with a thin dressing gown over her chemise and night dress. What was more, the flickering flame of her candle barely illuminated the space around her and Thomas was moving around in the dark.

'As are you.'

They had been stiffly polite at dinner, engaging in stilted conversation largely driven by Mrs Williamson, who had done her best to make the whole affair seem less painful.

Isobel had felt herself sinking into a deep melancholy, unable to believe she had let herself hope there might be something between her and Thomas. He had desired her when they had kissed on the path by the stream, but he had looked disgusted about the fact once he had managed to pull away.

She wondered if he would ever be able to forgive her. Ten years on she still hadn't forgiven herself for making such a terrible mistake. No doubt his hurt stung as vividly as her own.

'I couldn't sleep, I thought I might choose a book to take to bed with me for a while.'

'There isn't much to choose from.' She gestured at the half-empty shelves.

'What happened? Your father always had a wonderful collection of books.'

Her father had never approved of her friendship with Thomas and as such they mainly met outside the house, playing in the fields and the woods surrounding Battle. Yet sometimes on a rainy day when there wasn't much else to do Isobel would sneak Thomas into the library and they would pore over the books and maps and pretend they were planning a trip somewhere exotic.

'My father sold whatever was valuable a few years ago.'

'I am sorry, Isobel, I know how much those books meant to you.'

She shrugged, trying to summon a smile. 'At the time it was more important we could afford to eat.'

'Still…' he murmured. He reached out and for a moment Isobel thought he was going to take her hand. Her heart began thudding in her chest and she swayed forward ever so slightly. Instead he paused and then murmured, 'May I?'

Isobel glanced down, realising he was gesturing to the book in her hand. She nodded and he took it and studied the cover and spine before opening to a random page.

'I remember this one,' he said with a smile, 'It always was one of your favourites.'

'Thankfully the bookseller did not think it was valuable.' She shook her head ruefully. 'I disagree. Do you have a library in your home, Thomas?'

'Yes, one almost as large as this, You'd love it, Isobel,

the shelves are full of world maps and tales of adventure and exploration. One day…' He trailed off.

Isobel tried not to show how much his slip hurt. They both knew there was no chance she was ever going to see his library. The truth of the matter was that they were no longer friends. Even if they were slowly finding their way back to civility, life didn't hold much more for them than that.

Quickly she turned away. Part of her believed it was exactly what she deserved. These last ten years she had done whatever she could to sabotage her own happiness. The dreams of a husband and a family had died when she realised she had pushed away the only man she had ever wanted, the only man she could ever love, and she had been choosing the difficult path ever since.

As she went to take a step away, meaning to walk past Thomas and make her way to her room, Thomas caught her wrist. The contact was unexpected and sudden and Isobel heard herself take a sharp intake of breath.

'Don't go,' he whispered, his words barely audible.

For a long moment she did not move and then she slowly turned back towards him. She longed to throw herself into his arms, to bury her head in his chest and never let go, but Isobel knew that was an impossibility.

She searched his eyes, saw the conflict there and wondered what would happen if she rose up on her tiptoes and kissed his lips. The thought, once there, was difficult to dismiss and she found herself moving ever closer as if in a trance.

'Isobel,' Thomas murmured as she reached up and trailed her fingers across his cheek. Everything she wanted was standing in front of her, yet still she hesitated. It would be too painful to kiss him again and then be pushed away. She wanted more than a brief liaison, more than one final reminder of what they used to have.

The decision was taken from her hands as Thomas bent his neck and kissed her firmly on the lips. His arms pulled her to him, holding her tight, and for a moment she could imagine he never wanted to let her go.

Her body was tense, on edge, and she was waiting for him to realise his mistake and push her away. It was what had happened before outside in the snow—he had given in to the desire he felt, but once his mind had started working again he had regretted his actions.

This time he didn't pull away, holding her body closer to him, seeming to want to make them one.

'Thomas,' Isobel said, murmuring his name against his lips, 'what does this mean?'

It was self-sabotage of the most basic kind, but Isobel couldn't stand to open her heart and then have it shattered once he realised he wanted nothing more than a kiss from her.

'I don't know.' For a long moment his eyes searched hers and she could tell he was looking for an answer in them. 'I don't know.'

Isobel's heart began to pound in her chest, beating even faster when he dipped his head and kissed her again. She felt as though she was floating a few inches off the ground, her whole body weightless, her hopes soaring.

'Let me light the fire,' Thomas said. 'Come sit with me.'

She watched as he expertly stacked the firewood and kindling, using the tinderbox to set a taper alight and then coaxing the fire to life in the grate. It gave the room some much-needed warmth and the crackling and snapping of the dry wood took Isobel back to happy winter days spent in this room reading with Thomas.

He didn't get up as she expected him to, instead pulling a few cushions from the chairs and positioning them in front of the fire. When he was happy he held out his hand for Isobel and she took her place beside him.

'I need to talk to you about something,' Thomas said, his expression serious now.

A thousand thoughts ran through Isobel's mind, each more catastrophic than the last. She imagined him telling her he was secretly married or that he was planning to leave England for good, never to return, or that he had been told he had only months to live.

He leaned forward, studying her face, reaching out to tuck a stray strand of hair behind her ear.

'I know you and your father are struggling financially,' he said quietly, surprising Isobel with the direction of the conversation. His expression was serious and sincere and all she could do was nod in agreement of his words. 'It is a common topic of gossip locally and in London, and it is easy to see the depths of your financial issues here at Senlac House. I am now lucky enough to be very wealthy.'

'I don't want your money, Thomas,' Isobel said quickly.

He nodded, but pushed on anyway. 'If we married,' he said, a faint tremor in his voice, 'you and your father would be rescued from poverty. As your husband it would be expected that I provide for you, but also help your family, too.'

Isobel pressed her lips together, her heart sinking as she wondered if he was about to tell her he couldn't bear to rescue her father financially.

'It would be a good solution for you and your father.'

'There is no denying it,' Isobel said.

'If we were to marry, I think I would spend my whole life wondering if the only reason you had agreed to be my wife was monetary.'

'Thomas, no,' she said, but he held up his hand and pushed on.

'Ten years ago you turned me down, Isobel, despite us being madly in love with one another. You turned me down because your family, your father, did not approve of me and had greater expectations of his daughter. Yes, you were young, and perhaps placed too much importance on other people's opinions, but you were the one who said no to me.'

'Something I have regretted ever since.'

'Now I am wealthy, I can offer you a life of comfort that you no longer have here at Senlac House, I can alleviate all of these hardships.'

'And you worry the only reason I would say yes to you would be because of the comforts you can give me.' Many women would be offended by the way he had raised the delicate subject, but she could see how much it had cost him to speak of it at all. She turned so she was looking fully at him, her eyes holding his.

'I love you, Thomas. I have loved you from when you fell out of the horse chestnut tree at the bottom of our garden and I thought you were some mischievous faerie sent to spy on me. I loved you when I was ten and I loved you when I was twenty and no doubt I will love you when I am thirty and forty and fifty. That love has nothing to do with your money. You could be the poorest man in England and it would not matter.'

She silenced his protest with a stern look. 'I have not finished, Thomas. If I could go back ten years, I would counsel my younger self against making the worst mistake of my life, but not because in the change in our circumstances, but because it meant I lost the man I loved. I do not care for your money. I would choose a life of poverty—and believe me, I am well aware how difficult that life is—if it meant having you by my side.'

Thomas leaned forward from the cushion he was sat on and gripped her tightly, kissing her as if there was no tomorrow. He pulled her on to his lap, encircling her with his arms and holding her so close she felt completely enfolded in his affection.

'I have missed you so much, Isobel,' he said, trailing his lips across her cheek to her earlobe. He caught the soft skin between his teeth, making her let out a soft moan. A shudder ran through her whole body as he sucked and nipped and then continued the trail of kisses down her neck. 'I thought of you every single day and every single night we were apart.'

'That is a lot of days and nights.'

'Far too many. Do you know what I dreamed of doing?'

Breathlessly Isobel shook her head.

'I dreamed of everything,' he murmured in her ear. With strong fingers he quickly rid her of her dressing gown and pulled her nightgown up over her head. The air in the room still had a chill to it and Isobel shivered as the coldness touched her skin, but soon Thomas's hands were on her, warming her everywhere he touched.

Ten years ago they had struggled to remain chaste in one another's company and had often shared an illicit kiss, both thinking one day soon they would enjoy their wedding night. It had never come and now ten years of pent-up desire was bubbling to the surface.

'You are more beautiful now than I have ever seen you before,' Thomas said as he leaned over her, kissing her fiercely.

'I am an old maid.'

'A beautiful old maid,' he teased her.

Isobel knew she was being reckless. Thomas hadn't renewed his proposal of a decade ago and here she was, giving in to her primal desires. He could take her virtue and then walk away, no promises broken. She thought it unlikely and found to her surprise she also didn't care. If he did decide she was too much of a risk, at least she would have tonight, at least she would have one evening of pleasure with the man she loved.

With shaking hands she reached up and tugged at his shirt, pulling it off over his head. She paused for a second, her hands on his chest, loving the intensifying fire in his eyes as she touched him. Then he kissed her again and for a few minutes she lost all sense as he gradually teased the rest of her layers from her body.

When she was naked Thomas paused, his body held above hers illuminated by the flickering flames of the fire burning in the grate.

'What are you doing?' she asked, frowning.

'Savouring this moment. It is even better than I ever imagined.'

Isobel giggled, pulling him down towards her again. 'Stop savouring and start living it,' she whispered in his ear.

'Your wish is my command, my lady.'

He teased her with his lips, trailed kisses over her chest, circling her nipples before moving lower. She groaned, trying to guide him to where she wanted him the most, but he took hold of her hands and held them above her head.

'I am going to take my time with you, Isobel. You always were impatient, but tonight you will see the beauty of anticipation.'

He toyed with her, kissing her, nipping her skin, until she was a fraught mess, begging him to touch her, begging him for more. When she thought she could take no more he sat back, a satisfied smile on his face, and ever so gently touched her between her legs.

Isobel let out a low moan, petrified he would withdraw his touch, but it seemed he was done with teasing as he began to circle his fingers, making her writhe. Instinctively her hips rose to meet him and soon Isobel felt a wonderful tension begin to build deep inside her. She wanted to hold on to it, to keep it close, but let it go at the same time.

Soon the decision was out of her control as she felt as if something burst inside her and wave after wave of pleasure flooded through her.

It took a minute for Isobel to regain enough composure to open her eyes and realise Thomas was there, smiling down at her. She pulled him close, kissing him deeply, and felt his hardness pressing against her. At first he was gentle and slow, but as she relaxed and began to meet his thrusts with her own, his pace increased and soon Isobel found herself crying out again, clutching him to her. This time Thomas did not stop and Isobel was carried from one climax to another before she felt him tense inside her.

Breathing heavily, Thomas collapsed on to the floor beside her, pulling her to him and wrapping his arms around her. Isobel felt a wonderful warmth come over her, a happiness she had not felt for a long time. Tomorrow they could talk, they could work out what the future held for them both, but tonight she just wanted to be cocooned in the arms of the man she loved.

At some point an hour or so later Thomas lifted her from the floor and covered her with her nightgown before carrying her through the house to his bed. She revelled in the smell of him on the pillow, the warmth of him next to her under the sheets. As she drifted off to sleep she allowed herself to hope, to dream, to think this was what her life could be like if only they could find some way of letting go of the past.

Chapter Eleven

Thomas woke early, unaccustomed to having someone else in his bed. For a long moment he allowed himself to revel in the warmth of Isobel's body beside him and the lingering contentment he felt from the night before. None of it had been planned. When he had gone downstairs the night before he hadn't ever expected the evening to end the way it had, but right now he was finding it hard to regret his actions.

He looked down at Isobel, her long hair spread over the pillow and her cheeks rosy from the warmth of the bed. Gently he leaned over and kissed her forehead. It was tempting to close his eyes, to bury himself under the covers beside her, and let fate direct his course, but Thomas needed to be more decisive than that.

He owed it to himself to make the decision as to whether he had a future with Isobel and he owed it to her, too. He didn't want to wake up one morning five years from now and realise he had fallen into a marriage he didn't want and equally he might regret it if he let Isobel slip through his fingers again.

Quietly he rose and pulled on his clothes, taking his boots outside so he wouldn't make too much noise. The rest of the house was silent and he was grateful for it. The last thing he wanted was to have to make polite conversation with Lord Senlac or explain to his mother why he was up and about so early in the morning.

He retrieved his coat and stepped out into the snow. There had been fresh snowfall overnight and everything looked white and pristine again. He grimaced as he thought of the snow falling into his mother's cottage without the roof, but put the worry aside. The Loweridge brothers were going to have a look at the work needed today and there wasn't anything more he could do about it right now.

Outside he picked a path that took him through the back garden and out through the garden gate to the orchard beyond. There were views here over the rolling hills of Sussex and he was taken back to when he and Isobel first realised they had feelings for one another.

They had been walking through this orchard, although it had been summer rather than winter, and Isobel had turned to him and there was something in her expression that hit him like an arrow to the heart. He had told himself then and there she was the woman he would marry.

They'd shared their first kiss under the boughs of one of these apple trees and spent many a romantic evening strolling at dusk out of view of the house, away from the prying eyes of anyone in the village.

Thomas walked slowly, allowing the memories to come, the good mixed with the bad. For the first time in ten years he allowed the pain of Isobel's rejection to rip through him again, to remember the words she had spoken, the expressions on her face. If they were to have a relationship going forward, there could be no holding on to guilt or bitterness. It would have to be a completely fresh start or it wouldn't work.

He asked himself if he could do that, if he could finally

forgive Isobel for rejecting him all those years ago, if he could trust her not to break his heart again. It was a difficult question to answer.

Isobel awoke feeling rested for the first time in a long time. Normally she woke in a panic, worrying about everything there was to do that day, but today she felt different. It took her a moment to realise where she was as she stared up at the unfamiliar canopy above the bed in one of the guest bedrooms. In a rush everything came back to her—the encounter in the library with Thomas, the kiss and then their intimacy by the fire. She half remembered him carrying her upstairs and holding her in his arms until she fell asleep again.

There was no Thomas in the bed this morning, even though the light that filtered through a crack in the curtains was still muted and dull. It couldn't be much past dawn, yet there was no sign of the man she had shared everything with the night before.

Quickly she pushed away the devastation that threatened to overwhelm her. She had known there was a risk of this. Thomas had been caught up in desire the night before, responding to his needs rather than thinking about what was the most sensible thing to do.

She had been the same, she couldn't lay the blame solely at his door, but it would have been nice if he was at least here to tell her he had made a mistake.

'You will survive,' she murmured to herself, refusing to cry any more.

Even though there were a thousand things that needed doing, and the house to decorate for Christmas, Isobel flopped back down on the pillows and lay unmoving for a long time. She couldn't summon the energy she knew she would need to tackle everything in her day and she felt a heaviness settle on her. If Thomas had decided he didn't want to be with her, that the night they had spent together was a mistake, then there wasn't much she could do about it.

Eventually, after a whole host of self-recriminating thoughts, Isobel hauled herself out and bed and began to dress for the day. It was Christmas Eve and in many house-holds around the country people would be making prepa-rations to celebrate the festivities.

When she had been younger her mother had decorated the whole house for Christmas, bringing in festive plants and buying beautiful-smelling delicacies. She had spent time in the kitchen with Isobel baking biscuits for the whole family to enjoy on Christmas Eve. Isobel would have a new dress and then on Christmas Day they would exchange gifts. There was still a beautifully carved rocking horse in the nursery upstairs from one childhood Christ-mas that Isobel couldn't bear to be parted with.

Things had been different since her mother passed away, but over the years Isobel had strived to keep some of the traditions. She had long ago let go of any hope of her father buying her a small gift or contributing to the festive season, but she still liked to do a few things to make it feel special.

Every Christmas Eve she would decorate the dining room with holly and mistletoe and then she would spend some time baking biscuits in the kitchen. It wasn't much, especially not compared to some of the grand celebra-tions other people had, but it was her way of remember-ing a happier time.

Downstairs was quiet as she set about lighting the fires, the repetitive task allowing her to focus on her work rather than think about Thomas. She wondered how he would be with her when he reappeared and knew she would have to summon every ounce of composure so she didn't break down when he told her there was no future for him.

She had heard her father beginning to stir and set the kettle above the fire to warm when there was a strange scrabbling noise in the corridor outside the kitchen. She wiped her hands on her apron and went to investigate.

'What are you doing in here?' she murmured, frowning at the chicken that was strutting its way along the tiled floor, not seemingly perturbed to suddenly found itself inside. Catching sight of something on its back, she crouched down and untied a piece of ribbon that was holding a folded note on the bird's back.

Come out to the horse chestnut where it all began.
Wear a coat. It's cold.

Isobel read the note three times before she took in the words. The handwriting was Thomas's, the short command giving no clue what he wanted. She crouched down again and scooped up the chicken, grabbing her coat from the hook by the door before she went into the garden. Only once the hen was deposited back in the coop did she make her way slowly to the front of the house, to the horse chestnut tree where she had first laid eyes on Thomas.

He wasn't there, instead there was only another piece of paper tied to a low branch.

Do you remember that evening when we shared our
first kiss?

She refolded the note, a smile playing on her lips. She felt a surge of hope and anticipation. Surely he would not be playing games if all was bleak.

Quickly she hurried to the back of the house and went

through the gate to the orchard, her eyes flicking over the trees until she saw another note, this time pinned to a thick tree trunk. She opened it, looking around and wondering if Thomas was watching her.

The rose is red, the violet is blue, honey is sweet and so are you.

Isobel tucked the note away and set off as rapidly as the snow would allow. Senlac House was set away from the village, but they did have a neighbour a hundred feet down the road. When Isobel had been young that neighbour had been a keen beekeeper, often giving Isobel and Thomas little jars of honey to taste.

Mr Montague had passed away a few years earlier and his house was falling into disrepair while his relatives contested his will, but the beehives were still in his garden and on a summer day you could still hear the buzzing of the bees as they flew backwards and forward.

She slipped into Mr Montague's garden through the dilapidated back gate and soon found the fourth note, wondering how long the trail was likely to be. She wanted to see Thomas, to hear what he had to say, but she could not deny he was skilled at building the anticipation.

Once I asked you a question on Christmas Eve...

Isobel drew in a sharp breath, reading the words to see if there was anything else she was missing. Ten years ago today, on Christmas Eve, Thomas had asked her to marry him. They had been stood on the little bridge over the stream. It had been a day much like today, with the stream frozen solid and snow on the ground.

For the first time since beginning the hunt Isobel paused,

knowing that the events of the next few minutes would shape the rest of her life. In her chest her heart was thumping and she felt as if every muscle was tense, as if ready to flee at any moment. Almost overcome by nerves, she made her way along the icy paths to the stream, following it for a few minutes until the bridge came into sight.

Thomas was standing there on the bridge, stamping his feet to warm them up in the cold. Isobel paused, knowing these next few minutes could change the course of her life entirely.

'You found all the clues.'

'I did. You attached one to Guinevere.'

'The chicken is called Guinevere?'

'She is.'

'Yes, she was a willing messenger.'

Isobel stepped up on to the bridge, her eyes searching Thomas's face for a clue to what he was feeling.

'What is all this, Thomas?'

He waited for her to come to a stop right in front of him and then reached out and took her hands in his own.

'I woke up this morning and you were gone,' Isobel said, her fingers warming a little as he rubbed them. She had brought her coat but no gloves in her rush to follow the clues.

'I needed a little time to think, to clear my head,' he said softly. 'I wanted to make sure I was making the right decision. I am sorry I disappeared. It was never my intention to leave you not knowing what was happening.'

'What is happening, Thomas?'

He took a deep shuddering breath and then gave her a half-smile. 'I love you, Isobel. I have loved you since we were children, before I really knew what love was. When we were young I never doubted we would spend our lives together.'

Isobel nodded. She had felt the same.

'These past ten years without you have not been happy ones. I have made a success of my business, I have travelled the world, bought a beautiful house and turned it into a home, but there has always been the feeling that something is missing.' He brought one of her hands up to his lips. 'Last night I finally admitted to myself it was you. You were what was missing from my life.'

'I know it is my fault…'

'Hush. No more blame. For too long there has been this bitterness between us. We need to rid ourselves of it. I understand why you did not feel you could marry me. It was a lot to ask a girl of eighteen to give up her family, her home, everything she had ever known. I think I never really appreciated what I was asking of you. I should have given you a little time, returned after a few months and discussed it again.'

'I started to write to you so many times,' Isobel said, thinking of the screwed-up pieces of paper strewn across the floor of her bedroom where she had thrown them in disgust.

'Instead I let my hurt grow into this darkness that I could never shake.' He shifted a little and Isobel could see the concern in his eyes, as if he was uncertain about what he was going to say next.

'I know now what I want from my life, Isobel, but first there is a question I need to ask you. If you take away the guilt you feel for how things turned out ten years ago, all the history we share, if you take away the dire circumstances you find yourself in, would you still want to be with me?'

'Oh, Thomas, of course I would,' she said, reaching up and placing a hand on his cheek. 'Never doubt it. I love you, only you.' She could see Thomas had spent his time this morning reasoning through all his doubts and now it was her turn. 'I feel such guilt, Thomas, for what I did to both of us. That is my main fear—that our relationship might be different because of my past actions.'

'No, we shall not let it. We need to look on this as a second chance and forget what has come before. I love you, Isobel, more than you could ever know. Coming back to Battle and spending these last few days with you, I feel as though I have awoken from a long sleep. Finally our lives can begin again.'

Isobel felt her heart soar as Thomas leaned forward and kissed her.

'I do have one last question for you. Isobel Partridge, will you marry me?'

Isobel threw her arms around Thomas's neck.

'Yes, yes, a thousand times yes.'

He reached into his pocket and withdrew something, taking her hand. 'I hope it fits. I had this made ten years ago when I asked you then. If you don't like it, we can change it for something different.'

It was a simple band of gold with a perfectly round, small ruby set on it. The ring was delicate and perfect and Isobel knew she would never take it off from this day forth.

'How did you afford it?'

'I saved for two years—every job I took I put a little aside for the ring.'

'I love it, Thomas. It could not be more perfect.'

Chapter Twelve

'I thought it was bad luck for me to see you before the wedding,' Thomas said as Isobel sneaked up behind him and covered his eyes with her hands.

'Then make sure you do not peek.'

'You clearly do not know how tempting you are.'

She laughed, allowing him to turn to face her. His eyes were dutifully closed and she kissed him long and hard on the lips.

'Tell me, what does my beautiful wife look like on our wedding day?'

'You're charming, but I am sure everyone tells you that.'

The door opened and Mrs Williamson bustled in, tutting when she saw Isobel had sneaked past her defences.

'It is bad luck for the groom to see the bride before the wedding,' she said, shaking her head with an indulgent sigh. 'And you should be at the chapel, Thomas.'

'He has his eyes closed,' Isobel reassured her future mother-in-law.

'I am not sure if that makes it acceptable.'

Thomas kissed her again and then quickly left the room. Isobel watched him leave, feeling the excitement and anticipation bubble and surge inside her.

'I have bad news, my dear,' Mrs Williamson said quietly. 'Your father has sent word he is not able to come.'

Isobel nodded, unsurprised. It had been difficult to know whether to invite him to the wedding, but in the end Isobel had decided she didn't want to be ruled by pettiness on her wedding day, so had extended him an invitation, half expecting him not to come. She wasn't disappointed that he hadn't wanted to make the hour's journey to see her married.

'I expect he is worn out after moving out of the house,' Mrs Williamson said charitably.

'Or that he just didn't want to come,' Isobel shrugged. 'It is his loss. I refuse to dwell on my father on my wedding day.'

She and Thomas had thought long and hard while discussing what was best to do with her father and his debts. Senlac House held good memories for Isobel as well as the bad, so she was reluctant to push her father to get rid of it entirely. In the end they had agreed Thomas would settle Lord Senlac's debts if he agreed to move to a much more modest dwelling in the village and Senlac House would pass to Isobel.

Lord Senlac had eventually agreed with much grumbling, but Isobel thought he must have seen the hard determination in Thomas's eyes and realised he would get no sympathy from his future son-in-law. The plan was to slowly restore the house to its former glory and Isobel had already started to hunt down some of the books that had been sold from the library a few years earlier.

'You look beautiful, my dear,' Mrs Williamson said, offering Isobel her arm. 'But you will need a coat for the ride to the chapel. It is still cold.'

The snow had melted a few weeks earlier, but it was early February and the weather was still icy. Isobel didn't mind, eschewing the idea of a longer engagement and a larger spring wedding. All she wanted was to finally be married to the man she loved.

There was a carriage waiting outside ready to take them to the chapel and Isobel felt the flutter of nervous anticipation in her belly as she climbed up and took her seat. Mrs Williamson came and sat beside her and took her hand.

'I know your mother would be very happy today if she could see you,' she said.

'I wish she was here.'

'I wish Thomas's father was here, too,' Mrs Williamson said with a tight smile. 'But the best way we can honour those who are no longer with us is by living our lives to the full.'

Thomas could see the carriage carrying Isobel and his mother rounding the bend as he alighted from his, greeted by his closest friend, Leonard Hearth. Thomas was tempted to stay where he was, to grasp hold of Isobel before they even entered the church, but Leonard ushered him inside.

The chapel was almost empty, a few friends of Isobel's having travelled from Battle and some of his from London, but they had opted for a small ceremony away from the eyes of society. He didn't want the inevitable questions and curiosity—all he wanted was privacy with his new wife.

As Isobel entered the church he felt something inside him lift. Even though it was irrational, he had fostered a fear these last few weeks that something might happen to change Isobel's mind. Now he had her he was determined he would never lose her again.

The ceremony itself was quick and within fifteen minutes they were walking down the aisle of the church, this time with their fingers intertwined.

'I have a surprise for you,' Thomas said, leaning in close to murmur the words to Isobel.

'A surprise?'

'Yes, in the carriage.'

She looked at him, intrigued. He loved to see the happiness in her eyes, the smile on her face, and vowed he would do anything to keep it there.

It felt as though it took an age for their guests to wish them well when all he wanted to do was get Isobel to himself, but eventually he helped her up into the carriage.

'Why is my trunk on top?'

'That is part of your surprise,' he said, then handed her a package. With a question in her eyes she carefully unwrapped it, gasping as she saw it was a book of maps they had pored over when they were children. It was one of the books sold a few years earlier, but he had managed to track a copy down.

'The business is in safe hands for the next six months and my housekeeper is perfectly capable of looking after the house, so all you need to do is open the book and pick a page.'

She looked up at him as if not quite able to understand his words.

'You mean…?'

'Yes, wherever you wish to go.'

'Just like we dreamed of.'

'Just like we dreamed of.'

Together they opened the book, studying the maps and turning page after page until Isobel paused and pressed her finger against one beautiful illustration.

'Here,' she said with a smile. 'This is where I'd like to start.'

* * * * *

HER DUKE UNDER
THE MISTLETOE

Helen Dickson

Dear Reader,

Tristan Osborne, a penniless duke who is looking for a rich wife, enters into a marriage of convenience with Sophie, a wealthy American. But Sophie has conditions of her own. She agrees to marry him, to pay all his debts and bring his estate back to its former glory if he'll disappear. She will release him from all the commitments that have dogged him since his father's death so that he can indulge his passion for archaeology—far away—in Egypt. There will be no correspondence between them.

Tristan agrees, but to Sophie's horror—as a woman who has a deep-rooted fear of childbirth—he comes back, after a tragic, life-changing experience, determined to make their marriage work.

Will they be able to forge a new life together?

After many years of writing lengthy historical romance novels, writing a short story is something quite new to me. I hope I've got it right and that you enjoy *Her Duke Under the Mistletoe*.

Helen Dickson

Chapter One

1817

'There,' Sophie said, pirouetting in front of the cheval mirror. 'Will I do, Maisy?' she enquired of her maid, satisfied that the turquoise silk she had chosen to wear for an evening at Carlton House set off her figure to perfection, enhanced the diamonds she wore and brought out the lights in her rich, auburn hair.

Maisy stood back, taking pride in her handiwork, although the Duchess was already beautiful. Tonight she looked positively breathtaking, daring, elegant and special. 'Indeed you will, Your Grace. Any gentleman seeing you tonight, looking as you do, will surely find his heart going into its final palpitations—as will Prince George himself.'

Sophie laughed happily. 'I don't think so, Maisy. The Prince has so many ladies buzzing about him all the time, he will fail to notice me.'

'Don't be too sure about that. He may not be as handsome as he once was—his gargantuan appetite has seen to that—but he cuts a fine figure in his military uniforms and the sumptuous clothes he wears. He is still charming and has an eye for a pretty face.'

The preparations complete, with her velvet cloak folded

about her shoulders to guard against the chill of the cold December night, Sophie proceeded down the stairs of the Almesbury town house to where her dearest friend Caroline Hatherton and her devoted husband Duncan, the Third Baron Hatherton, awaited her. Duncan was a handsome, brown-haired young man with warm hazel eyes. He was easy to please and the most amenable of men. Caroline, small and slender, golden-haired and blue-eyed, openly adored him.

'You look lovely as always, Sophie,' Caroline said, greeting her friend with a kiss on the cheek. 'Is there no one you would want to partner you tonight? It's a regular occurrence these days for us to go places in a threesome—be it the theatre or a soirée.' She followed Sophie to the door, which was being held open by a footman.

'That's the way I like it, Caroline, and it's so good of you to take me on. No gentleman means no entanglements—no complications.'

'I'm sure one of my friends would be more than honoured to accompany you,' Duncan suggested.

'Thank you, Duncan, but I would rather not. I am content with the way things are. Truly.'

'Very well. Come, ladies,' he said jovially. 'We have the whole evening to enjoy ourselves.'

Sophie laughed, pulling on her gloves. 'That's what I like to hear, Duncan. Consider yourself fortunate to be attending such a splendid occasion with two ladies on your arm. Why, you'll be the envy of every gentleman at Carlton House tonight.'

Sophie was excited about going to Carlton House and meeting English royalty. The house was the most beautiful, the most glamorous in London. Vibrant and lavishly decorated, it was the most stylish house in England.

Prince George was a splendid host, at his happiest when

entertaining on a grand scale. The whole of society aspired to be invited to his fêtes. The banquets were always glittering occasions, the point of the proceedings to admire, for the Prince, who spent weeks planning the setting of the next event, liked to show off his aesthetic taste and imagination.

Feeling decidedly gay and definitely light-hearted, Sophie had been looking forward to the party for days and intended to enjoy every minute of it.

On reaching Pall Mall, they alighted the carriage and the driver moved on to find somewhere to await the end of the evening's entertainment. Sophie's expensively shod feet barely touched the ground as she passed beneath the portico of towering Corinthian columns that led to the foyer of Carlton House and then into the great hall of classical elegance. The house was ablaze with light. Disposing of their cloaks, they joined the throng milling about in the rooms.

Taking two glasses of champagne from a silver tray, Duncan handed them to his companions, then took one for himself and surveyed the glittering company.

'Rather splendid, isn't it?'

Sophie nodded her agreement. Thousands of candles illuminated the surroundings and enhanced the equally brilliant gathering that thronged the many rooms of Carlton House. Ladies sought to outshine each other with their magnificent ball gowns and gems. 'It's what you expect at Prince George's parties. I haven't seen him, but he will be somewhere in the throng.'

In no time at all they were surrounded by friends and admirers, leaving Sophie little time to look around. She saw a few faces that were familiar to her and she bowed and smiled politely. It was not the first time she had been part of such a grand assembly. There were honoured guests from all over Europe—never had she heard so many languages spoken under one roof.

She smiled to herself, taking a sip of her champagne with a feeling of excitement. How could one fail to enjoy oneself in the presence of such interesting and vibrant company? It was with some semblance of gaiety in her manner when she accepted her first partner of the evening to dance.

Having arrived early and trying to work up some enthusiasm to mingle with the guests here to enjoy the banquet, which he imagined would be tedious and infinitely dull, Tristan Osborne, the Duke of Almesbury, a dark-haired handsome gentleman, lounged on the edge of the room against a pillar.

As the long line of carriages in the Mall—a solid block of equipages stretching all the way to St James's Street—deposited the glittering cream of London society at the door, with a thoroughly bored expression on his face he had already decided that he would exit the house early if the lady he had been told was to be present failed to appear. Then he saw her.

The Duchess of Almesbury. His wife.

He was unprepared to see how much she had changed since he had last seen her and had no doubt whatsoever that she would not be pleased to see him.

His gaze was drawn to her standing with her companions. The light from the chandeliers bathed her in a golden glow. From across the room he studied her stunning figure and flawless beauty. Her heavy, fiery auburn hair had been twisted into burnished curls at the crown. Her turquoise gown with a tightly fitted bodice forced her breasts high and exposed a daring expanse of flesh adorned with a diamond necklace with a single diamond drop that captured the eye.

Entranced, he stared quite openly, unable to do anything else. She was so embedded in his heart that he was dazed by it, by its intensity, and he could not believe that she did not know it. Like forked lightning it tore through his senses and he knew quite unequivocally that it would never diminish.

During the years of their separation he had thought of her constantly, wondering what this defiant, stubborn woman with a spirit to match his own was doing. All the years they had been married and all the women he had known, there had been no one like her.

A cool vision of poised womanhood, she was undeniably the most magnificent woman he had seen in a long time, though it was not the way she looked that drew his eye, since the distance between them was too great for him to see her features clearly. It was the way she tossed her imperious head, the challenging set to her shoulders and the defiant stare that did not see the lowlier beings about her.

He stood and watched her as she slowly walked around the room with her companions—although walked hardly described the way she moved, for she seemed to glide effortlessly, her body eternally female in its fluid movements. As they disappeared into another room, with a frown he stared into the crimson depths of the ruby on his finger. Gleaming with a regal fire, it seemed to motivate him into action.

Drawing himself upright, straightening the folds of his black evening coat, with a knowing smile he followed in the wake of the Duchess of Almesbury, looking forward to the moment when he would make his presence known to her. Please God, he prayed, let her be as happy to see him as he was to see her.

Escaping near death in the Sahara Desert, Egypt had finally lost its appeal. All he could think of at that time was home and his wife. He was desperate to reconnect with her, Sophie, the woman who had consumed his thoughts for four years. He wanted a shared partnership, a proper marriage, the joy and comfort of a wife and in the future a family. If she would have him.

As the evening progressed and Sophie had dined and danced her way through the night, watching couples waltz about the floor, she was distracted when masculine voices drifted towards her and she turned slightly to observe a group of gentlemen who were clearly enjoying themselves. Some of their exuberance rubbed off on to her and she smiled.

But then her gaze shifted past them to where a man stood with his profile to her, leaning in a negligent pose against a pillar. He must be foreign, she thought, although she didn't know why she should think that, except that his skin was tanned and his hair, drawn back to his nape, was black, as black as his coat. He was either foreign or burned by the sun in an exotic country. Every other man looked pale in comparison.

The stranger was forgotten when Caroline appeared by her side, an excited glow on her face.

'You appear to be enjoying yourself, Sophie. Have you managed to dance with Prince George yet?'

'I have not and nor do I wish to. Anyway, there are so many ladies here tonight he has plenty of choice.'

Again the stranger drew her attention. Shrugging himself away from the pillar, he began walking away, momentarily turning his head to acknowledge an acquaintance before moving on. Something about his stance, about the way he held his head and devil-may-care demeanour, seemed familiar.

Suddenly she froze. He was tall, taller than most—in

fact, there was only one man she knew who was as tall. Caroline was still speaking to her, but she heard not one word of what she was saying. Everything seemed to melt away around her, for she only had eyes for the stranger.

Her breath caught in her throat and for a moment the world seemed to stand on its end. Something in her coiled and tied itself into a knot, something small but significant, for though she was aware that she should not be daydreaming on the edge of the dance floor, it was thoughts of *him*, of this man, her husband, which had taken her senses and made her foolishly dazed. The blood drained out of her face as she stared at him, unable to comprehend that he was here.

'Sophie, what is it? You're as white as a sheet. You look as if you've seen a ghost.'

'I—I think I have, Caroline. Excuse me—I must...' Without finishing her sentence, she hurried away, trying to catch a glimpse of the stranger—if indeed that was what he was.

'But—where are you going?'

'Tristan,' she whispered, ignoring her friend. But it couldn't be. He'd promised her he wouldn't come back.

There were so many people in her path she had difficulty moving quickly and when at last the crowd thinned out she could no longer see him. Where was he? she asked herself with a feeling of desperation. He couldn't just disappear into thin air. Had she been mistaken? And then there he was, striding in the direction of the conservatory. Once again her path was obstructed by people, hampering her progress.

Trying not to draw attention to herself, she hurried through sumptuous rooms with walls lined with silk and ceilings elaborately stuccoed and from which huge crystal chandeliers hung, their delicate glass pendants casting prisms of dancing lights. Losing sight of her prey, she looked in every room she passed. He had to be somewhere.

By the time she reached the conservatory, which was surprisingly devoid of people, she walked round the potted palms and the rows of clustered, carved pillars supporting arches, from which sprung the fans and tracery that formed the roof. Frustrated that she had let him slip away, utterly despondent, she turned to go, when a voice halted her.

'Hello, Sophie. Are you looking for me, by any chance?'

She spun round and, when she met a pair of silver-grey eyes as cold as Antarctic ice floes, she knew she had not been mistaken. This was Tristan Osborne, the Duke of Almesbury. Her husband.

For a moment she was paralysed, unable to speak. She was occupied for several heart-stopping moments with trying to bring her mind and her emotions under control. It was the moment he moved which jerked her from her frantic thoughts and it was as if, dwelling on him as she had done interminably for the past four years, she had conjured Tristan Osborne up with the strength, the longing and the despair of her thoughts.

It unnerved her, especially when those silver-grey eyes locked on her. The reality didn't frighten her. She was shaken, yes, alarmed, too, and beneath the overwhelming joy at seeing him after such a long time which she stifled as best she could, she was as angry as hell.

'Tristan.'

'The same.'

He smiled with the ingrained arrogance of a true aristocrat, which only served to confirm the awful, yet wonderful, truth that her husband of four years really had come back.

'What are you doing here?' she demanded more sharply than intended as, with great difficulty, she tried to hold her emotions at bay. 'Why have you come back? You're supposed to be in Jordan or Egypt or wherever it is that you dig for your ancient relics—not here.'

He shrugged, averting his eyes. 'Things happened to me out there—something quite dreadful that changed me. I got tired of digging up ancient relics. I decided it was time I came home.'

'But—you can't,' she said, doing her best to sound ordinary, to be calm, to be as unconcerned as he appeared to be, yet she wondered what it could be that had happened to him to bring him home. 'It wasn't part of our arrangement. We had an agreement, if you remember.'

'Yes, I remember—and I am sorry to renege on the bargain we made. But things happened to me that change everything. It's been a long time, Sophie.'

His voice had the same rich timbre she remembered and she began to wonder if he had any flaw she could touch upon and draw some strength from. She had imagined the harsh life he led in the Egyptian sun would leave its mark and it had.

It was evident in the sunburned skin and the lean, hard planes of his handsome face. She had seen it in the easy way he had of walking and the long lines of his body. There was a health and vitality about him that was almost mesmerising. In all, he was even more handsome than she remembered. Yet there was something in his eyes, a shadow of something dark and troubling, that drew her curiosity.

'I—I thought it would have been for longer than four years, Tristan.'

'I imagine you would—but as I said, things change, Sophie, things we have no control over. We need to talk—'

'Yes, of course, but now is not the time,' Sophie cut him short disdainfully. 'If you have anything to say to me, you may write me a letter.'

His dark brows rose, also disdainfully. 'Really? I seem to recall you telling me there would be no correspondence between us. I haven't time for writing letters—although I did intend calling on you. I trust you will not turn me away from my own house.'

'No, of course not. You must have seen me earlier?'

He nodded. 'I did.'

'Then why didn't you make your presence known to me?'

'It was too public. Meeting my wife again after four years' absence I prefer to do in private—besides, it was obvious you were enjoying yourself. You were with our neighbours—the lovely Caroline and Duncan. They are married now.'

'Yes. It was a summer wedding.'

He grinned. 'As you know Duncan and I go way back. Caroline is delightful—in fact, they make a delightful couple.'

He was right. Caroline was delightful. She had been a friend of Tristan's first wife Dianna, who had died in childbirth. As handsome as he was, she could imagine that Tristan had grown quite adept at swaying besotted women of all ages to do his bidding.

He did seem to have a way about him and she could not fault any woman for falling under his spell, for she found to her annoyance that her heart was not as distantly detached as she might have imagined it to be. Even his deep mellow voice seemed to act like a warm caress stroking over her senses.

'Caroline has become a good friend—and Duncan. He is charming and most considerate. When we go down to Surrey, and with them living close to Kingswood House, we see a good deal of each other. Duncan is a charming prankster—and mischievous, which drew Caroline to him in the first place. As you know, my own nature is less trusting.'

He looked at her, his eyes softening. 'I'm sorry to hear that. I'd like to think that the time we will spend together in the future will help to change your mind.'

'I won't do that.'

'No? We'll have to see. You're looking very well, Sophie. I'm glad to find you are not so enamoured of any particular gentleman that you have forgotten your husband altogether.'

She looked at him, startled. 'No, there isn't, but how on earth do you know that?'

'I make it my business to know.'

'You laid down conditions of your own if you remember, Tristan—that what I denied you I would not give to another. You insisted that I did not tarnish the Osborne name with scandal. I respected your request.'

'Yes, I knew you would. However, there are matters we have to discuss. The sooner the better.'

'As far as I am concerned we have nothing to talk about.' Considering the turmoil within her, her voice was curiously calm. Her proud, disdainful blue eyes met and held his without flinching.

Shaking off the effects of what his presence was doing to her, Sophie took herself mentally in hand and reminded herself of the bargain they had made four years ago. Where she was concerned, nothing had changed.'

'So, when were you going to inform me you were back in England?'

'Probably tomorrow.'

'You have left Egypt—or wherever it is you spend your time—for good?'

He nodded. 'Yes.'

'That must have been difficult for you.' After four years he was changed. The Tristan Osborne who had returned to England was very different to the one who had left four years ago. Where Sophie had known him to be light-hearted with many pleasant sides to his character, she now perceived an air of seriousness—of suffering about him. He displayed nothing of the easy, fun-loving man she had known before he had gone away. Perhaps the hardships and tribulations he had experienced abroad had stripped all humour from him.

'Four years ago you were glad to marry me, Tristan. You were in dire straits. You had a mountain of debts and your creditors had called in your loans. Everything that was not entailed was about to be taken from you. None of it was of your doing, I grant you, but your grandfather and then your father were reckless and made some bad investments.'

'It was more than that. My father exhibited a proclivity towards all manner of expensive vices. He gambled all the time—it had nothing to do with having fun, it was an addiction. He lost astronomical sums—he even thought of offering his estate in payment. Thankfully it didn't come to that. Your father knew all this when he approached me and offered me a way out—that if I married you, in exchange for a title, all my worries would be over.'

'And you agreed.'

'What man in his right mind—a man with nothing to lose—would turn down such a tempting offer? But that was before I knew you had conditions of your own attached—that six weeks after our wedding I would disappear.'

'And you were happy to comply.'

'I knew you weren't offering marriage because you desired me,' he remarked drily. 'We were strangers after all, but I confess it was rather a blow to my vanity at the time.'

'I was relieved you didn't allow your masculine pride to get in the way and that you were glad of the opportunity to go off and indulge your passion for poking about in ancient temples and digging up whatever there is to dig up and never come back.'

'Four years is a long time, Sophie. Situations change—people change.' He moved closer to her and looked down into her dark blue eyes. 'Our marriage wasn't consummated.'

'No,' she said, becoming flustered at the mention of such intimacy and looking away. 'That—that was another part of the bargain.'

'Why me, Sophie? Why did you choose me? There were other peers equally as impoverished as I was.'

'My father chose you, not me.'

'Maybe, but you fell in with his wishes. So, why me?'

'Because you were desperate and because you had all the prerequisites that suited my plan.'

'Had I been portly and ugly, would it have made any difference?'

'I don't think so. It didn't matter what you looked like if you were willing to fall in with my plans and disappear. I am now beginning to think I chose unwisely.'"

'What a mercenary heart you have, Sophie.'

'That makes me sound cold and uncaring when I'm not,' she replied on a note of sadness and regret that he should think that of her. 'There was no way out for you at that time—or for me, as it happens. You were about to lose everything—and I…' She bit her lip, unwilling to be drawn on her reason for marrying him. 'Face it, Tristan, you were relieved to be rid of your irksome duties.'

'And you—for reasons that are still a mystery to me—were as desperate in your own way as I was. All you wanted from me was my name and a title. I hope buying me was worth it.' He smiled crookedly at the sudden hurt that flooded her eyes.

'I didn't buy you. Please don't think that.'

'No? That was how it seemed to me. But now I am back I sincerely hope things will be different.'

'You—you mean you are home for good?'

'Yes. I have no intention of going back.'

'I see. You have broken your promise to me.'

'My circumstances have changed. Things happened to me—terrible things that made look at my life. I didn't like what I saw. I have come home to take care of my estate, to take care of my wife—if she will have me.'

Curiosity stirred within Sophie. What could have happened to him that was so terrible it had driven him from Egypt? 'I don't need looking after, Tristan. I am capable of taking care of myself.'

'Yes, I believe you are. You have learned to do nicely on your own, but it is not as cut and dried as you would like to think. We are man and wife, Sophie. Married couples are not meant to live apart. I was hoping that, given time, we will see a way through this quagmire of conditions set down when we married. I have expectations of this marriage.'

'Are you saying you have conditions or your own?'

'No. No conditions. I am heartily sick of conditions. There shouldn't be any conditions between a man and his wife.'

Feeling suddenly nervous and unsure of herself, Sophie swallowed. To confuse her totally, he had swept back into her life, just as handsome, just as intriguing, and with him he had brought an offer to set things right between them, for them to have a normal marriage. He knew too well how difficult it would be for her to refuse such an offer, but she must.

'So—what is it you want?' she asked, peering at his well-chiselled profile.

He looked at her long and hard before saying, 'I want to get to know my wife—to live a normal married life—if she will have me. I also miss Kingswood. I didn't realise

how much a part of me it was until it was no longer there.'
His eyes locked on hers.

Stubbornly Sophie shook her head, rejecting his state-
ment. 'But—I said…'

'I know what you said, what you wanted, that ours would
be a marriage in name only, but that is no longer acceptable to me. I want a wife, Sophie—a normal married life—
with you. We don't have to rush matters. I will not apply
any pressure. All I ask is that you think about it. To give
us a chance.'

Dumbfounded, Sophie stared at him in appalled disbelief. He hadn't mentioned children, thank goodness. The
thought of bearing a child was abhorrent to her. Unbe-
known to Tristan, it was at the root of everything that
separated them. Her mother had had six children. Sophie
was the first, the others she either miscarried or they died
shortly after being born. Her mother was of a weak dis-
position and suffered terribly.

Sophie remembered the heartbreak of it. She had watched,
had seen with her own eyes, and when she had been old
enough to understand and seen the demands her father made
on her mother, after losing yet another child due to a disease passed on to her by her father, she had held her mother
in her arms while she cried her despair. Sophie vowed she
would not let that happen to her.

Tristan's first wife, who carried a child for just five
months, had miscarried and died. According to Caroline,
who had shared the confidence with Sophie before her
marriage to Tristan, Tristan and Dianna had had an almighty argument, with Tristan telling Dianna he didn't
want a child—which made him all the more suitable a husband for Sophie. Knowing this, she had hoped her union
with Triston Osborne would be a union of convenience

and that their relationship would be conducted outside the bedroom.

The painful details of all her mother had gone through at the hands of her father made her cringe. He had used her as if she were a dumb animal, without feeling or emotion, unworthy of tenderness. Sophie never wanted to experience anything like that—hence her arrangement with Tristan Osborne, the Duke of Almesbury.

As if sensing her withdrawal, Tristan moved closer to her. 'I don't think I am being unreasonable. Every man wants to have a normal relationship with his wife—otherwise what is the point of marriage?' Frowning, he looked at her closely. 'Do you not agree?'

Unable to look at him lest he saw the horror in her eyes, she turned and walked away from him. 'Of course— but it has to be on equal terms, Tristan.' The words were strained, but she could think of nothing else to say.

'I wouldn't want it any other way. I belong to you as you belong to me. What we have is no longer enough. You were not so ill disposed to me during the time we were together before I went to Egypt,' he said, his tone silky, easy, his eyes regarding her with fascinated amusement.

'In fact, you were rather amiable, as I remember—when we kissed, just the once. Remember?' He let his eyes dwell on her lovely face and caress the long, graceful throat and the proud curves revealed by the low-cut bodice of her gown.

Sophie flushed as the memory of that kiss came flooding back, poignantly, vibrantly familiar. Of how his warm lips had moved on hers and she had become lost in a stormy sea of desire, confusion and yearning.

Watching her reaction closely, he cocked a satisfied brow. 'I'm glad to see you haven't forgotten entirely.

'No,' she retorted suddenly. 'I remember.'

He smiled crookedly at her under drooping eyelids.

'This is the most affecting moment,' he stated with heavy irony. 'Two people who are married to each other, together again after so long an absence—especially after believing themselves parted for ever. My dear Sophie, you should be glad to be reunited with the man you married.'

Sophie had had enough. The infuriating smile that quirked at the corners of his mouth made her want to slap it from his handsome face. She was shocked at the violence of her emotions. She had never been given to unladylike and rude impulses. Yet Tristan, by just a flick of an eyebrow and quirk of his lips, a gleam in his eyes, could raise her to fury.

'That will do,' she retorted sharply. 'You are amazingly impertinent.'

Tristan shrugged, but his eyes shifted to avoid Sophie's sparkling gaze. 'It was you who laid down the terms of our marriage—and I have kept them to the letter.'

'And I hope you continue to do so.' When she turned and walked away, his next words made her pause.

'You look exquisite, by the way—a lady of distinction.'

It was a comment casually thrown, but it took her off guard. She stood for a moment and then turned and looked back at him, her expression one of contempt. 'Why, what's this? Flattery from you? Coming from you it is insincere and I prefer you didn't use it on me.'

'It's not flattery. I am sincere in what I say. You make me almost sorry for staying away so long. You were beautiful in the past, but now, with a new maturity about you, you are more so. No man could help but desire you. It suits you to be angry. It makes your eyes sparkle.'

For what seemed an eternity, Sophie stared at the incredibly handsome, virile man who had imposed himself in her life again. His face was leaner than she remembered, though still proud and arrogant, and there was an implacable authority in the strong jawline, and cold determination in the thrust of his chin. But she would not succumb to his authority.

She had fought too hard and for too long for her independence to forfeit it on the whim of any man. 'If we are to remain married, we will have to find some way to exist together that will suit us both.'

'I agree. It will be interesting to see if the arrangement we made will outlast the testing of the flesh.' A warm gleam entered his eyes as they lingered on her lips, then he smiled.

'I cannot escape the fact that you have intrigued me from the moment we met. You have no artificial airs and graces and you possess a kind of courage that is unusual in a woman. You are also proud and independent, with bold, forthright ways which I admire. Looking at you now, what I see in your eyes quickens my very soul, stirring my mind with imaginings of what life married to you would be like.'

'That is not what I want. I will not consign myself to that kind of marriage I did not want in the first place. We have been married four years and yet we are strangers.'

Tristan stared at her, knowing exactly what she was saying. 'Neither of us knows what will happen in the future. We can find a way that suits us best.'

She shook her head, holding his gaze. 'I cannot possibly trust myself to you the way a commitment like marriage will require me to. I cannot give over the control of my life, left alone give you my heart, if I don't really know you.'

He nodded. 'I understand what you are saying. I am staying at the Pulteney Hotel at present. I will call on you tomorrow before I go down to Kingswood. However, since we are here, we might as well enjoy the party.'

'Together?'

'Why not?'

Sophie stared at him hard. He seemed to have everything worked out. There was no softness in his gaze, only the calculating gleam of a man on a mission. 'I can think of plenty of reasons. Please do not pressure me now. This is not the place. Excuse me, Tristan. I must go and find Caroline. She will be wondering where I've got to.'

Without another word she turned on her heel and walked away. Now he was back—four years older and wiser, and even more handsome and desirable, her heart and her head were telling her. Dear Lord, she prayed silently, let her have the strength, the power to resist his offering.

What had happened to him in Egypt to bring about this change in him? she wondered. There was a hard, hawklike shrewdness in those cold, silver-grey eyes that told her he would not be as easy to manage as he had been in those days of desperation before their marriage.

Chapter Two

Tristan watched her go, more determined than ever to win her over. She had matured admirably in four years—very much a woman with skin as smooth as cream and lips that begged for a man's kiss. Reflecting on those early days when he had met her, from the very beginning he had admired her boldness and audacity.

He had been puzzled at first by her father's offer of marriage to his daughter, for he couldn't imagine how a twenty-one-year-old woman could help him—unless she was as rich as Croesus. Which, he soon learned, she was—or her father was—and he was prepared to lavish more money than Tristan could have imagined to secure her the title of Duchess of Almesbury.

And then had come her arrangement, which had almost knocked him off his feet. She had offered to pay all his debts, to repair and refurbish Kingswood House and other properties he owned, to bring the estate back to its former glory if he disappeared.

In other words, she would release him from all the commitments that had dogged him since his father's death ten years earlier, so that he could indulge his passion in his archaeology. Suddenly it had seemed to him that the gates of heaven had been flung open to him here on earth.

He had hesitated, but only long enough to ask what was in it for her—apart from becoming mistress of a stately home and the title of Duchess. She had told him he would never understand and he hadn't asked, but she insisted that he cut all family ties—which included her when she became his wife—and there would be no correspondence between them. The bargain would protect her. They would both benefit from it.

Her voice had been matter of fact, the smoothness of her countenance giving nothing away as she told him what she expected of him, her discretion unrevealing of any secrets she might have, that everything she did was deeply thought out and set in stone. Initially he had taken her impassivity to mean that she was without deep feeling. It hadn't taken him long to realise the opposite was closer to the truth, that there was a well of passion there, just below the surface.

He remembered the anger he had felt, wondering at her upbringing and what kind of man her father was, that he could inflict such emotional upheaval on his only daughter by bringing her across the Atlantic to marry her off to a titled English lord in a strange land and then leave her.

The more he got to know her, the more tainted his feelings for her father became. After the wedding, relieved that he had achieved a perfect marriage for his only child and she was off his hands for good, her father had hotfooted it back to America to make himself even richer.

For the six weeks they were together at Kingswood House, things began to change. Tristan found himself married to a beautiful woman, with a strong and clever mind. For his part it confirmed what he already suspected about her—she was extremely well read, intelligent and witty, and yet there was a naivety about her that he found completely appealing.

When she smiled she lit up a room and when she laughed

he was transfixed by the beauty of the sound. She had captivated him, dazzled him—baffled him. She had something in her that he could not get hold of—a brilliance, a magical something that had made him unable to look away. There was also a strength of character in her he admired, an alertness which he had never seen before in a female—not even in his first wife Dianna.

A darkness entered his heart when he thought of Dianna. When she had died, the last thing he had wanted was another wife. Marriage to her had taught him many things—most of them unpleasant—and he was in no hurry to repeat the experience, until Sophie had come along and he was unable to resist what her father was offering.

But he chafed at the constraints she had put upon him. The fact that she did not want him began to matter a great deal, and for reasons that had nothing to do with his masculine pride. Every day he was with her and unable to touch her became a torture.

The last night they had been together, he was unable to resist her a moment longer and had kissed her. It had been a kiss like no other and she had melted in his arms, only to recollect herself and pull away. Unable to endure living with her and not having her drove him to leave Kingswood House two weeks before the designated six.

Taking up his life in Egypt, he had tried to put her from his mind. His excavations were all that mattered and he would not let anything distract him from that—not even Sophie—even if she did have the face of an angel and the body of a goddess.

However, it had proved to be impossible. She was too deeply embedded in his heart and mind for him to do that. He had always been a disciplined man, be it dealing with his business affairs, putting over his point in the House of Lords, dealing with his stewards on the estate and a thousand other matters that took up his time, never allowing himself to be distracted by a woman. But he had not reckoned on a woman like the one he had made his wife. Her image had remained in his mind and desire for her often overwhelmed him, taunting him in the most inappropriate moments.

Now he was back and determined to stay. Living in the same house, seeing each other day in and day out, it would be impossible for her to avoid or ignore him. If he was patient, he would succeed in breaking down her resistance and make her want him. But he would not pressure her. Yes, he wanted her, but she had to want him also. She must come to him of her own free will.

Leaving the conservatory, he went in the direction of the music. Leaning on a pillar, he scanned the chattering throng. He saw her almost immediately. His breath caught in his throat at the sight of her in her shimmering gown, her auburn hair warming and softening the delicate features.

He'd expected the vision he had carried in his head for four years to be tarnished with age, but now he had seen and spoken to her that was not so. He had thought no woman could be as exquisite as he had imagined, but he was wrong. She was even lovelier and, from the looks the other men cast her way like a pack of hungry wolves, he was not the only one.

He battled against the primal urge to stride over to her and take her away from so much temptation. In the end he lost, unable to bear seeing her dance with another adoring swain. Shoving himself away from the pillar, he made his way to her.

Caroline hurried to Sophie's side when she reappeared.
'So here you are, Sophie. Where on earth did you disappear to? You look distracted. Has something happened?'

'Yes, Caroline, you might say that,' she replied, tight lipped.

'Did I hear you mention Tristan's name before you rushed away?'

She nodded. 'My husband has come back, Caroline. He is here.' Caroline and Duncan knew about their separation, but not the reason why Sophie had insisted on it. No one knew that but herself, but Caroline had a way of picking away at the issue and making her own conclusions.

'Goodness!' Her eyes full of excitement, Caroline glanced around the room, as if expecting Tristan to materialise at any minute. 'I can't wait to see him. It must have been a shock seeing him again.'

'It was. Did you know he was to return, Caroline?'

'Of course not. Had I known I would have told you. He has written to Duncan now and then—his letters always about his latest finds. You know Duncan is almost as fanatical about that sort of thing as Tristan.

'The last I heard, he was to leave on an expedition into the desert to see a burial ground that had been discovered. But that was months ago. Not having heard anything since, I think Duncan would have gone to look for him but for the baby.'

It was early days and Caroline was hardly showing yet, but she had taken on a warm glow with her pregnancy. 'I'm glad he didn't go, Caroline. When your time comes you will want him here. I know he's excited about the baby.'

'He's over the moon. He wants a boy of course. But then, doesn't every man?'

'I suppose so,' Sophie murmured, averting her eyes. She was relieved Caroline didn't refer to her own marital situation. She was in no mood to discuss that with anyone. Caroline had been as bemused as anyone when Tristan had disappeared on one of his expeditions just a few weeks into their marriage and shown no enthusiasm to return to the marital home.

'Where is Tristan now?'

'I really have no idea, although I suspect I haven't seen the last of him tonight. No good will come if this, I just know it.'

'But—he had to come back some time, Sophie. I can hardly wait to see him again. I know the two of you have your issues, but men like him are few and far between. You cannot deny a man his home indefinitely.'

'No—I can't. But that does not mean I have to like it or share it.'

'Oh, dear, Sophie, you cannot blame him for wanting to come home. Things were difficult for him married to Dianna—'

'You told me that, Caroline—and about his anger when he realised she was carrying his child—'

'Dianna told me that—but it was never credited. I only knew what she told me. I have no idea what went wrong between them and now he's home I think it's about time you asked him yourself.'

'It's none of my business what occurred between him and his first wife, Caroline.'

'Yes, it is. Until the air is cleared between the two of you, how can you hope to be reconciled?'

Sophie threw her a startled look. 'Reconciled? How can we be reconciled when we were never together in the first place?'

'When he was married to Dianna it was—difficult for him. Some regarded him as a cold, unapproachable individual—and you have accused him of being cold and aloof yourself, Sophie. He was always an exacting master who demanded only the very best from those in his employ—at least that was the case before you banished him to Egypt.'

'I did not banish him, Caroline.'

'Forgive me, Sophie, but it seemed like that at the time. He can't be happy with his situation and because of it he can be just as easily hurt as anyone else.'

Sophie's heart softened. 'I am not intentionally cruel, Caroline, and I can well imagine how difficult it must have been for him leaving Kingswood. I will try to be more understanding.'

Before Caroline could reply, a gentleman she had promised the next dance to came to claim her. On a sigh Sophie moved to the edge of the room, content to sit this one out and watch them. The room gleamed with light and colour and careless gaiety, and the musicians began to play a waltz.

Suddenly the room seemed to contain too many people. It had grown noticeably warmer. Colour flushed her cheeks and her blue eyes seemed to have become luminous. But it was not the heat but rather the uneasiness and tension within her that was responsible. Someone came up behind her. Warm breath caressed her ear.

'Dance with me, Sophie.'

'I do not want to dance with you. Please go away,' she said quietly.

'People are watching us. Oblige me—unless you wish to create a scandal and have everyone gossiping about us over breakfast in the morning. It is the last thing either of us wants.'

There was a harsh note in his voice that made Sophie shiver in spite of her fury at his high-handedness. He was being positively obnoxious, she thought viciously, realising her predicament. Yet she knew enough about London society to know how it thrived on rumours and the more outrageous the more titilating the scandal, the more it was enjoyed.

She took a step to one side, thinking only of flight. With deceptive negligence his arm shot out and she felt the strength of steely fingers about her wrist, halting her. Forcibly he turned her so that she was facing him.

'You cannot refuse to dance with your husband. It's a pleasure I have long looked forward to. They are playing a waltz. You used to enjoy dancing as I remember.'

He was deliberately taunting her, goading her. With a feeling of helplessness and frustration and not wishing to make a scene, Sophie felt one hard, muscular arm go around her waist, holding her firmly. His other hand grasped hers, not permitting her to pull away as he drew her on to the dance floor.

'You really must learn to mask your feelings, Sophie,' Tristan chided as he took her in his arms. 'For your own sake, if nothing else. Try to look pleased to have me back after such a long period of absence.'

'And pretend what I don't feel,' she snapped while pinning a stiff smile on her face. She could feel the fascinated stares of everyone in the room as Tristan whirled her into the waltz.

At that moment everyone seemed galvanised to attention as they took to the floor. Already the air was abuzz with whispered conjectures about the return of the handsome Tristan Osborne, the Duke of Almesbury. By breakfast he would be being discussed in every household in London.

Tristan was surprisingly light on his feet. Sophie tried to keep her mind on the music, willing it to end, but as if to spite her it went on and on.

'Why are you here, Tristan? Did you know I'd be here?'

'As a matter of fact I did. I wanted to see you before calling at the house. When I found out you would be here tonight I couldn't stay away.'

Sophie stared up at him, searching his eyes for the truth behind his words. 'Are you being serious?'

'Absolutely,' he replied, twirling her round. Making a quick sweep of the room, he was not unaware of the attention they created. 'We've become something of a curiosity among the crowd,' he said softy, his palm firm against the small of her back, his breath warm and smelling pleasantly of brandy on her cheek. 'I've been told that you are extremely popular among society, that your presence at any event is much sought after.'

'Yes, I suppose it is—when I'm in town. I prefer to spend my time in the country.'

'Kingswood is a lovely old house—the park and surrounding countryside unsurpassed.'

There was a wistful look in his eyes and a softness in his voice when he spoke of his home. For the first time in four years Sophie felt a stirring of guilt when she realised how much he must have missed it.

'You dance divinely, by the way. In fact,' he said, his eyes devouring her face, 'everything about you is divine, Sophie. I'm looking forward to taking up permanent residence at Kingswood—which is my right. I think it is time for some plain speaking between us.'

Sophie lifted her chin. 'What do you mean?'

A black brow flicked upwards. 'I think you know exactly what I mean. We have played out this farce of a marriage long enough. We have the whole of our lives ahead of us. It is time to decide how best to move forward.'

'Have you any idea how cold and heartless your proposition makes you sound?'

Tristan's brows snapped together over ominous silver-grey eyes. 'Quoting your own words, Sophie,' he said, his voice dropping to a low, cold whisper, 'you said ours would not be a bond of marriage, but an arrangement, and as such that is how I treated it. It also suited me perfectly—until now.'

What he said was true. He really was discussing the terms of their marriage as he would a business arrangement—cold and without emotion—as she had done four years earlier. She was relieved that he said nothing about how he planned to move forward and hoped that was how it would remain until she'd had the time to gather her wits and consider what it would mean for her and what she was going to do about it.

Content to let the music carry them along, they fell silent. As the dance progressed, couples dipped and swayed, but Tristan and Sophie were unaware of them. They made a striking couple. There was a glow of energy, a powerful magnetism that emanated from the beautiful, charismatic pair.

Sophie stared up at Tristan's handsome face and into his bold, hypnotic eyes, lost in her own thoughts, before she realised that his gaze had dropped to her lips and his arm tightened around her waist, drawing her against the hard rack of his chest.

When the dance was over he escorted her back to Caroline, who was positively delighted to see him back from wherever it was he had been. She always did have a soft spot for him, Sophie thought with irritation as her friend gave Tristan an unrepentant smile.

'You are just as pretty as I remember, Caroline,' he murmured, raising her hand to his lips.

'And you are still the charmer I remember. In fact, I cannot decide which of you is the worst—you or my husband. Duncan will be pleased to see you—he's engrossed in a game of cards at present—he's not one for dancing as you know. He always says he has two left feet and I have to agree with him.'

'I'll go and find him. It will be good to renew our acquaintance.'

As soon as Tristan had excused himself and gone to find Duncan, Sophie turned to Caroline. 'It would appear he's back for good, Caroline. He is missing Kingswood. It would appear I have much to think about.' She gave a sigh of exasperation. 'I've had enough of dancing for one night. I would like to leave. I'll take the carriage and send it back, if you don't mind.'

'What on earth for? What will I tell Tristan when he comes looking for you?'

'Tell him anything you like. His return has come as a great shock to me and I want time to get my head around it before I see him again.'

'Very well. I'll come out with you and wait for the carriage.'

Later, in the privacy of her bedroom in the Osborne fashionable town house in Mayfair, Sophie paced the carpet, too angry and on edge to sleep. How dare Tristan come back and ruin all her carefully laid plans? What would it mean for her? She had created a new life for herself, one that suited her admirably, and to simply do as he asked and fall in to married life was unthinkable.

Thinking back to the frantic days of their courtship and the importance of marrying an English duke along with the barrage of fawning of Tristan's relatives and friends, she'd had little time to consider what it would mean for Tristan, to hand his estate over to a perfect stranger—a woman at that—and to disappear for good. But before that they had married, to halt the gossip they had lived together at Kingswood House in Surrey. Alone, in such a wonderful setting, they had spent time together. Each morning they met for breakfast and made plans for the day.

Fortunately they shared a love of horses. Due to his circumstances, Tristan had been forced to shrink his stable, but they managed to find two suitable mounts, enjoying leisurely rides in the Surrey countryside. Tristan proudly showed her the estate, introducing her to tenant farmers and local landowners. They dined together, even laughed together. In fact, they did everything together except sleep together and she was relieved that Tristan had made no attempt to consummate their marriage.

But as the days passed and Sophie had drawn closer to him, she had begun to feel a hot, searing need inside her, exacerbated by the kiss they had shared on that last evening they had spent together. She should never have let it happen. It was not part of the agreement. A nameless panic began to take hold of her and she had been relieved when he decided to leave before the appointed time.

Now he was back for good. She was trapped in a snare of her own making. She would have to replan her future. Divorce or annulment was out of the question. She could leave him and return to America—to her father. She shuddered. No, she could not bear that.

Her father, Gerald Granger, was an Englishman who had gone to America and made himself obscenely rich. Lacking the pedigree and status of a nobleman, he had learned that the cut of one's coat was the single, most obvious factor separating the common man from his betters and that an extravagant wardrobe was the hallmark of a true gentleman. He had lost no time in acquiring one.

He had sat down to cards and diced with nobles and millionaires alike, and dined and entertained according to the high stratum of New York society into which he had projected himself.

The one regret in his life was his inability to sire a living son, just the one daughter. They were constantly at odds.

On the death of Sophie's mother, when his eyes met hers it seemed that she could see into the heart of him, marking his failings as a husband and measuring his guilt, blaming him for the death of her mother.

Not long after her death he had booked passage on a ship to England with his daughter, determined to marry her off to a titled Englishman. It hadn't taken him long to pick out Tristan Osborne, the Duke of Almesbury.

It was not what Sophie wanted, far from it, and long before she had left New York her mind had been working constantly on how she was going to deal with an unwanted husband. Marriage would gain her a measure of control over her own life. If the Duke of Almesbury was indeed as poor as the proverbial church mouse, then in exchange for the wealth she would bring to the marriage, money that would go a long way to enabling him to rebuild his empire, he might not be averse to the conditions she would insist upon.

Not having gone to bed until the early hours, the following morning Sophie slept late. Hearing noise coming from downstairs, curious as to what could be happening, she donned her robe and went to see. She was shocked to see several housemaids carrying clean linens up the stairs along with baggage and lighting a fire in the connecting room to hers. Another pile of baggage was being delivered at that very moment.

'What on earth are you doing?' she asked one of the footmen.

'We're getting everything ready for the return of His Grace,' the housekeeper said, as Sophie's mind went blank and she tried to comprehend what had just been said, and what it meant.

'His Grace?'

'He sent his valet on ahead. Apparently he's back in England and will be arriving shortly. You—you didn't know?'

'Yes, of course,' Sophie said quietly. 'I—I saw him last night, but I didn't realise he would be here so early.' She sighed, turning away. 'I'll have breakfast in my room, Mrs Walker.'

'I'll have your maid bring it up right away, Your Grace.'

Sophie went back to her room, anger searing through her. Her husband was losing no time in taking up residence, but he'd said nothing about doing so this morning.

Chapter Three

When she had eaten and dressed and went downstairs, a load of crates was being delivered and deposited on the black and white marble tiles in the hall.

'His Grace has arrived, Your Grace,' one of the footmen told her, who was hoisting a large wooden crate on to his shoulder.

'I see. Where is he?'

'In the library.'

Sophie crossed to the library and flung open the door. It was a large room with floor-to-ceiling windows that overlooked the terraced garden below. Early morning frost glistening on the grass would soon disperse beneath the winter sun.

With its carved and gilded doors, marble chimney-piece and floor-to-ceiling shelves lined with rich scented, leather-bound volumes, the library had always been Tristan's favourite room. He was seated behind a large desk, his head bent over an open ledger—looking very much in charge, she thought irately.

She took a moment to take in the sheer male beauty of him. A tingle of excitement trickled down her spine at the sight of his dark head bowed over the ledger, his hair charmingly tousled, as if he had combed his fingers through. He really was an attractive man. The elegant line of his masculine features, eyes as brilliant and perfect as a clear day and seemed to see everything, his dark wavy hair that held the gloss of polished jet, blended to create nothing less than a masterpiece.

Already she was seeing a change in him from the man who had left four years earlier. He was thinner and there was a darkness in his eyes. His manner towards her was polite and courteous, but what really lay beneath it, she wondered. Unease stirred and she could not still her anxiety. She was totally unprepared for his unexpected return. She certainly hadn't thought she'd feel this powerful awareness that made her heart do strange things and her stomach to clench in pleasure.

Closing the door, she walked over the Persian carpet that shimmered with gold, reds and blues towards the desk and stared down at his bent head. He hadn't even bothered to look up when she entered.

'I am surprised, Tristan. You told me you were coming to call this morning. Not moving in with all your—your paraphernalia.'

Raising his head, he looked at her and smiled, not in the least put out by her reproach. 'So I did, but then I got to thinking. Why should I be paying for a hotel when I have my own residence here in Mayfair. Although,' he said, looking back down at the ledger, 'your expression tells me you are not pleased.'

'Of course I'm not pleased,' she retorted crossly. 'I'm not pleased about any of this. I will not accept it, Tristan. I will not have it.'

He studied her with a hooded gaze. 'No? Then what do you suggest?'

'I—I'm not sure.'

'I do not doubt you will think of something. One thing I

have come to learn about you, Sophie, is that you are a very resourceful woman. 'Although,' he said, fixing her with a steady gaze, 'it matters to me what you think. If you object to me being here, I will find accommodation elsewhere.'

Taken by surprise by his unexpected offer, Sophie hesitated, then sighed, shaking her head. 'I could not ask that of you. This is still your home, Tristan.'

'Thank you—but worry not. I have no intention of encroaching on your privacy. Most of my time will be taken up with sorting out what I have brought back with me.'

'When are you going to Kingswood?'

'I haven't made up my mind, but the sooner the better. I find London stifling—especially now the gossip has started as to my whereabouts for the past four years. Our presence at Carlton House last night has not gone unnoticed and I would like to remove myself before all and sundry come knocking at the door. I look forward to some country air and I want you to accompany me. I'm interested to see what changes you have made in my absence.'

'I don't think you will be disappointed.'

'I don't suppose I will if what I have just read in the ledger is anything to go by. As you have seen, some of my possessions have been delivered—some that will arrive later are to be taken directly to Kingswood. Most of them are artefacts I've collected during my time away. A large number I will donate to the British Museum here in London. Perhaps you would like to see them.'

'Not now. I have more pressing matters to attend to.'

'Such as?'

'How to rid myself of an unwanted husband.'

He gave her a tiresome look. 'Why are you being so difficult, Sophie? Yes, I am home, but I have no intention of encroaching on your life. You must carry on doing what you have always done and if we come together now and then, so much the better.'

Closing the ledger he pushed his chair back and walked round the desk to where she stood. 'Why do you feel the need to fight me all the time? I realise my sudden appearance will have come as a shock to you, but it doesn't have to be like this. I will endeavour·to make myself agreeable to you, in which case you might find being married to me is what you want and have no wish to leave. See, I have something for you.'

Removing a small box from inside his coat, he handed it to her. Nonplussed, she stared at him and then down at the box. 'It won't bite. Open it?'

Gingerly she removed the lid to reveal a brooch. It was beautiful, a gold scorpion inlaid with sapphires. 'It—it's beautiful, but I can't accept it,' she said, thinking she had probably paid for it.

'Why on earth not?' Knowing what she was thinking, he smiled thinly, his eyes hardening. 'Don't worry. *I* paid for it. I know we agreed that you would support me in my ventures and any family dependents, but I paid for the brooch myself. It is not unusual for a husband to give his wife gifts. Besides, when I saw this brooch it reminded me of you.'

'Why?' she uttered drily. 'Because it's a deadly insect—with a sting in its tail.'

'No—because the sapphires are the colour of your eyes,' he said softly.

'Oh.' She was taken aback, not having expected that.

'If you don't like it, you don't have to wear it. Put it in a box and shut it away.'

'No—I won't do that.' Touched by his gift and that he had thought of her when so far away, she smiled. 'It's far too beautiful and precious to be shut away. I shall wear it.'

'I'm glad.' Returning her smile, he perched his hips on the edge of the desk, folding his arms across his chest in a relaxed pose. 'When we married we went directly to Kingswood, so how do you find living in London?'

'Like you I prefer to be in the country. What excites so many people about London society I actually find an ordeal. The Season that excites so many people to me resembles an obstacle course of so many events. To respect the custom, it must be got through and must be dreadfully arduous to the participants. Personally I have found some of the events excruciating and a dreadful bore.'

'I imagine New York isn't so much different in the upper echelons of society. Your father must have moved in such circles.'

'Yes, he did—he still does.'

'When he came to England he was determined to marry you off to an aristocrat.'

'He was—and he succeeded.'

'And because I was struggling to survive, I had to reconcile myself to being a kept man. It did nothing for my pride or my ego at the time.'

'No, I don't suppose it did. And now you're back, I could stop providing you with an income if you insist on remaining here.'

'That doesn't matter any more.'

'It should. You would be lost without it.'

He looked at her hard. 'You would do that, would you—see me destitute?'

That hit a nerve. 'No,' she conceded. 'I wouldn't do that. I'm neither heartless nor cruel.'

'That's good to know. As a matter of fact, I'm not as destitute as I was when I married you. Things improved for me considerably.'

'They did? Why did you not tell me?'

'No correspondence, you said—remember?'

'Yes, I do.'

'The money you gave me I invested in several projects—diamond mining in Africa and coal over here. The dividends are healthy and I am beginning to reap rewards. I intend investing more. So you see, Sophie, I no longer depend on your money.'

'I see. Then you will be pleased to know Kingswood is also thriving, so you can put your financial worries behind you.'

'It is because of you that I can do so. I am grateful. Our reasons for marrying were hardly the reasons on which to build the strong foundations of marriage.'

Sophie took a deep breath, not knowing what to say, but she felt the bite of cruel truth in his words.

'God knows I didn't want to marry anyone—not after my experience with Dianna,' he went on, 'but at the time, to save Kingswood from being taken from me, I had no choice.'

'And you hated yourself for it, didn't you, Tristan?'

When he looked at her, Sophie stepped back in alarm from the unexplained violence glittering in his eyes.

'Yes, I did. Very much as it happened. But I didn't walk into our marriage with my eyes closed. Wishing to know all about you before committing myself, I sought out a friend of mine at the Foreign Office.'

'You did?'

He nodded. 'He told me you had been showered with admiration from every eligible male in New York society and had received proposals from several, yet your father turned them down.'

'Because he wanted me to have an English title—even though it meant buying one,' she said, unable to hide the bitterness in her tone. 'Do you still hate yourself for accepting what my father offered you?'

'Now—when I look at you and see what you have achieved—I don't.'

'I'm glad. You know, I also had no choice in the matter at the time. My father is a hard and exacting man. I was not free to do as I wished so I had to comply to his wishes. When he told me what he intended for me, before I came to England I must confess that I tried to familiarise myself with everything English by immersing myself in a study of your newspapers and anything that would enhance my standing when I was introduced to English society.'

Transfixed, Tristan stared at her sagely, strangely moved as he listened to her confession of how she had tried to learn about everything English before leaving America. 'That was a very wise thing to do, since the English aristocracy is confusing to even the best people—even to the aristocracy.'

'Even you?' she asked, gazing into his unfathomable silver-grey eyes, seeing the cynicism lurking in their depths.

'Even me. Tell me, Sophie. Do you miss New York?'

'No, I don't.'

'But your father lives in New York. Would you not like to see him?'

'I haven't seen him since he left London following our marriage.' Her eyes hardened. 'As you know we were never close. I have no wish to see him.'

He nodded. There was a knock on the door and when he told whoever it was to enter, it was a footman come to inform him more crates had arrived.

'Goodness,' Sophie said as Tristan strode to the door. 'You appear to have brought the whole of Egypt back with you.'

'They will take some sorting out. They will all have to

be dealt with carefully, each article cleaned, sketched and catalogued.' He looked at her. 'You might like to give me a hand. I shall need some assistance when I get to Kingswood.'

Sophie stared at him in mock amusement. 'You would trust me to do that?'

He laughed. 'Why not? Unless you are so put out at my return you might be tempted to throw them at me instead.'

'But I know nothing at all about ancient relics and I don't know if I'm all that interested.'

'It's fascinating. You might surprise yourself and enjoy learning.'

Sophie gave him a dubious look and marched past him. 'I very much doubt it.

The days before going to Kingswood were taken up with Tristan sorting through the packages and crates. A few were to remain in London, a large number were to go to the British Museum, and others were to be sent to Kingswood and stored in the *antika*—a building close to the house he used for storing such things. Each artefact was as precious as the next and had its place.

Tristan would seek Sophie out to show her interesting mosaics, broken pieces of amphorae, statues and all manner of frescos. Despite showing her reluctance, Sophie found herself being drawn in, quietly and annoyingly wanting to learn more. She also found herself taking more time wither her toilet each morning and hoping he would be present at breakfast.

He was looking forward to going to Kingswood to begin his own dig on a site that was thought to have been a Roman villa which had been found in the grounds. Perhaps he would become so absorbed with his dig that he might forget he had a wife indoors.

* * *

It was a lovely December day, though very cold, when they went down to Surrey. Sophie, seated across from Tristan with a warm rug over her knees, chafed under his scrutiny. Neither of them broke the charged silence until they were close to Kingswood.

'I'm not at all sure that I should have left London at this time,' Sophie said, wishing the journey would end. 'I had some appointments to keep with Caroline. She'll think I've deserted her.'

Tristan gentled his gaze when he saw her downcast face. 'Caroline will understand perfectly. It will be good for us to be together at Kingswood—to spend some time together. You have nothing to fear.'

Sophie bristled as though he had given her some great insult. 'Have I not?' She shook her head. 'No one can promise that.'

'No, they can't. But I meant what I said, Sophie. I don't want you to feel under any pressure,' he answered, with a half-smile. It was obvious that he had touched a nerve. 'I am not perfect. Far from it, in fact. But I will do all in my power to make you happy.'

'How?' she demanded, her deep blue eyes glittering with ire. 'How can you claim you will do that?'

'Because I know you.'

'No, you don't,' she countered petulantly. 'Six weeks is hardly enough time to get to know one another.'

'Which is something I intend to rectify—at Kingswood.'

'Despite my desire to remain in London at this time.'

'As a matter of fact, it matters to me a great deal what you want. You are a remarkable young woman, Sophie. I have thought of you often over the years we have been apart. You are beautiful and wise—and you have confidence, too, as well as a sense of humour—although I have seen very little of that of late. You are also brave.

'The fact that you have taken on Kingswood, picked it up and—according to the ledgers I have worked my way through—made it the prosperous estate it once was is commendable and bespeaks your determination and good sense.'

'Goodness me! That is praise indeed,' she uttered with a trace of mockery, which her husband ignored.

'It makes me feel that I can trust you, trust in your integrity, which is a rarity for me. It's not often I come across a person I can trust. I'm an ungrateful wretch and I don't think it even occurred to me to thank you for all you have done—but I do. Just don't ask me to believe you are indifferent to me because I won't believe you.' He smiled, encouraged that she did not look away.

He spoke the truth. Of course she wasn't indifferent to him. No woman could be. She looked at him, rendered speechless by his words. It was difficult to argue with a man who praised her not for superficial things, but for the very qualities that she most valued in herself. It would seem he did understand her a little better than she had given him credit for. The tantalising channels in his cheeks deepened as he offered her a smile that seemed every bit as persuasive as it once had been. She breathed a sigh of relief as the coach finally swung in through the gates.

Tristan ordered the coach to stop. Climbing out, he held out his hand. 'Come. The view from here is worth seeing.'

Sophie took his hand and stepped down, pulling up the collar of her coat to shield her neck from the cold. Despite the wind blowing off the park, they stood looking at the wonderful vista that stretched as far as the eye could see. Turning to their right, they could see the house, the diamond-paned leaded windows glinting in the sunlight. She had known what to expect, having seen it many times, but as always the breath caught in her throat. Kingswood was the ancestral home of several generations of Osbornes, comprised of woods, parkland and fertile fields.

'It really is quite beautiful,' she breathed.

'Yes, it is. The timeless splendour of all this never fails to move me. I had to come back—to see this. I always feel as if I am in the grip of something I cannot name—or escape.'

Sophie glanced at him, knowing exactly how he felt. She turned and looked at the lush green acres, impressive and heartbreakingly beautiful. The fresh wind carried the smell of the pines in the forest and the damp smell of wet earth, winter scents of the countryside she had grown to love. When she had first seen Kingswood it was like nothing she had experienced before and she had felt herself ensnared by this lovely old house and its surrounding park and farm land.

At that moment she'd had no doubt that Kingswood was part of her destiny, that she belonged here, that she could be happy here. She'd shaken herself back to awareness, telling herself that these were fanciful thoughts and such things were not possible, that things did not happen like that, but then when a woman was as wealthy as she was, perhaps it was possible to make such things happen. In no time at all the fabric of the great house had seemed to close itself around her and claimed her for its own.

Tristan moved closer to her side, his voice soft and warm to her ears.

'The house never changes,' he murmured. 'It smiles, it beckons, it invites and welcomes. I have loved it since I was a child. There is nowhere quite like it.'

'And yet you chose to leave it.'

He looked down at her. 'I didn't choose to leave it, Sophie. The way I saw it I had no choice. If you hadn't taken it over I would have lost it for ever. So you see you did me a favour—even though it didn't seem like that at the time. I have much to be grateful for.'

Settling back inside the coach, she glanced across at Tristan. As their eyes met she realised how he must feel returning to his home after so long an absence. Already she could feel the situation changing between them. She was no longer on neutral ground, and in control of the situation.

Tristan received a warm welcome from the staff at Kingswood. They were happy to see him back where he belonged. Leaving him to find his way to his own suite of rooms, Sophie went to her own. With a sigh of relief she leaned her back against the door. Well, she was home now. It felt strange to think her husband was here in this rambling old house once more—where he belonged. This she could not deny, even though—for her own peace of mind—she would rather he was still in Egypt.

She had to admit that running a house and estate as large as Kingswood had been difficult and had given her many headaches. Now Tristan was back, she thought as she eyed the large bed, she prayed he would be considerate and not insist in exerting his conjugal rights. A shiver of fear ran down her spine at the thought of her husband in her bed, but he had assured her she was under no pressure to take their relationship further.

The next morning, impatient to see the changes Sophie had made and to reacquaint himself with his tenant farmers, Tristan had suggested she accompany him. Looking forward to a good gallop herself, she'd agreed. When she was mounted, he brought his horse alongside her dancing mare, eager to be off.

'Shall we go?'

The day was bright but cold, with gusts of wind that billowed out the skirt of Sophie's dark blue riding habit and played with the tendrils of hair about her face that had escaped her hat. Her horse was spirited and eager and needed a firm, attentive hand on the reins. She was deeply conscious of her companion as he rode beside her, letting his body roll easily with the surge of the powerful mount beneath him. Watching him with admiration, she realised how much she had missed these daily rides they had taken together before he left.

Tristan stole an admiring glance at her. He stared at her profile, tracing with his gaze the classically beautiful lines of her face, the sweep of her lustrous ebony eyelashes, the delicate curve of her cheek. She represented everything most desirable in a woman.

There was a passion in his wife. He'd sensed it when they had been together in those early days of their marriage. Brief glimpses, perhaps, but he knew enough about women to know he hadn't been mistaken. He just had to work out how to ignite that passion so that it burned for him. Now that he had managed to get her alone at Kingswood he would have more chance to do that, without the distractions that filled her time in London.

Suddenly he found himself actually looking forward to his future for the first time in a long time. In the beginning, as part of their arrangement, he had been prepared to wait patiently, as it was in his nature to be, for Sophie to become his wife in the full meaning of the word. Now he'd had time to reflect, if he had anything to do with it would not be long in coming. But he would not force her. It was important that she came to him of her own free will.

Tristan immersed himself in his work, the excavation in the park dominating his attentions, which meant he spent little time at the house. There wasn't a day went by when Sophie's curiosity didn't draw her to the *antika*.

Tristan tactfully encouraged her and was pleased when she found herself helping him unpack crates containing all manner of relics collected on his travels in the deserts of Africa, Arabia and Mesopotamia, sorting them into groups and carefully cataloguing each item.

He observed that she surprised herself for she actually enjoyed unwrapping theses treasures, excitedly anticipating what was inside. She found the work needed all her attention and she listened with interest as Tristan explained the objects' places of origin.

He was expecting an excavation archaeologist any day to inspect the site of the Roman villa in the park so he could begin excavating. Already a small part of a mosaic floor had been uncovered. Duncan, Caroline's husband, a close neighbour and amateur antiquarian, was to come over and help with the dig. It was all very exciting.

'Are you happy doing this work, Sophie.' Tristan asked when he came in to the *antika* and found her wrapped in warm winter clothes, painstakingly trying to cement together some crumbling mosaics.

Looking up, she smiled. 'I have to confess that I do find it interesting. I've surprised myself.'

'I'm glad. I'll make an antiquarian out of you yet.'

'I'm learning—or trying to,' she replied absently—piecing the mosaics together required her full attention. 'I always thought I was a woman of the present, yet here I am, familiarising myself with the far distant past.'

'Which is far more interesting than the present.'

'And there speaks a man who knows.'

'I, too, have much to learn, Sophie. The more one learns about the past the hungrier one becomes to know more.' Perching on the edge of the table on which she was working and folding his arms, he smiled down at her. 'You look different—with your hair all mussed up and a smudge of dirt on your cheek.'

'Have I?' she said, rubbing at her cheek with her hand.

'The other one.'

'Oh, you might have said—but it doesn't matter. I'll have a bath when I get to the house.'

'I'll walk with you.'

'I'd just like to finish this before I go.'

Tristan looked down at her head bent over her work and smiled, amused and pleasantly surprised by the interest she was showing. 'As you wish. I'll come back in half an hour.'

'Mmm—oh, yes,' she said distractedly. 'All right.

The horror of the nightmare hit Tristan when he fell into a deep sleep in his bed. Insidiously, like one of the snakes he had seen uncoiling and slithering out of rocks in Egypt. It was the horror of the recurring nightmare of being in the desert that unfolded, of being hungry and thirsty and watching his friends die of it. In a moment of lucidity he threw back the covers and, getting out of bed, paced the room, raking trembling fingers through his hair.

Thrusting his arms into his robe, he poured some brandy into a glass and tossed it back, willing the horror of the nightmare to leave him. Stopping outside the connecting door to his wife's bedroom, frustrated and angry and consumed with a desperation not to be alone, without thought he opened it and stepped inside.

Sophie was drifting on the edge of sleep when she had a strange feeling that someone was in the room, watching her. Her eyes snapped open. Tristan was standing quite still at the bottom of the bed, the glow from the embers of the dying fire behind him. With his black tousled hair and attired in a midnight-blue robe, he was a strangely threatening figure as he stood motionless as a dim statue, all his attention riveted on her.

With a gasp of fear and indignation she sat up and got out of bed, grasping a bedgown draped over the back of a chair close to the bed.

'Tristan! What are you doing here?' Her mind was in complete turmoil.

He did not speak, but stared at her with a remote brooding look. He moved towards her. Lean of waist and hips, with strong muscled shoulders, Tristan Osborne was undoubtedly a handsome man, but his face in the mellow light was too strong, his mouth too stubborn and his chin too arrogant for Sophie's liking just then. In fact, the sheer power emanating from him brought a fluttering to her stomach.

He took a step towards her and then another. Sophie retreated step for step, until the backs of her legs bumped the bed. Unable to go forward and adamantly unwilling to fall back on to the bed, she stood in mutinous silence, her heart pounding in her chest. Tendrils of alarm wrapped themselves round her heart. She caught his eye as he watched her.

There was a strange expression on his face, sad, she thought. It was a tormented face, a beautiful face, a face that carried the weight of tragedy, the eyes heartbreaking. Those eyes, framed with thick long lashes, only seemed to betray his sorrow. His mouth, wide-curved and passionate, was drawn thin.

He stopped a few inches from her, a darkness in his eyes. They were close, closer than they had ever been before. Sophie was aware of nothing but the vigour of him, the power of him, the faint scent of his cologne and the aroma of brandy on his breath that fanned her cheek.

'It's very late, Tristan, and time you were in bed.'

His gaze swept over her, turning to amazement at the heavy mass of her hair that rippled down her back, crackling and alive in the light from the fire.

'Forgive me. I couldn't sleep.' His voice was toneless, flat, dead. He touched her curling hair. 'You have beautiful hair, Sophie – so soft.'

Unconscious of the vision she presented in her clinging robe and her hair tumbling over her shoulders in loose disarray, Sophie's cheeks flamed, but at the same time her heart missed a beat. Her husband was beginning to alarm her nervous, awakened senses.

She felt the weakness attack the level of her knees, quivering up her thighs to her stomach. She thought she would experience bitterness, anger, some strong emotion which would strengthen her, but all she could feel was his pain. There was no flippant humour in his strong mouth, no warmth in his eyes. His face was ravaged, tormented, the blue of his eyes dimmed, indifferent to all but what was inside him.

'You may have come back, Tristan, and this is your home, since we are husband and wife, but our sleeping arrangements haven't changed. I would be obliged if you would return to your own room.'

The expression on his face, the blank expression that told her that nothing she might say or do could penetrate his mind, did not alter. He ran a hand across his eyes and looked at her, agony and torment hot in his eyes. She had never seen him look like this—as if someone else had taken him over.

'Yes,' he replied, his voice hoarse.

The room was hushed and dark and still around them. He was looking at her directly, a look that searched her face, with tenderness. She felt compassion. Then she felt his hand. It rested on hers, gently, folding over until it encompassed hers. She did not pull away but held it, for what comfort it could offer.

'Tristan—whatever happened to you in Egypt that brought you home—for what comfort I can offer, I am sorry.'

It was then he looked beyond her and then back again, as if remembering where he was. 'It is I who am sorry. I should not be here. I don't know what brought me to your room, only I cannot rid myself of what happened—of my grief. Each time I remember it worsens, yet I must rid myself of it for I will know no peace until I do.'

'Then—tell me, Tristan. It might ease your burden to share it.'

'No—it is too raw.'

Sophie looked at him mutely. She could think of no words of comfort. Raising her hand, he pressed his lips to her fingers, then let it go. Turning from her, he walked across the room to the door. Then he had gone, like a ghost of the night, leaving behind consternation and a need in Sophie for a deeper understanding of that proud and lonely man. What she did feel was a closeness between them that had never been before.

Like a sleepwalker, numb, stunned by what had just happened, Sophie turned to the bed. Still in her robe, she crawled beneath the covers and curled herself in a tight ball, hugging her knees. Yet the haunting look in Tristan's eyes would not leave her. What had happened to him in Egypt that had been so terrible it had brought him home?

Chapter Four

The following morning they met at breakfast. What had occurred during the night was not mentioned. Suggesting she accompany him on a ride before he became immersed in his antiquities in the *antika*, Sophie agreed.

They galloped together over the springy turf, rejoicing in the freedom this gave them. In absolute abandon, Sophie's laughter bubbled to the surface like fresh spring water. Stopping to rest on a hill overlooking the parkland, the lake belonging to Kingswood glinting in the distance, Tristan sprang athletically from the saddle, helping his wife to dismount. They strolled towards a large oak and sat on a log beneath it.

Leaning his back against the trunk and draping one arm over his raised knee, Tristan was content to sit there and look at his wife. His thoughts had a habit of turning to lust whenever he looked at the woman who insisted on keeping him from her bed.

As he listened to the breeze gently weaving its way through the branches of the trees, his heavy-lidded gaze feasted on the vision of the lovely creature in a warm lavender dress. The richness of her loosely brushed-back hair emphasised the creamy whiteness of her fine skin and the brilliance of her blue eyes. She looked enchanting. Sophie was warm, loving and giving. She was made for love and having children and everything else a husband and wife could contrive in a successful marriage.

The restraints she had forced on his nature were in danger of breaking and the force between them had grown powerful and impatient in its long captivity. But he must be patient with her, he must wait for her to come to him.

Resting on her knees and sitting back on her heels, idly plucking at the grass, Sophie looked at her husband closely. For a moment she forgot the accumulated tension that had beset her since his return. His intrusion into her bedchamber and the torment he had revealed of his inner self—suddenly she felt curious to know a hundred different things about him.

What kind of man are you, Tristan Osborne? she wondered and realised she had no idea at all.

A light blazed briefly in his eyes, then was extinguished. She gave him a speculative look, deeply conscious that his easy, mocking exterior hid the inner man. There was a withheld power to command to him that was as impressive as it was irritating.

'What are you thinking?' he asked. 'You're looking at me as if you're wondering whether to ask me a question or keep it to yourself.'

She laughed. 'I find I am curious about you. Why did you come back, Tristan? Was it really to take up your old life here at Kingswood, or did something happen to you when you were away that drove you back?'

A sudden shadow fell across his face. 'I had been thinking of coming back for some time, then something happened to me—something life-changing.'

Sophie looked at him compassionately. Beneath his

smooth façade was something dark and savage kept on a tight leash. 'I'm sorry. I shouldn't have asked.' An unexpected emotion made her voice tremble. She glanced at him. He was sideways on and all she could see was his stony profile, which seemed to be deep in thought. She lowered her face. 'Please forget I mentioned it.'

Tristan turned his head and looked at her. 'But you did. I can imagine the bewilderment my sudden return has caused you—the questions you must have asked yourself when I left your room last night—for which I apologise, by the way. I suddenly felt the need for company, for the presence of another human being.'

'It isn't any of my business why you did, but it was clear to me that it was of a vicious nature."

Tristan didn't answer at once. He sat a while, his head bowed, as if meditating. He hesitated, as if thinking to refuse this sudden, surprising curiosity. Then he relented.

'Since we are to live together for the rest of our lives, it is only right that you know what happened to me. It may help you to understand me better and to realise why I had to return.

'It was when I was in Alexandria with like-minded people whose minds had been opened to the wonders of ancient Egypt. A couple of explorers, who had come in from the desert, professed to have found an ancient tomb to the west of the Nile. Greedy for anything at all that concerned new unexplored tombs and treasures, we listened to what they had to say.

'They were full of excitement at what they had seen. They had found steps leading to a tunnel filled with rubble. When they cleared it out, they came to a solid wall guarded by two life-sized statues.

'Through a small breach in the wall, with the light of a candle they looked inside, claiming to have seen wonderful things—a tomb filled with gilded antiquities that hadn't seen the light of day for centuries. They also saw evidence of a further chamber—a burial chamber. They gained our interest.'

'Did they show you where it was?'

'That was their intention. The project was so big they could not do it alone.' He sighed, his expression set, his eyes hard as he looked into the far-off distance. 'The thrill of looking into the sarcophagus in which the body of a pharaoh might rest was too tempting for us to resist. There were eight of us who set out on the expedition into the desert. When we set out we had no idea how long we would be gone.

'We went deep into the desert. Unfortunately we experienced the worst—sandstorms, freezing nights. After one particularly bad sandstorm, when it cleared it was to find we had become separated from the two men who were guiding us. We were two weeks into the journey and no idea where we were.'

'But—had you no map?'

'The maps were with the two men—along with our compass and four of the camels. We were left with just two.'

'And—did you find the tomb?'

He shook his head. We were in the desert for four weeks, going round in circles, although at the time—with little food and water, as one day ran into another—we lost all track of time. We were exhausted and sick with pain as the horizon swam sickeningly ahead of us. We had to press on. Every day was the same.

'After many days it was impossible to think or even to try. The water was gone and the sickness in all of us was worse. People suffering from dehydration start to hallucinate—to imagine we saw water ahead of us—a mirage. I was dying. This I knew. We all needed to rest, but we knew if we did we'd never get up again.

'The two camels died, along with three of the group.

By some miracle we met some Bedouin who took us to a village where we were taken care of. By some miracle I survived and managed to make it back to Alexandria.'

Silent, wide-eyed with horror, Sophie stared at him as if seeing him for the first time. There was no longer any anger in her, only an immense sadness and pity which welled up from the bottom of her heart towards this man whose sufferings must have been great indeed. She preferred not to think of what agonies he had gone through.

A heavy silence replaced Tristan's strangely calm, slow voice, broken only by the sound of birds in the air. A lump in her throat, Sophie struggle to find words which were not hurtful, for she sensed in him a raw and quivering sensitivity. She was the one who broke the silence, speaking in a voice that was controlled, but unconsciously tinged with respect.

'The memories of that time must pain you greatly,' she whispered.

'Yes. I consider myself fortunate to have survived—as do my two companions. Suddenly what we had set out to achieve in Egypt and beyond had lost its appeal.'

Sophie looked at his serious, proud face, his restless eyes bright. With his hair falling over his brow and his features in repose, he fell silent and his gaze drifted to her, which gave Sophie a moment to dwell on what he had told her. As she looked at him she felt drawn to him in a way she never had before.

Yes, he had reneged on their arrangement, but he was not her enemy. He never had been. In fact, he made her want to get to know him better, to step beyond the terrible things that had happened to him. But in a vulnerable state herself, where this man was concerned she must proceed with caution.

'What a terrible experience you must have gone through. How afraid you must have been.'

'I am not ashamed to admit I was—every day I struggled in that desert. It's how you survive. Fear keeps you alert—it keeps you safe. You think only about the moment. That's the only thing that matters.'

A scowl darkened his brow for a scant second, then his mood changed with the purposefulness of a strong will. He looked at her and smiled and placed his hand on her arm. 'And before you ask, we never did find the two men who lured us into the desert with tales of wonders. They might have perished—we never did find out.' He smiled bleakly. 'There. Does that appease your curiosity, Your Grace?'

Sophie was stirred by the depth of passion in his voice. Silence fell once more between them. Tristan sat very still, but it seemed to Sophie that his broad shoulders bowed, as though under the force of some strong feeling. For a moment she was tempted to reach out to him, but she was too wary, too much on her guard.

His hand still rested on her arm and she moved slightly so that he had to remove it. The warm, strong grip disturbed her, making it more difficult for her to regard him as an enemy who might have ruined any chance she had of keeping her freedom.

'Thank you for telling me, Tristan. I can understand how difficult it must be for you to talk about it.'

'The truth never is easy.' His gaze settled on her face. 'So, what now, Sophie? What does this mean for us? We shall have to learn how to live together.'

Sophie looked down at her hands folded in her lap. 'Which I hope will not prove too difficult—given your unpredictable temperament.'

'I promise I shall try to be patience personified in the future.'

Perhaps it was the quietness of the countryside, or perhaps it was the odd combination of gentleness and solemnity in his eyes as they gazed into hers, but, whatever the cause, Sophie's heart quickened.

'However our marriage came about, whatever differences there are between us, could we put it aside, do you think, and behave like any normal husband and wife?'

Mesmerised, Sophie stared into his fathomless eyes while his deep, soft voice seemed to caress her, pulling her under his spell. For some reason, his request did much damage to her resistance, but not entirely. With his face in repose, he looked far too handsome for her peace of mind. The curve of his lips and the way his eyes roamed appreciatively over her face aroused curious sensations deep within her. Sensations she desperately wanted to deny.

There was something thrillingly feral and vastly appealing about him as he regarded her steadily. The sunlight caressed his compelling features, making her breathlessly aware of the strength of his character inherent in his face. Her emotions were in chaos and she could feel herself being drawn in in a way that was far from comfortable.

She admitted helplessly that he was the most beguiling and infuriating man she had ever met. To her alarm she was conscious that, beneath her determination to keep him at arm's length and not to let her emotions become involved, there was a growing excitement that she actually enjoyed being with him.

Getting to her feet and taking hold of her horse's reins, she looked down at him. 'Not now, Tristan. Please don't speak of it now. It's too soon. I have to get used to having you home.'

Standing up, Tristan put his arm about her shoulders and drew her close, giving her no time to draw away. Sensing the tension in her body, when she looked at him he saw something in her eyes that was akin to fear. He regarded her attentively, his suspicions beginning to work overtime as he wondered what it was that she was afraid of.

Aware of his scrutiny, Sophie ran a nervous hand over the back of her neck, tucking non-existent strands of hair behind her ears. 'Why are you looking at me like that?' she whispered.

'It is difficult not to look at you, Sophie. You are very beautiful. And very frightened.'

He said it so coolly, so unemotionally, that it was a long moment before Sophie was certain she'd heard him correctly. But then it was too late for her to react. Tristan turned to her horse, taking hold of the bridle. Then abruptly he stopped and faced her, blocking her path. 'Why?' he demanded in a terse, frustrated voice. 'Why are you frightened?'

'I—I'm not,' she denied, startled.

'Yes,' he said harshly. 'You are.'

Sophie stared at him. Despite his harsh tone, there was a gentleness in his eyes and calm strength in his features. 'It—it's just that there has been so much to do of late— you coming home—all your paraphernalia which I have to say I have found so excessive...'

A lazy smile touched Tristan's lips and he curved a hand behind her head. 'So, convince me that is all that is worrying you,' he murmured, bringing his mouth even closer.

Sophie's hand glided up his chest in an attempt to push him away, unaware that the devastatingly tantalising caress made his muscles tense and his breath catch in his throat.

'And how long do you think it will take me to do that?'

'About two seconds. A kiss, Sophie. Just a kiss.'

When she didn't pull away and let her eyes drop to his lips, she surprised herself by raising her face to his. Taking this as her consent, Tristan captured her lips and proceeded to kiss her long and deep, leaving her breathless. She melted against him, the fire in her response igniting the flames deep within him. When he raised his head, he placed his arm around her shoulders in an intimate embrace and together they stood gazing wistfully across the lake to the distant hills.

Sophie felt the peace of the countryside. A sudden explosion of starlings lifted across the sky. The rain of the day before had left a freshness, a sweetness, a sparkle to the vista spread out before them, and the essence of it settled on her heart, finding a place there which she knew it would never leave.

'Did the kiss cure you of your problems?'

Sophie's long curling lashes fluttered up and her eyes, soft and a warm deep blue, were captured by his. 'No, but I didn't find it unpleasant.'

He grinned. 'Then that's a start.' Helping her to mount, he placed a hand on her leg. 'Don't you care,' he said, 'what is usual between a husband and wife and what isn't?'

His hand remained on her leg and for some reason she could not move away.

'Sophie, you're not like other women. We both know that. Somewhere, at some time, you've been through a kind of hell. Each of us has our own kind—and you now know mine. Most of us never admit it exists. But you and I—we know it does. We have to be honest to ourselves.'

Removing his hand from her leg, he mounted his horse and they rode back to the house in silence.

With that strange knowingness of his he did not press her further. He knew there was a fear of marriage within her, yet he did not shrink from the knowledge and demanded no explanation. Something stirred in Sophie—the wildness of joy and excitement and at the same time fear of committal.

That night as Sophie prepared for bed, each time she looked at the connecting door she could not trust her own senses because of the turmoil inside her. Everything told her not to fall in love with Tristan, that to love him would be a madness—a mistake, both a mixture of torment and pleasure. But the wildness of this reasoning made her delve further into her feelings. Torment she already had. Why not reach for the pleasure? Would he come to her?

Curling up in a high-backed chair by the hearth, she let her thoughts wander to what Tristan had told her about what had happened to him in Egypt. How terrible that must have been when he had been lost in the desert, affecting him so severely that his thoughts had turned to home. Her face was soft and wistful as she gazed into the glowing embers. Her arms hugged her slender waist, as if they sought to simulate a lover's embrace, which she had yet to experience.

Breathing deep and closing her eyes, she felt again the ache inside her when she remembered their closeness when he had come to her room and the tenderness of his lips when they had kissed. It had done strange things to her sensibilities, things she could not understand.

Suddenly a sound from behind the door intruded into her thoughts. Her eyes snapped open and she listened to the footfalls that were familiar to her now. She had listened to them every night and only once had Tristan entered her room through the connecting door. The warmth of the fire relaxed her body and as she continued to listen to him moving about, again she felt the awakening of pleasure deep within her. It was strong and disturbing, flooding her body with a pulsing warm excitement.

Dear Lord, what was the matter with her? Why was she so afflicted? She had lived with the fear of intimacy between a man and a woman because of the pain and that awful disease her father had inflicted on her mother. Yet now her mind envisioned the dark, handsome face of the man behind that door.

She resented the hold he had over her so that she didn't know what to think any more and she withdrew in horror from the bold, unmistakable urging of her body. She knew she would not be free of this torment until she had given him what he wanted from her.

What she wanted?

The footfalls fell silent, but a light still shone from beneath the door. Her husband was waiting for her on the other side like a big black spider intent on luring her into his web, this she did not doubt. He was challenging her, testing her, wanting her to go to him.

It was as if some mystical presence were embodied within that room, for she was caught for a moment by a yearning so strong and physical she found it hard to draw breath. Uncurling her body, she stood up and padded to the door. She looked at it long and hard before putting her hand on the brass knob and slowly turned it.

Was it locked?

Her heart lurched when it yielded. For a moment she wanted to turn and flee to her bed, but somewhere in her tormented mind, she knew Tristan was right and that their marriage should be more than in name only. Gently she pushed the door and it opened silently into a room of large proportions and dimly lit.

Sophie saw the shadowy shape of a huge bed on a raised dais and then, very much at ease, seated in a large armchair by the fire, was the room's inhabitant. The image of relaxed elegance, Tristan was calmly watching her. He had discarded his coat and waistcoat and neckcloth, and his fine white linen shirt was open at the throat to reveal a firm, strongly muscled throat.

His eyes smiled at her, touching her everywhere, and

the mocking grin gleamed with startling whiteness against his swarthy skin—in fact, there was a health and vitality about him that was almost mesmerising. Something awakened in her, something strange and alien to her nature—longings she had never felt before.

With her silk dressing gown draped about her and with her hair unbound in a single great fall down her back, Sophie stood staring at him, her eyes dark and huge in her pale face, burningly aware of the reasons that had brought her here. Now she was here, she knew there would be no going back. The figure, which was already rising with a cool nonchalance that did not seem appropriate to greet her with a deep, profoundly mocking bow, had succeeded in luring her into his bedchamber.

'Come in, Sophie, I was expecting you.'

'I know.'

'Although I did not expect you quite so soon. I thought the struggle with your inner self would have taken longer.' He met her expectant gaze with a cool, crooked smile of mild amusement. 'I'm glad you've decided to brave my chamber—and with it, discard your state of abstinence.'

'My state of abstinence I intended to diligently pursue as my only means of escape from…'

'What happens in bed between husband and wife,' he stated calmly when she faltered. 'And yet here you are, confronting your husband in his lair—a man you bought.'

'Please don't keep reminding me,' she snapped, her concern more with her own response than with his lingering, hungering gaze.

He smiled leisurely, infuriatingly sure of her. 'Do you recall me saying that it would be interesting to see if the agreement we made would outlast the testing of the flesh?'

'Yes. Why?'

'I have been home a mere four weeks and already you are showing signs of weakness.'

'And no doubt you think because I am here in your room that you have found a chink in my armour.'

His chuckle was low and deep. 'No, my dear wife, not a chink, but a massive hole.'

Purposefully he reached out and loosened the belt of her robe. Sophie put up no resistance. She met his gaze directly and her body tensed as he worked it off her shoulders and it fell to her feet, revealing a sheer white nightdress. One soft and lovely shoulder was temptingly bare.

Her body was covered and yet revealed everything and Sophie saw a quickening of passion spark in her husband's eyes as they slowly perused her from head to toe. Stripped naked by his bold gaze, every bit of the courage she had strived so hard to erect was shattered in an instant. She was too close to the muscular chest, too close to the scent of him, of everything that was masculine.

For a moment she was assailed by the memory of her father and her mother's misery. Her flesh went cold. Then a darker fear pierced her fear. Had her father mentally scarred her, left her unable to respond to a lover's touch? Her mind rebelled, but a trembling set in. Seeing her hesitation, Tristan sensed it and questioned it with a frown. Reaching out his hand, he caressed her cheek with featherlike fingertips.

'You tremble. Do you fear me, Sophie?'

Sophie waited for the screaming denial to come from the dark recesses of her mind—and this time she was determined to quell its intrusion and the trepidation that had arisen and surged within her. Tristan was not forcing her. He was awaiting her consent. The knowledge stilled her panic.

'What are you afraid of? Are you afraid of what happens between a man and woman?'

'Yes,' she told him flatly. 'I'm sorry. I can't help it.'

Placing a finger beneath her chin, he tilted her face up to his. 'Then don't be. There's no need. I promise you, Sophie, your worries are needless.'

'But you and Dianna—your first wife—what happened between the two of you… I don't want…'

'What happened between me and my first wife will not happen to us, Sophie. I promise you that. I'm aware of your fears and I do understand. Trust me.'

Relief flooded over her. Along with many other things to do with the opposite sex, Caroline had explained there were certain things men could do to prevent children being born. Sophie could not even imagine what these certain things might be for matters of a sexual nature were never discussed openly, but she believed Caroline implicitly.

Thankfully, Tristan understood her fears. She was confident he would take care of everything, and he had nephews aplenty to carry on the title after him.

'Please don't be despondent,' Tristan murmured. 'Especially not now. We have been married four years—four years we have missed. Now is a time to make amends—a time for happiness—a time to look forward for us both.' He drew his finger gently down the bare flesh of her slender neck. 'The time for talking is ended. Now it is time for loving.'

'It is my intention to be your wife in every way, but—it is all so new to me, so I ask you to show patience, Tristan.'

He raised a quizzical brow. 'And you won't run scared and change your mind?' She shook her head, but he could see the uncertainty in her large eyes. His expression softened, understanding more about what was going on in her mind than she realised. 'You will find what we do neither distasteful nor undignified. This I promise you. You will find pleasure, not pain, in my arms.

'Making love is a time for giving and sharing, not taking. I will not hurt you. But I must warn you that what happens between us—that what you will find and experience in my bed—may bind you more eternally than anything else in your life.'

He wrapped her in his arms, their bodies clinging together, hers slender and silky, his hard, long and lean. Taking her face between his hands and threading his fingers through her silken hair, he kissed her mouth and trailed featherlight kisses down her neck to her breast, slowly drawing her down on to the bed, finding her lips once more and deepening the kiss.

'You are like a bird of paradise with a body made for love,' Tristan murmured, raising his head, his breathing deepening as he felt her respond to his caress.

Sophie closed her eyes and slipped her arms around his neck. 'You'll have to show me how it's done,' she whispered against his lips. 'I've had no practice, you see, so I would not know.'

'I will teach you. I will awaken all the passion in that lovely, untutored body,' he murmured, well aware that it was her first time and determined to be gentle with her.

They stroked and kissed, exploring each other and languidly enjoying the experience. Tristan groaned with pleasure, deepening his kiss, almost losing control completely. She moved against him as his caresses grew bolder, exploring the secrets of her body with the awareness of a knowledgeable lover.

He was gentle, infinitely so, his hand wandering with deliberate slowness over every part of her, as if savouring what he found, and she trembled beneath his touch. Sophie felt as if her body were on fire, melting and flowing, and a sob of startled pleasure escaped her.

Reluctant to leave her, but impatient to remove his

clothes, Tristan stood and divested himself of his clothing. Sophie slid off the bed and slipped her nightdress over her head. Then like a celestial being she moved towards him. She lay on the bed and Tristan knelt beside her in reverence. The pull of his gaze was too strong for Sophie to resist. It was as though he were looking into the very depths of her heart and soul. She felt the touch of empathy like healing fingers touching and soothing her pain like a balm.

Her fear of what was to come was like a cutting edge and yet sublime, and when it left her she was wide open to a flood of wondrous emotions. When she tasted the warmth of his lips, she felt all the love, the compassion, the respect he carried for her in his heart and, when he finally took her, the pleasure transcended anything she had known before.

She held him to her, floating on a sea of mindless pleasure. His body was as lean as an athlete's, bold, virile and golden brown. Entwined, they merged together, the firm, slender body beneath his like a yielding, living substance as she gave all her desire, her passion and her love. They became one, fulfilling each other in a most sublime, exquisite act of love.

Tristan raised his head and looked down at her. She was flushed and satiated with loving. Her hair was spread out in shimmering waves across the pillows and she was staring up at him with wide, searching eyes that had taken on a strange, deep hue, amazement etched on her flushed face.

The woman in his arms had fire and spirit and she was also charming and innocent. She had given him exquisite pleasure and when the moment of his release came, he couldn't have said who clung to the other most desperately. It was as though the very life source was being wrung out of him. He had turned her into a passionate, loving woman, a woman to fill his arms and warm his bed and banish the dark emptiness within him, a woman to fill his life with love and laughter.

The whisper of a sigh escaped her as she lifted her face to meet his, wanting to hold on to this moment in time lest she lose some portion of it to the oncoming forces of normality. Her trembling lips parted as his mouth possessed hers with a gentleness that was nothing like the fierce kisses of a moment before.

'My God,' Tristan murmured, his eyes smouldering. 'You are wanton beyond belief and quite magnificent, Sophie.'

Completely captivated by the intimate look in his eyes and the way a stray lock of crisp, dark hair fell across his forehead and the compelling gentleness in his voice, Sophie swallowed and said, 'So are you.' All the doubts she had expected, all the qualms of gnawing shame she imagined would torment her, were not there. More unnerving and frightening to her was the strange sense of contentment, of rightness she felt being in his arms, as if it were where she was meant to be.

'Are you content now I have fulfilled my word?'

'Nay, Sophie, far from it,' he murmured, nuzzling the hollow in her throat where a pulse was beating a tantalising fast rhythm beneath her soft flesh. 'The night is far from over and I intend to make the most of you while I have you in my bed, to give you such pleasure you can never have imagined.'

Later, little remained of the woman who had been a victim of her father's treatment of her mother. Sophie was a woman of the past. The mysterious alchemy of her inner self mixed with elements inside Tristan had worked the miracle of transformation. The change in her was clear and for the first time in years Sophie felt at peace with herself.

Chapter Five

The following days that ran into weeks were filled with loving. Tristan was completely enamoured of his wife. They made love with a fierceness, unable to control the tormenting demands of their bodies, as if to make up for the time they had lost from being apart.

Their bodies did the most wonderful things, lovely things, and a shivering ecstasy pierced Sophie's entire body, sending streaks of pleasure curling through her. Her sighs were soft and seductive as she stretched out alongside this man she now adored. Not only had she a husband, but a lover. His irrepressible carnality enthralled her.

They were days to treasure and remember. Sophie was so happy. Now that they were not just man and wife, but lovers in the true sense, she had discovered a new happiness which was a revelation to her. The compulsion to know all there was to know about this enigmatic man who had turned her life upside down from the moment she'd set eyes on him long ago was so strong it couldn't be denied.

They did everything together—eating their meals together, riding and immersing themselves in Tristan's work. They enjoyed a quiet Christmas together and Sophie was learning all the time about this ancient world that so absorbed him. His interest and knowledge astounded her. He would talk vividly of his travels and bring the past to life with such clarity that she could almost see it before her eyes.

This closeness to another person, this newly found intimacy, of having someone to reach out to, to be his first consideration, to share her bed and her life, was exciting and so wonderful. She vowed that she would make him a good wife and that she would please him in every way.

Her complete happiness came to an abrupt end when they were walking back to the house from the *antika*. Sophie could feel Tristan's eyes on her. Laughing softly, she turned her head to look at him.

'What are you thinking that makes you look at me like that?'

His grin was almost salacious. 'I cannot tell you that without offending your sensitive ears, my darling. But I was thinking how very lovely you are and that our offspring—if we are blessed with a daughter—will look exactly like you.'

Sophie felt the blood drain from her face and her heart began to race. 'A daughter?' The word began to howl like a banshee in her brain. 'But—what are you saying?'

'That if we have a daughter, I would like her to have your hair—your eyes… Of course, a son would be most welcome.'

Sophie's mind registered disbelief. It started to shout denials—even while something inside her slowly cracked and began to crumble. 'But, Tristan—I—I thought you understood.'

Bemused, he stared at her. 'Understood? Understood what?'

'I don't want children,' she burst out, her voice almost unrecognisable, brittle and frantic. 'I—I thought you didn't either.'

Tristan's eyes narrowed. 'Have I given you reason to think that?'

'Yes—I mean...'

'What? What do you mean?'

'That day—before we—we...'

'Made love?'

'Yes. You said you understood.'

'What I understood was that you were afraid about what would happen between us when we did finally make love. Are you telling me it was something else?'

Wringing her hands in front of her, Sophie looked at the anger kindling in his glittering eyes. 'Yes.'

'Sophie, why were you so certain I didn't want children?'

'Because—because Caroline told me you didn't want children,' she uttered wretchedly, unable to keep the truth from him. 'She—she told me you...' She trailed off at the sight of the murderous look on his face.

Gripped by something unexplainable, his body stiffened and his eyes were hard and probing when they looked at his wife. 'Caroline should have known better than to...'

'I thought you were like me,' she cried, 'that neither of us wanted children.'

That was the moment Tristan understood. It was as if a veil had been lifted. This explained Sophie's cool behaviour towards him when she had laid down the conditions for their marriage.

'So, that's what all this is about. Children. You don't want children, do you, Sophie?'

She stared at him, almost bursting with the emotions that were killing her. Of course she wanted children—the words screamed inside her head. She just didn't want to go through the process of having them. Her fear was silent, too painful to talk about. 'Caroline told me when your first wife was pregnant you didn't want her baby—

and that she was so upset that she lost it—that she was so ill she never got over it.'

'And you blamed me, didn't you?'

She nodded, gulping down the tears that threatened.

'I didn't want it. At least Caroline got that right. The child wasn't mine,' he told her brutally. 'I would not accept another man's child.'

Sophie stared at him, appalled. 'I didn't know. Caroline didn't tell me your wife had been unfaithful. How—how dreadful for you.'

'Caroline didn't know Dianna before our marriage, so I very much doubt she knew about the other men in Dianna's life—the more the merrier,' he ground out bitterly. 'When I found out she was pregnant our marriage was already over. I no longer cared what she did.'

'But—you must have loved her when you proposed marriage to her.'

'It was a marriage of convenience. She was wealthy, but not wealthy enough. She already had a lover when we married. She never did want my children. She was the most corrupt woman I have ever known.'

'I'm sorry. That must have been difficult for you. It is plain the memories of your former marriage are still raw.'

'Small wonder,' he said tightly. 'So, assuming I didn't want children, that was another reason that made me a suitable candidate for a husband.' His eyes turned to shards of ice and the muscles of his face clenched so tight a nerve in his cheek began to pulse. 'Your desperation not to bear a child must be very strong indeed for you to do that.'

'Yes.'

He had thought perhaps she was suffering from a love affair that had gone wrong or some such thing that affected the heart of young ladies, but he was wrong. It was more deep-rooted than that. 'So all this has been brought on because I failed to understand the true reason why you didn't want any closeness between us.'

'But I thought you knew that my fear was that I would become...'

'What? Pregnant?' She nodded. 'Sophie, we have made love every night for the past two weeks and you have shown no fear of pregnancy.'

She flushed, embarrassed. 'I—I thought you would... I mean, I know there are things that can be done...'

'Why didn't you tell me this? There are precautions than can be taken, but there is only one sure way to prevent the conceiving of a child, which is abstinence,' he told her coldly.

'No,' she cried, suddenly distraught, her fear and her emotions running high as she wrapped her arms about her waist in a protective manner. 'There are other ways. There has to be. I will not—cannot—allow myself to be dragged down to the status of a breeding animal, subject to the whims and fancies of any man. I do not want children,' she cried, quite distraught. 'I will not have them.'

'I think I get the picture,' Tristan said in an awful, silky voice. Thoughts of his first wife sprang to mind. She didn't want children either—at least, not his children. It would appear Sophie was yet another woman who didn't want children—a woman who didn't consider him worthy enough or good enough to father her children. "So what is to be done? Separate beds, separate rooms? Is that what you want?'

Unaware of the turn his thoughts had taken, she shook her head. All she wanted to do was fling herself on his chest, to beg him to help her, to make things right for her. But she couldn't. 'Of course it isn't. I don't know the answer. But if that is the way it has to be, then there is no other way.'

'I cannot live like that,' he said, his voice low and ice

cold. 'I'm human—a man with needs. I want to make love to my wife. I will not play the monk. I cannot believe that you thought we were of like minds. I expected you to be fearful of the first time—but I never expected anything of this magnitude. I do want children, Sophie. I want an heir to inherit Kingswood after me.'

'I'm sorry—I—I can't… I don't want…'

'You do realise I could divorce you for this.'

'Yes—but—you wouldn't.'

'I could, if I so wished. The grounds of your refusal to withhold from me my conjugal rights in order to prevent the conception of a child would be sufficient to grant me a divorce. But admit it, Sophie. You married me believing I didn't want children. But I'll be damned if I will stand up in court and tell the world that my wife refuses to share a bed with me. So, believing I didn't want a child, that made me an ideal candidate for a husband.'

With a bitter smile he looked at her hard, then, as if he couldn't bear to look at her a moment longer, he turned and walked to the door. 'No doubt you consider this marriage a mistake, Sophie, in which case I shall do you the favour of disappearing once again.'

'No, Tristan—but I really do not want a child—I cannot…' The mere thought of it made her shudder.

Seeing it, Tristan opened the door. 'Enough,' he said. 'I have heard enough. I will not listen to any more of what you have to say on that subject.'

In desperation she crossed the distance that separated them. 'Tristan,' she said, stretching her hand out in a gesture of mute appeal, then letting it fall to her side when her beseeching move got nothing but a blast of contempt from his eyes. The tension between them was so thick she could barely stand to breathe as she pleaded and hoped.

'I don't want you to go. I realise you must despise me for what I've done.'

Hearing the pain and desperation in her voice, he gave her an odd, searching look. 'I don't despise you. Quite the opposite. I just happen to love you—fool that I am. I just wish I understood. What I have to do right now is put some distance between us so that I can try to make some sense out of it.

Sophie stood still and watched him go, knowing nothing she could say would change his mind.

She had not seen Tristan again that day. The following morning he left for London before she was up. As one day passed into another, she wondered what he did when he was away from her—probably spent his time at the houses of his friends, socialising and drinking the night away in the company of other women. And why shouldn't he? she asked herself. He couldn't be blamed for seeking that which his wife denied him.

No matter how busy she kept herself, she missed him. She missed him at mealtimes, she missed him when she went to the *antika*, seeing him flushed and excited from his exertions. But most of all she missed him in her bed and the wonder and magic of when he had been a considerate and tender lover—when he had called her his love and praised her ability to please him and she had expected—what?

Not protestations of love. Not his constant presence nor his attention even, which he had given her since she had become his wife, but a little of his time, of the discussions, the laughter, the interests they seemed to find agreeable to them both, all leading to that magical time at the end of the day and the joy they shared.

Her mind dwelt constantly on what he had told her about

Dianna and the hurt and pain she must have caused him. Her heart wept for this man who had known nothing but pain and humiliation and betrayal at her hands. If he felt bitter by her betrayal, he could not be blamed.

Battered with a torrent of conflicting emotions and self-condemnation, and aware that, having trampled on his pride, Tristan would not come near her unless she made the first move, she realised that to make things right between them her pride was going to have to suffer now.

Besides, she now had good reason to seek him out—the very thing she had feared since she had been old enough to understand had happened and there was no running away from it any longer. She was going to need her husband. She would not let her fear ruin her life and destroy her chance to have a warm and happy marriage. She would have to go to him and try to explain as best she could her fear of childbirth.

Alone in London Tristan had plenty of time to think. He desperately wanted to understand why Sophie was adamant about not wanting a child—his child. He would have given anything to understand, but he had no idea where he should begin to try to break down the barrier she had erected around herself.

Why was she doing this? That was an agonising thought and an infuriating one. But only for a minute, for in the purple light of deepening dusk creeping over London, he couldn't actually believe that a young woman as tender and gentle as she was wouldn't want a child of her own without good reason.

Perhaps he had got it wrong and she was simply afraid of bearing a child—any man's child, and, if so, why? Or did she genuinely not wish to be a mother? He'd been so wrapped up in his own need, misery and anger that he hadn't even bothered to ask, to get to the bottom of it.

It might have been the solitary time he spent in his London house with no one for company other than the servants, that had this mellowing effect on him, but it seemed to him somehow that for whatever reason she had married him, she had come to care for him deeply. He thought of the short time they had been together at Kingswood before the subject of children had driven them apart, of the way they had passed their days in quiet talk and laughter and unbridled passion. No woman alive could have tried to give him as much pleasure as he was giving her if she didn't care for him.

It was past midnight when Tristan arrived home from his club. When the butler informed him that his wife had arrived, he went directly to his room. Taking a moment to remove his coat and cravat, he quietly entered her room through the connecting door and crossed to the bed.

Seeing her now gave him the most piercing joy of his life. As he gazed down at his wife's sleeping features, his thoughts grew tender as he remembered the golden candlelight upon creamy, silken flesh, still moist from making love, soft curling hair flowing across a pillow as it was now.

What was there about her that made him unable to forget her, that twisted his emotions, that left him with the desire to taste again the sweetness he had known on the nights so recently shared at Kingswood? He could find no answers.

She had served his pleasures well, more than any woman before, and from that first moment he had held her in his arms she had held his every thought so tightly that, even in his sleep, he could dream of nothing else but her.

As these thoughts beset his mind he would turn over and strike his fist into his pillow in mute frustration. My God! he thought. My wife denies me and my very soul crumbles. But in his heart he knew he could not keep away from her much longer. Already he had been contemplating his return and what he might do to win her back. He'd bide his time carefully, he'd mused, play the suitor all over again and court her tenderly, then perhaps she would turn to him.

And now, here she was.

Sophie had eaten a solitary supper in her room and retired to bed, only to be woken when she sensed someone in her room. Opening her eyes, she saw Tristan standing by the bed, looking down at her. Her heart gave a joyful leap.

Sitting up and rubbing the sleep from her eyes, she peered up at him. He was so tall that she thought he must have grown since she had last seen him. She gazed at him wonderingly, forgetting for a moment all that she had suffered because of his absence.

'Tristan!'

'Yes—Tristan. Your husband.'

Shoving the covers back and reaching for her robe, then wrapping it around her, she crossed to the hearth and sat beside the still-glowing fire.

'You're not angry with me for coming to London without telling you?' She tilted her head and stared into his fathomless gaze while he came and stood in front of the fire, looking down at her.

'It is not my intention to berate you, Sophie. I am not so insensitive that I don't know what you must be going through. There are things to be said—matters to be settled between us.'

'I know,' she said quietly. 'I—I missed you when you left.'

'I missed you also—in fact, I planned on returning to

Kingswood in the morning. When are you going to tell me the real reason you have come to London?'

'I—I wanted to see you—to speak to you—to explain as best I can why I decided a long time ago not to have children—which I am finding extremely difficult.'

'It clearly pains you to speak of it. But if we are to move forward you must. We have to be open and honest with each other. I remember my mother telling me that a trouble shared is a troubled halved—that two can bear a cross more easily than one.'

Sophie drew a tortured breath, trying not to show her trepidation. Tears were forming in her eyes. 'Yes, I am sure your mother was right.'

'It became my problem when you married me. Share it with me, Sophie.'

Conscious of his scrutiny, suddenly agitated, she got to her feet. 'How can you be so sure that telling you will make me feel better—that it will resolve everything?'

'I'm not saying that. But it will make me feel a damn sight better.'

With tears spilling over her lashes, Sophie looked at him long and hard before turning away, wrapping her arms around her waist as if to contain her awful secret. She realised that it was important for Tristan to know. In the end she turned to confront him and a flicker of sanity lit the chaos of her thoughts. Dashing her tears away with her hand, she took a deep breath.

'I know you are right. I have to tell you. What I have to say is significant to our future and may well go some way to resolving—or at least to giving you an understanding of my fear of…' She fell silent. His eyes locked on to hers, understanding exactly what she was saying.

When Tristan saw the tears and the fear steal into her eyes, he wanted to go to her and pull her into his arms, but he held back. She had to do this on her own. 'Go on,' he coaxed gently.

Her lovely, luminous eyes were saturated when she looked at him. 'I have to do this. My salvation is in my own hands. Only I can cure myself of what has become a virtual obsession. You must bear with me' The silence in the room was profound. Tristan's granite features were an impenetrable mask.

'It—it concerns my mother,' she uttered quietly. 'I spoke with the doctor when she died—she died in childbirth. She had lost several babies—six in total. I was the first and the only one to survive. The pregnancies weakened her, but my father was so intent on having a son he—he... He wouldn't leave her alone. She suffered terribly—and I bore witness to each of her losses.'

'It is not uncommon for some women to suffer so in childbirth, Sophie. That does not mean it will happen to you.'

Sophie swallowed and nodded. 'I know that. But when I married you the only knowledge I had of childbearing was of pain and blood. I was there when she suffered the miscarriages. I was young—too young to understand what was happening. After the last time, when she died, I swore I would never have children if I had to suffer like that to bring them into the world. I know that some illnesses are inherited from one's parents and I truly believed I had inherited my mother's inability to bear children.'

'Your mother gave birth to you, Sophie—a perfectly healthy girl.'

'Yes, I know, which confused me as I grew up. I thought if she could have me, then why not another healthy child? How could I possibly have known then that it was my father who had contaminated her.'

Tristan stared at her. What she told him horrified him. 'I see. And then you found out.'

She nodded, swallowing down the tears. 'How could he? How could he do that to my mother? She was such a gentle, caring, loving woman.'

'Who told you about your father?'

'Back then I could hardly go around asking people if they happened to know whether my father was respectable or not. I began listening to the servants. I heard them talk among themselves and then I knew.'

Her face grew flushed and she averted her eyes. When she next spoke her voice was barely audible. 'When my mother died the doctor told me she—she wasn't clean—that she had syphilis. You—you know what it is?'

He nodded, feeling her pain. 'It's a common enough affliction among those who visit brothels.'

'For some, perhaps. Not for a gently reared woman like my mother. My father handed her a death sentence. It was fortunate the babies were born dead. It's a terrible affliction to give a child.' She did not look at Tristan, but she would have seen he was listening intently as he began to piece together what had tortured her for so long, and with it at last there came understanding.

'I realised it was through no fault of my mother's that she failed to produce another healthy child. More than anything I wanted to have a baby to love and cherish, but the fear was constant. The long agony of the birth of my mother's babies would not go away. It was something I could not put into words. My mind and brain recoiled from it.'

Tristan's heart went out to her. Opening his arms, he said, 'Come here.'

Like a sleepwalker, Sophie's legs moved to obey his summons, but, unable to wait, Tristan met her halfway and pulled her against hm, wrapping his arms around her.

Turning her face into his chest, having emptied her heart, she could not stem the grief and anguish that burst from her in a sea of tears and emotion. Tristan let her weep, hoping that by doing so she would cleanse her soul of all the ugliness that had defiled it for so long.

When her weeping subsided, she looked up at him, the pull of his gaze too strong for her to resist. It was as though he were looking into the very depths of her heart and soul. She felt the touch of his empathy like healing fingers touching and soothing her pain like a balm. She had seen in his eyes the reflection of her torment, and now, as though he were God's own advocate, he was offering her redemption.

'Despite everything, I was so wretched when you left me at Kingswood. I've missed you so much. I was never afraid of love, only of its consequences. I love you, Tristan. There are no reservations.'

'What about regrets?' he murmured, placing his lips against her hair.

'I have no regrets. And I shall be very happy to prove it to you if you stay with me tonight.'

Tristan's arms tightened round her. 'God help me if you don't mean it,' he warned fiercely, 'because I'll never let you go or be parted from you again. At this moment I can't possibly imagine how I could love you more than I do right now, or, for that matter, have loved you since I left you for Egypt four years ago.'

Holding her from him, he touched her chin, turning her face up to his. Tenderly he wiped away the strands of hair clinging to her damp face and tucked them behind her ears. 'Do you know what I thought when you told me you didn't want children? I thought it was *my* children you didn't what—you see, Dianna didn't want my children either.'

Appalled, Sophie stared at him. 'How wrong you were

about that. I was simply afraid of bearing a child—of losing it like my mother did all those babies.'

He gathered her to him, holding her tight. 'Thank God for that. First and foremost it is you I want, Sophie. A child would be a bonus.'

'Then I think you will have your bonus fairly soon, Tristan,' she murmured, 'in approximately seven and a half months' time, in fact.'

Tristan stared at her in stunned disbelief, an array of fleeting, conflicting emotions crossing his face. His concern for her was sharp, then he pulled her into his arms once more. 'Dear Lord, Sophie,' he said, his voice sharp with dawning alarm. 'This is just what you didn't want. How do you feel?'

Sophie felt his warm breath on her face and, seeing his worried gaze, she forced a reassuring smile. 'I have this fear that all may not be well—but despite that I am pleased, Tristan—if a little apprehensive. Truly. I have suffered enough because of my memories. I have to try to put it behind me now—and with you by my side I hope to succeed.'

Gently, he stroked her hair, his fears for her welfare overriding all else. His love for her made him hold her close. 'You must take every consideration of yourself, Sophie, and rest at every opportunity.'

Sophie laughed and kissed him lightly, but the apprehension lurked in her eyes like a dark shadow. 'I have not the patience to make myself an invalid and I beg you not to treat me like one. But I need you, Tristan. I don't think I can get through this on my own.'

Her confession wrenched his heart and he wrapped his arms about her. 'I think you underestimate yourself, my darling,' he murmured against her hair. Then, holding her from him, he stared at her for a moment in wonder, and then he smiled.

'You will manage very well. But worry not. I have no intention of going anywhere. You will have the finest doctors, the finest care, and I shall be beside you every step of the way. We will get through this—together.'

He wrapped her in his arms once more, his heart filled with such anguish that he held her tighter. 'All will be well, my darling.' He closed his eyes in a fervent prayer.

The doctor came and, after examining Sophie, he told them both that there was no reason why she should not carry a child to full term—that it would be a Christmas baby, in fact. As Sophie's pregnancy progressed through the long winter months and into spring, when she felt the first fluttering movement of the baby she placed her hand protectively over her stomach. She must remain calm and not worry unduly lest it harmed the child. She followed this doctrine to the letter, willing everything to be well as the baby's movements became more frequent, but the treacherous fear would not be stilled.

Tristan knew the fear of childbirth still haunted her and her pregnancy gave him little joy, yet pregnancy suited her. She bloomed and positively glowed with health. Despite this he continued to view the birth with trepidation and yet he was impatient for it to be over. He hid the fear which overrode his joy, his emotions always under control when they were together. He was so afraid of losing her.

Epilogue

All Tristan's anxieties proved needless. Edward James Osborne, the future Duke of Almesbury, was born a shortly before Christmas Day. The speed of his birth took everyone by surprise. After Sophie felt some discomfort the day previous to his birth, the pains were quick to follow. Tristan immediately sent for the doctor and shortly after he arrived the child slipped effortlessly into the world.

Tristan, already a besotted father, cradled his son in his arms. He was astounded by the suddenness of it all. The room was bathed in a golden glow from the winter sun. It washed over Sophie, who was sitting up in bed watching him. Her eyes were bright with emotion and happiness, her cheeks soft and rosy.

Sitting on the bed facing her, he placed their son between them. Reaching out, he cupped her chin in the palm of his hand and, leaning forward, kissed her tenderly on the lips. 'Thank you, my darling, for this most precious of gifts—a wonderful Christmas gift. Although I have to say his impatience to be born astounded me. And you look radiant. No one seeing you now would credit you had just given birth.'

Sophie laughed. 'Flatterer.' She sighed as she looked

down at their son. 'He's beautiful, isn't he, Tristan? I can't believe how afraid I was.'

'With good reason. Your fears were justified. But it's behind you now. You can look to the future...'

'And imagine all the babies we will have, for I mean to add to our family just as soon as I can. I did not think it was possible to be this happy.'

Drawing their son into the crook of his arm once more, where he settled down willingly since this was where he already most liked to be, Tristan placed a finger under Sophie's chin. He searched her eyes for a moment, then shook his head. 'You are quite remarkable, do you know that?'

Sophie wasn't certain, but she thought it might be a compliment. It flustered her to have him looking at her so, as if she had accomplished some great deed rather than bear their first child, and his simple words flustered her more.

'Thank you,' he said, his voice low and tender, warming her as she gazed into his eyes. After this day, Tristan was certain he had never experienced such happiness. He also knew he wouldn't have traded his freedom for his darling wife, his mate for life.

* * * * *

*If you enjoyed these stories,
you won't want to miss these other
Historical collections*

Regency Christmas Liaisons
*by Christine Merrill, Sophia James
and Marguerite Kaye*

Snow-Kissed Proposals
by Jenni Fletcher and Elisabeth Hobbes

Under the Mistletoe
by Marguerite Kaye and Bronwyn Scott

Regency Christmas Parties
*by Annie Burrows, Lara Temple
and Joanna Johnson*

A Gilded Age Christmas
by Amanda McCabe and Lauri Robinson